PINT-SIZED PROTECTOR

A Bad Boy Inc Story

EVE LANGLAIS

Copyright © February 2017, Eve Langlais

Cover Art Razz Dazz Design © February 2017

Edited by: Devin Govaere, Literally Addicted to Detail, Amanda Pederick, Brieanna Robertson

Produced in Canada

Published by Eve Langlais ~ www.EveLanglais.com

ISBN: 978-1-988328-60-7

CHAPTER ONE

I HAVE COMPANY.

The door to the balcony didn't make a sound as it eased open, sliding in its track.

Awake in his bed, Darren sensed rather than heard the disturbance and wondered why the house alarm didn't go off. Despite being on the second floor, all the windows and exterior doors were hooked to sensors and completely wireless, which meant nothing to snip.

Of interest, as well, was the fact someone had made it onto his property unnoticed. Between the cameras, motion detectors, guards, and dogs, someone should have noticed something.

Bribery or incompetence, it didn't matter either way. *Someone's ass is getting fired.*

Heads would roll later, though. First, he wanted to see what the intruder planned.

Darren didn't move a muscle. Barely breathed as the filmy curtain billowed at the trespasser's entrance, the fabric clinging for a moment to a body barely visible in the dim illumination provided by the weak lights in the yard.

Had the person come to rob him? He had plenty of wealth for those with avarice in mind. Yet, why not wait until a more opportune moment, like when Darren was away from his abode? Plus, he had plenty of things to pawn on the first floor alone, so why go through the trouble of climbing to the second?

He could think of only one reason why someone would dare penetrate his most private sanctum, a reason that probably involved deadly consequence.

I think he's here to kill me.

Cool, and not the first time it had happened.

There was no denying that Darren had acquired his share of enemies over the years. So many people wanted to see him fail. To see the rich and mighty Thorne family fall.

Or was this person here because of his hidden life? He'd done things under other guises that would engender strong hatred and a need for deadly revenge.

As a secret part owner of an academy, inherited from his father, that trained elite specialists—assassins and hackers and thieves who stole not just items but also knowledge—he could probably name at least a half-dozen individuals who would love to see his operation shut down.

Too fucking bad.

The academy existed for a reason, money being only part of it, with justice as another piece. Darren's father had created the academy and its specialized programs to give people a choice when it came to fighting, whether it be drug lords with a stranglehold on cities, governments with agendas, or even rich businessmen who didn't care for their employees. People sometimes needed a champion, especially when law enforcement couldn't help. There were instances when you needed someone who flouted the laws and could provide solutions.

After his father's retirement, Darren continued his father's tradition of training elite people, hand-chosen because they had the right mentality and skills to help those who needed it.

What most people didn't know was that Darren had trained at the academy, too.

Holding still, Darren waited, hearing the soft whisper of steps on the plush carpet. Forced himself to breathe slowly as the intruder came to a halt beside his bed. Only then did he suddenly open his eyes.

A knife flashed down, but expecting it, he'd already rolled. As he did, he grabbed the wrist of the person attacking and rammed the arm sideways, slamming it into the headboard and forcing the fingers to open and drop the blade.

"Fucker!" The expletive emerged on a definitely masculine note, not that it mattered. In life-or-death situations, there was no difference between man or woman. Just survival.

The defensive moves he'd learned so long ago returned, kind of like riding a bicycle, a skill never completely forgotten. Darren twisted around, locking his legs around the torso of his attacker, feeling the wiry strength of his opponent.

A climber, he'd wager, someone nimble and adept at finding crevices on the outside of buildings and entering where they shouldn't. A skill they taught at the academy.

In the midst of grappling, Darren couldn't help but wonder if he would recognize the face if he pulled off the mask.

Is this one of my students come to pay some final respects?

It wouldn't be the first time.

Despite all the screening done before admittance and the help the Secundus Academy gave to those selected for their program, there were always some who failed. If they were not deemed harmful, and understood the penalty if they talked, they were released. But resentment could come after the fact. Sometimes, those who passed and graduated the tough school, decided to find umbrage later on—mostly because they didn't understand how to monetize the skills the academy gave them. The academy didn't guarantee them success. The graduates had to take responsibility for that.

But...the ways of the human mind were intricate, and those taught to kill even more complex. Sometimes, teaching someone to fight and defend caused a person to revert to more primitive actions and ways of thinking.

Was his attacker an idiot who'd decided to blame his own shortcomings on Darren?

It would be the last stupid thing he did.

Darren struggled with his assailant, giving thanks

that he worked out daily to keep in shape, unlike other guys his age—just shy of forty—who let work get in the way. But strength and skill against someone younger didn't help in this case.

His assailant wasn't a novice or a guy without skill. Darren would need an advantage.

Throwing himself sideways, Darren reached for a bedside lamp. Every bedroom should have one. It provided the perfect weapon in plain sight. His hand curled around the base, and he yanked it toward him, using it to club the fellow on the side of the head.

Whack.

"Motherfucker," hissed the guy, his language skills seemingly rather limited. All Darren could see of him through the mask was the whites of his eyes. Of more interest were the intruder's hands reaching for and squeezing Darren's neck.

Wrong move. Choking took too long.

Still holding the lamp, Darren swung again.

Thud.

The hard blow caused his opponent to loosen his grip and reel away from Darren.

Rising from the bed, Darren noted, via the pale light filtering through the drapes, his intruder beating a retreat but only so he could regroup. With his knife lost, the guy reached for his thigh and the holster strapped there.

Dressed only in sleep pants, Darren wore no protection against a bullet.

Time to end this.

Before the guy could aim, Darren charged and yelled.

The noise served as a distraction as he abruptly halted and pivoted on one foot, his other arcing high and hard into the air, kicking the gun from the man's hand. Darren immediately followed with a quick left hook and then a right uppercut to the face.

His assailant staggered, but Darren didn't relent. Thrust. Jab. Kick. The guy couldn't handle the flurry of blows and hit the floor with a hard thump.

Darren pounced.

By the time the door to his room slammed open, bouncing off the wall, Darren had kneeled on his attacker, pressing his face into the plush carpet while twisting his intruder's arms behind his back.

"What the fuck is going on?" bellowed Marcus.

"About time you showed up, sleeping beauty. Not that I needed you, it seems." Darren wrenched a limb far enough to cause the intruder to yelp.

"Where did he come from?" Marcus snapped.

"The window. Seems someone likes to climb."

Darren's bodyguard, gun in hand, headed to the window and took a peek outside while asking, "Why didn't the alarm go off?"

"Good question, and one we'll have to find an answer to. But, right now, what do you say we take care of our guest?"

Sliding the gun into his waistband and cracking his knuckles, Marcus approached. "I'll dispose of him."

"Later." The gators living in the swamp bordering the back end of his property would appreciate the fresh meat.

In Darren's public life as a businessman, he killed his

opponents with paperwork, but when it came to his other line of work, that of a rogue CIA for hire, he operated under a veil of secrecy.

This guy had tried to kill him, and unfortunately for him, Darren didn't believe in second chances.

The intruder's failure to eliminate Darren would cost him his life and send a message to whoever had hired him. Because there was no doubt someone had sent the guy to eliminate Darren.

He planned to return the favor.

First, though, Darren wanted answers.

"Grab me a chair and some restraints," Darren barked as he hauled the fellow to his feet. He hung quite passively in Darren's grip, head hanging, body limp. A man defeated.

More like an opossum playing dead. The masked intruder jerked out of his hold and managed only one step before he met Marcus's very firm fist.

The fellow hit the floor, out cold.

A sigh left Darren. "So much for a quick Q&A."

"Don't blame the mighty fist." Marcus waggled it.

"So mighty that our visitor could be napping for a while. Might as well order up some food since we need to wait for our nocturnal friend to wake up."

Rubbing his belly, his giant of a bodyguard grinned. "I won't say no to a midnight snack."

The chef didn't grumble about the late-night order because that was his job, to feed Darren and his gang on demand. Given their sometimes erratic hours, Darren kept a pair of cooks on staff, one for the day, and one for the night. Never knew when a man might need sustenance. Not all business happened during normal office hours. Plus, guests had a tendency to drop by unannounced.

A few toasted paninis layered with shaved chicken breast, crisp, salty bacon, a slice of provolone, lettuce, and tomato with a smear of garlic aioli and lemon iced teas— because only morons drank alcohol during serious business— later, the fellow, now tied to a chair with a belt around each wrist and leg, woke up.

Quite predictably, he thrashed and tried to rock the seat over. The chair was made of sturdy wood and didn't even wobble. Realizing this, the guy didn't struggle long. The face, still covered in its fabric hood, lifted and turned toward them, brown eyes peering out through the slits. "What are you going to do with me?"

Darren, who'd taken a seat across from the intruder, arched a brow. "Shouldn't I be asking that question? After all, you're the one who rudely interrupted my sleep—"

"Which was rather shitty of you, considering the boss needs all the beauty rest he can get," Marcus interjected.

"—and tried to kill me. And all this without even introducing yourself first. Quite ill-mannered, I might say."

"Fuck you."

Darren shook his head. "I see you lack language skills, too. But that won't be a problem for long. Shall we start with introductions? As you probably already know, I'm Darren Thorne. And this is my friend—"

"Friend? I work for you," Marcus snorted. "And, I will add, I only stick around because of the benefits."

"Don't forget the awesome retirement pension. I reward those who serve me well." Darren chattered, knowing the discourse with his bodyguard would throw off the intruder. "Anyhow, as I was saying, this is my bodyguard, Marcus Rutledge. Say hi, Marcus."

"We already met." Marcus held up his fist.

Darren snickered. "Ah, yes, I'd forgotten. You really should thank Marcus for that lovely nap you enjoyed."

"Fuck you."

A tsking noise left Darren. "Did you never learn any expletives past the letter F? I have to say, your lack of cooperation really isn't to your advantage. But, then again, what can one expect from a cheap thug?"

"I'm not cheap."

"Maybe not, but you're certainly stupid if you thought you could come into my house and get away with murder." Darren's words emerged low and cold. "I can guarantee right now that whatever price you were offered wasn't enough." He clapped his hands, and the intruder visibly startled. "But we'll discuss that more in a moment. Marcus, would you please reveal our guest."

Now, it should be noted that Darren had already taken a peek while the fellow lay comatose. Marcus, too. The pictures they'd taken were currently being run through a secure computer. The software they had access to took measurements of facial features and then compared them against a massive database. If this guy had so much as a parking ticket, they'd know.

However, the fellow didn't know they'd already taken a peek because Darren had replaced the mask. When it came to getting answers and settling positions of power, actions counted. The more intimidating, the better.

With no pretense at gentleness, Marcus tore off the mask, dragging the intruder's head back hard, snagging the fabric on the man's nose. A rather unremarkable face glared at them, unshaven and sallow, topped by sparse strands of hair.

"Well, I think we can all see why you wear a mask. Not a pretty fellow, are you?" Darren wrinkled his features in disgust. "And your face is about to get even uglier courtesy of Marcus here unless you want to save us all some time, and yourself a lot of misery, by telling me who hired you."

"Fuck off."

Whack. The fist came from the side and rocked the guy's face.

The intruder shook his head. "Fucking cheap shot. Listen here—"

"No, *you* listen." Darren leaned forward. "I don't think you quite grasp the trouble you are in—"

"Clem," Marcus interrupted.

"Clem?" Darren turned to look at his bodyguard. "That's his name? What is it short for, Clementine? Did your parents love oranges?" Darren kept their prisoner off guard as Marcus swiped at his watch, reading a report. It would seem the computer had gotten a hit on their guest.

"I ain't saying shit. Call the cops. I'll be out by morning." Clem smirked.

He still didn't get it.

Darren's lips pulled into a slow yet very cold smile. "About the local law enforcement, they're not coming. No one knows you're here but Marcus and me. And Marcus isn't going to tell, are you?"

Hands tucked behind his back, his bodyguard smiled. "I saw nothing."

"You can't—"

Interrupting him, Darren laughed. "I can do whatever the fuck I like, Clem. Didn't your employer tell you about my reputation?"

Clem's lips remained tight, so Marcus answered for him. "Of course he didn't hear, because you have no reputation, boss, other than that you pay your staff well."

"Exactly, Marcus. Hear that, Clem? No one talks shit about me, and do you know why that is?" Darren leaned close. "Because the people who fuck with me die."

At that, Clem's eyes widened. "You won't murder me."

"Me, waste my time killing you? You think highly of yourself, Clem. Even Marcus has better things to do with his time, such as taking care of his pets. Did you know he tends to some gators on my property? And they are always hungry. Why, you no sooner drop in a chunk of meat than...poof." He exploded his hands. "It's gone. How long do you think it would take them to eat you, Clem?"

Apparently, Clem didn't want to find out, and he started to talk. And talk.

The answers he provided didn't contain enough

substance to save his life. Nothing would have saved it, but they did do one nice thing before tossing him to the gators. Marcus put a bullet in his head.

I'm sorry. I hope you didn't think we were really nice guys. Haven't you heard? Nice guys finish last.

Whereas Darren always won. As to the question of good and evil, he could live with his conscience. What he couldn't handle was sitting back and doing nothing.

By the time Marcus returned from dumping the body, Darren had had a chance to mull over what they'd learned, which wasn't much.

As his bodyguard entered his office, Darren leaned forward to hand Marcus a glass of brandy. "Thanks."

"Don't thank me. Because of my fuckup, you were attacked." Marcus took his duties seriously.

"Not exactly your fault. Neither of us heard about the bounty placed on my head."

"Because the hit wasn't on you specifically but anyone associated with the administration of the school." Marcus swiped at his watch and flung an image onto the screen. Found buried on the Dark Web, in a forum specific to jobs —including murder—was a new entry. The gist of it was: kill the owners and operators of Secundus Academy by any means necessary and get a wickedly large sum.

"Someone's got a hard-on for the academy," Marcus remarked.

"Who would want to fuck us? We provide a service to mankind."

"Exactly why some people want to see you and the

academy gone." Marcus tossed back the drink, and Darren signaled at him to hold it out so he could pour him a new one.

"This is rather inconvenient timing," Darren remarked.

"Glad it's all about you," Marcus said with a roll of his eyes. "You're not the one who's going to be camping on the floor."

"Whose floor are you planning to sleep on?" Although Darren already had a good idea.

"Save your stupid face for your enemies in the board-room. With what happened tonight, and until we elimi-nate whoever is contracting the hit, I'll be sleeping with you."

"About that, while we've known each other for a while, I don't think I'm ready for us to take this friendship to the next level." Darren couldn't help but tease his bodyguard, who, over the years, had become a close friend.

"Joking about it isn't going to change the fact that you need someone sticking close to you at all times, even when you're sleeping."

"I can defend myself, or did you not notice what happened tonight?"

"I did, and you got lucky. What if, next time, there's more than one assailant? Or you bring the wrong girl home?"

"It wouldn't be the first time a paramour tried to kill me." A certain ex-girlfriend came to mind. Though she hadn't actually attacked him with a knife, the pain she caused...

Arms crossed, Marcus adopted his stubborn face, which had a lot in common with a giant boulder that wouldn't budge. "I will protect your ass whether you like it or not."

"As your boss, I will tell you what protection I need."

"Then I'll quit so that, as your friend, I can tell you to fuck off. I will protect you whether you like it or not."

A moue of amusement pulled Daren's lips. "Asshole. You're just hoping to save my life so you can ask for a raise."

"I should get a bonus no matter, given I'm the one who's going to have to suffer through your snoring."

"I don't snore." Total lie. He did. But it never woke him up.

"Whatever makes you feel better, *rhino*," Marcus coughed in his hand.

Darren couldn't help but smile. "On other business, Clem never did explain how he managed to bypass our security. He obviously didn't have the right skills to do so." Few people would because Darren took his protection seriously.

"I've already got a tech team running diagnostics. So far, they're not showing any outside hits on our system. My thought is we either have someone working on the inside, or there's a secret backdoor onto your network."

Hands folded, Darren leaned back in his chair. "In either case, until we find the breach, our system is vulnerable." The whole house would require a top-to-bottom sweep for bugs and other possible electronic intrusions.

"I'm going to have an outside source run background checks on our staff. I'm also going to increase security on the grounds."

"That is all well and good, but we'll need to think of something for my upcoming trip." A business meeting in an unknown location, which meant he couldn't prepare much in advance.

"Cancel." Marcus didn't even hesitate.

Unfortunately, this wasn't something Darren could easily blow off. "I am not cancelling, but don't worry, I already warned them I'd be bringing you, so pack some swim shorts. We're going to tan those white tree trunks of yours."

"If you insist on being a moron, then I'll assemble a security team."

Darren shook his head. "Only one protective detail allowed per guest."

Marcus grimaced. "Figures. Better make sure you get two beds in the room. I am not sleeping on a cot or the floor. These bones are getting too old for that kind of shit."

"You're barely thirty."

"And my ass likes a bed. So make sure they put an extra one in the room."

At that, Darren snickered. "Because us sharing a room won't look strange."

"Big deal. They'll think you're into guys." Marcus shrugged. "At least you'll be alive."

Alive, and yet the rumors would abound. "I won't have you curtailing my love life. The threat is only temporary, and while I do admire your skills, you can't be with me twenty-four seven."

"Then what do you suggest?"

"A new bodyguard."

"You have one," Marcus snapped. "Or am I suddenly not good enough for you?"

"Of course you're good enough. Chill out. You're still coming with me."

"But you just said you could only bring one bodyguard."

"Exactly. But what I didn't mention is that I get to bring a plus one. Given I'm not married, I think I'll bring along a bodyguard who can pass as my girlfriend."

"Where the fuck are you going to find someone who can do that?"

Darren shot him a look, but Marcus shook his head.

"I know what you're thinking. You're going to poach from the academy. Bad idea. Not only are they kind of young for you, but they also lack field experience."

"On that, you are correct, which is why I'm going to hire a seasoned female operative. And I know just the man to call for help." A friend who owed him a favor. Time to call it in.

CHAPTER TWO

Talk about boring. Kacy tapped her blunt nails impatiently on the table as they went through the current business.

Nothing new to see. The meeting went like all the others. A room full of boys arguing about who was going to get what job. With one difference. Harry, her boss, wanted the gang to work in their home turf, busting some kind of drug ring.

Forget their rule about not working from home. Apparently, they were going to make an exception. And since it was about drugs, Kacy could already predict her role in the operation. She jumped into the conversation. "Let me guess, the Latina girl should talk to her *hombres* to see what they have to say about the rich kids and their designer drugs." The stereotyping continued, and Kacy couldn't help but roll her eyes.

"Actually," Harry said, "I need you to go shopping for

girly stuff because you're going to be assigned to a special security detail starting next week."

The description of the job brought her brows together. "I'm not a babysitter." Killer, thief, information gatherer, and pain in the ass, yes. Someone who protected soft, rich men from their just desserts? No.

"Are you sure about that? It pays more than your last two jobs combined." Anyone could see the devious delight in Harry's smile.

Twice the money? Twice the money would mean she could fix her mom's roof and help her aunt send her cousin Juanita to college. The struggle between annoyance at the job and the realization the cushy gig would pay off didn't last long. "Fine, I'll do it." Her acceptance emerged begrudgingly.

The protests by the boys in the room followed soon after. "How come she gets a gravy security detail job?" Declan interjected. Pretty boy Declan, who was a handy fellow with a keyboard, but who'd yet to best her in unarmed combat.

She stuck her tongue out at him.

"Would you like to shave and dress as a hot chick so you can pretend to be this guy's girlfriend while protecting him?"

Shaving? Hold on a second, and what was this nonsense about dressing hotly? This was supposed to be a bodyguard job, not an escort position. She glared at Harry, who ignored her.

Meanwhile, Declan shrugged and argued for the sake of arguing. "Depends on if I've got to put out."

"The right question," said Ben with a grin, "is, is the client hot? I'm in between boyfriends right now, so I'd do it, but I might have a hard time passing as a girl." A big and hairy man, Ben would need a tub of depilatory cream if he hoped to have baby-smooth skin.

"The client is heterosexual and already has a male bodyguard, so Kacy will be the secret one hidden in plain sight." Harry opened his leather folder, the one he carried with him everywhere, and slid a black credit card across the smooth table toward Kacy. "Go out and buy whatever you need. High-end stuff. Our man moves in important circles so you need to look the part."

Money or not, this job was starting to piss her off. New clothes, shaving, what else would she have to do? Wear makeup and heels?

The travesty!

Once the meeting had adjourned, Kacy followed Harry into his office, but she held off on haranguing him until the door shut. "Spill. I want details on this job. What am I doing? For how long?"

"Like I said, bodyguard duties."

"Since when does being a bodyguard require me to wear a dress?"

"Because you're going to be doing it undercover. The client needs you to be able to follow him in social settings without drawing attention. Therefore, you'll be posing as his girlfriend."

The job kept getting worse. "What am I guarding him against? Ex-girlfriend? Pissed-off employees who are mad the *hombre* is shafting them?"

"Actually, Darren is the good guy. But not everyone sees him that way. Someone put a hit out on him. He thwarted the first assassination attempt last night, but given the price, there'll be others."

"Who is this Darren person?"

"An old friend of mine."

Tapping her foot impatiently, she snapped, "What's his last name?"

"Not necessary."

"What?" At that, she recoiled and then glared. "Why can't I know his last name?"

"Because the less you know, the better. We don't know who's watching him. So, if we're going to make this work, then we're going to have to make this authentic."

"And exactly how do you plan to do that? I can't just suddenly show up and announce I'm his girlfriend."

"Exactly, which is why you're going on a blind date. Courtesy of my wife, who is setting you up."

"Like fuck." The black credit skimmed the top of Harry's desk as she pushed it back to him, and Kacy planted her hands on her hips. "Not interested. I am not going into this job blind." And she most certainly didn't want to pretend to be some a-hole's girlfriend.

Harry grabbed the card and tapped it on the mahogany. "You're not going in blind. I'm telling you, this guy is in danger. Who he is doesn't matter. What matters is that you get your attitude in check and do your fucking job."

She leaned forward and braced her hands on his desk. "I don't like it."

"You don't like shit. And I'll add that, while I might be sending you in light on info, how ignorant you remain once you meet Darren is up to you. You're a professional. Or, at least, I thought you were. Treat this like an information-gathering mission."

"I'm not putting out for this *hombre*."

"No one asked you to. And if he tries anything you don't like, you have my permission to knee him in the balls."

"Really? I thought he was your friend."

"He is, but I'm not pimping you out. Just so you know, I wouldn't give you this job if I thought he'd try anything. But you're the best I've got. The only one I can count on to follow this guy around and keep him alive. And trust me, you want this guy alive."

"I don't like it."

"I know you don't. I am asking you to please do this for me."

Ugh. Not the *P* word. Harry didn't ask much, and she owed him. She would do this, but she wouldn't give in gracefully. "Anything I buy for this isn't coming out of my check."

"Not a dime. I'll be billing him extra for it." Harry grinned.

"You'll keep an eye on Mama while I do this?"

"I always do."

With that promise, Kacy took back the black card and then had to suffer through the boss's wife taking her shopping, gushing about how much Kacy would like this guy she was going to meet.

"Darren is handsome. Rich. And so polite. I'm sure you'll like him."

"You can stop it with the sell job. I doubt I'm on anyone's radar yet," Kacy grumbled as they browsed through the store looking for stuff. It made her cringe to see the price tags. One dress in this place could have clothed her whole family for a year as a kid.

"You know, just because this is a job doesn't mean you shouldn't give him a chance."

The good Lord save her from matchmaking women. Wasn't it bad enough that her mama kept asking when she'd settle down? Now, Harry's wife, who regarded her as an unofficial daughter, seemed determined to have Kacy settle down, too.

"If he's as wonderful as you say, I highly doubt he's going to be interested in me." Rich guys had a type, and that didn't involve Latinas born on the wrong side of the border with baggage. So much baggage.

"You never know. Now, would you mind not looking as if you're about to step in front of a firing squad? It wouldn't kill you to smile a little. It's not every day we get to go on a shopping spree." Sherry held up a dress with more holes in it than Kacy's childhood T-shirt the mice had nested in. "You would look amazing in this."

"I don't wanna look amazing." Kacy's lip puckered, and she shook her head.

"Don't be silly. Every girl wants to look good."

Only girls who wanted attention. "I'm fine with my duds." In her public role at Bad Boy Inc., Kacy worked as their property inspector, which involved crawling around in dirty places and often justified some of her infiltration antics. When people found her in forbidden areas, she played the dumb Latina with a work order.

For those who might question her knowledge when it came to inner workings of buildings, her family had worked in construction for years, at least until her *papi* died. Then her brothers and cousins chose other careers. Lucrative ones when it went well, but when it went badly...deportation south was preferable to a stint behind bars. The irresponsibility of her male siblings was why Kacy took care of more than just herself.

Think of the money. Think of the good you can do with it.

Holding that at the forefront of her mind, she snared the dress from Sherry and held it up. Squinting at it one-eyed didn't add more fabric. "How do you wear it without falling out?" Petite and athletic didn't mean flat-chested and skinny-bottomed.

"Trust me. You'll look stunning. You'll need more than one dress, though." Sherry began to pile Kacy with clothes, more dresses than she'd ever owned. Then there was the torment of trying them on—a torture that Kacy wouldn't admit she enjoyed.

She might have grumbled going into the partitioned room at the back, yet there was something about sliding silky material over her skin and seeing the transformation from tomboy to woman—a woman with curves—that flustered.

Kacy rarely took time to draw attention to herself. Rarely did things to make herself more attractive to the opposite sex. Unlike many girls she knew, Kacy didn't thrive on that type of attention.

Still, she couldn't help but admire how she looked in some of the dresses and outfits.

But she had to draw the line somewhere. So when Sherry shoved her newest finds at her, Kacy shook her head. "Like hell. Put those back."

"Think of the mission."

"Ain't no mission should require me wearing this!" Kacy held up the matching bra and panties made of black lace, the quality so fine it felt silky instead of scratchy. "I'm supposed to be pretending to be his girlfriend. Key word being *pretend*, which means he ain't going to be seeing anything under the clothes."

"You know better than that. If you want this undercover op to succeed, then every part of you, including the lingerie, has to match the role."

Kacy did know better, which meant she lost that argument and got ridiculously impractical undergarments, but Sherry did relent and allowed her to add underpants that weren't just dental floss.

As for colors, Kacy tried to stick to plain stuff. Black dresses. Simple lines.

Sherry would have nothing of it, which meant the bags Kacy dragged home were full of things in shades of color she'd never buy herself. Silks and pretty pastels, stuff that required ironing and hanging.

It was wrong. So wrong. Why couldn't she dress in her regular gear? There was nothing wrong with her jeans—the hole forming in the ass hadn't reached any crucial spots. Or her T-shirt—won at a fair declaring she was the Unicorn Horn Ring Toss Champion. Great stuff for wearing around the house, or on property inspections, but a rich guy wouldn't date a girl in rags.

The blind date wasn't happening here in the city but in another state under the guise of her ferreting out some property information for the company—Bad Boy Inc. dealt in real estate around the world. In the process of packing her things, the phone rang.

"Yello," Kacy answered, knowing it would drive her mama nuts.

"When will you learn to answer the phone properly? It is h-ell-o," her mother enunciated, and yet it did nothing to eliminate her heavy Mexican accent.

"How are you, Mama?" Kacy asked, tucking the phone between her ear and shoulder as she held up a filmy negligee. Baby blue and practically sheer enough to see through.

"Fine. But that man was back again."

"What man?" A frown knitted Kacy's brow as she stuffed the silky item into her suitcase. Her new suitcase since, apparently, her duffel bag, repaired with duct tape, wouldn't do for the trip.

"Did I not mention him? Forget it."

"Mama!" Kacy put a warning tone in the word. "What's going on? What man keeps coming by?"

"I don't know his name, but he says Tito owes him money."

Dear brother Tito, who had a thing for not paying his debts. "Did you tell him to bother Tito for it?" Which wouldn't work so well given Tito was doing six months for possession. Again.

"I did. But he was quite insistent. Said someone had to pay."

And that someone wouldn't be either of her brothers because God forbid they take responsibility for their actions. Rubbing at the knot forming between her eyes, Kacy sighed. "Don't worry, Mama. I'll handle it." Actually, Harry would have to take care of it since he was sending her out of town. But then again, given they'd talked about handling the drug problem in town during their meeting today, perhaps that would work in everyone's favor.

To think she'd hoped by moving her mother out here she could avoid the problems in their old town.

If only she'd managed to keep her brothers from following. But Mama was too nice to them. She'd let them know her new address instead of taking Kacy's suggestion that involved pretending they'd both died.

"Listen, I've got to go away for a few days." Possibly weeks, but she didn't mention that.

"Are you finally taking a vacation?" Mama said hopefully.

As if. "It's for work. I'm flying out to Miami in the morning to check out the specs on a property."

"Take a bathing suit and go for a swim in the ocean. The salt water is good for your skin."

"I don't know if I'll have time for that, Mama." Kacy took little time for herself. In her world, it was all about the job.

"Make time. You work too hard."

So had her mother until Kacy stepped in. "I'll try, Mama." And then because she knew it would please her mom, even if it wasn't true, she added, "I'm going on a date."

"With a man?" The words were screeched.

"Yes, a man," she said with a grin no one could see. "But don't get too excited. My boss and his wife set it up since they have a friend who lives out there. I doubt we'll hit it off."

"Did you pack something nice?"

"Yes, Mama."

"That doesn't have holes?"

She couldn't help but laugh. "Yes, Mama. Sherry and I went shopping for some new things." And because she knew her mother would love it, she added, "We got some dresses."

"*Dios!*" Her mother lapsed into Spanish and then remembered herself. "I mean, that is nice. Don't let him sweet-talk you into doing stuff. I don't care whose friend he is."

"Don't worry, Mama." Kacy had a firm grasp of the word no.

That word was what had led to her whole life changing and how she'd met Harry.

Never would she forget that moment. Always tough, at fifteen, Kacy had thought herself rather invincible. As a bit of a tomboy, she had no time for the things other girls indulged in. She eschewed the makeup and slutty clothes meant to draw attention. Kacy lived in her worn jeans and T-shirts. As for bras, the stupid things hurt, so she refused to wear them. Not to say she wasn't cute. Kacy had her share of good looks. Boys hit on her all time, and she blew them off.

But that changed one day after school when a gang of boys surrounded her on the sidewalk. Only teenagers themselves, many had already become neighborhood thugs, but Kacy didn't fear them. These were kids she'd grown up around, guys who ran with her brothers and cousins.

Despicable pigs, who thought they could bargain her virginity for cash.

"Where you going, *puta*? I got something for you." A grab at the crotch brought laughs from his buddies.

She could still see every one of their tanned, leering faces. The dark hair slicked back on some, shaved on others. Not seriously believing them at first—that type of thing happened to other girls, not Kacy—she tried to push her way through them, but they'd formed a tight ring.

"Get out of my way." She still recalled her defiant demand. A request they wouldn't listen to.

"How much do you think we could charge for the *puta*?" A hand reached out to tug the hair she kept in a ponytail.

She slapped at it. "I'm not for sale. Go bother someone else."

"Mouthy bitch. You won't be talking much once you have a cock shoved in your mouth."

The crude threat brought fear, an anxiety she hated to admit. "My brothers—"

"Will do as they're told, or we'll cut them like we cut Jorge."

They were the ones who'd put Jorge, a gentle kid who dared to get straight As, in the hospital?

She couldn't help but succumb a little to the panic, especially as the boys pushed in closer, grabbing at her. Touching her.

They touched me in places that were private.

She'd slapped at their hands. Kicked.

But they'd slapped her back.

Tore at her clothing.

She couldn't help but call out for help. No one replied. In the *barrio*, people didn't like to get involved, especially against the gangs.

Hot tears of shame bled down her cheeks as they kept attacking her.

And then they were the ones crying out as a man, a *gringo* in a suit who used only his fists, taught the boys a lesson.

When the leader of the gang, Pablo, pulled his knife, the man, a grin on his face, pulled out a bigger one and said, "Would you like to die quickly or slowly?"

Apparently, Pablo didn't want to die at all. He ran off with the others.

Much as Kacy appreciated the actions of her savior, she couldn't help but moan as they scattered, "You do realize once you leave, they'll be back." Back with a vengeance.

"Then you should leave."

"And go where?" she exclaimed.

"What if I gave you a way to escape this life? To become something more? Someone who can fight against the thugs in this world?"

Kacy had thought he joked with her. No one could fight the gangs, and yet there was something in the man's eyes. Something that indicated he meant every word he said. So, she'd brought him home.

More like he'd insisted on following her and then spoke to her mama.

It didn't do any good. As if Mama would listen to the *gringo* in his suit when he claimed he wanted to help send Kacy away to a boarding school. A school for special children.

"Is that what they call the whorehouses now?" her mother had spat, not trusting him at all.

"I assure you, the school is real," he'd said. He claimed he could prove it.

Who would pay for it?

The school would subsidize Kacy's education, which seemed even more suspicious.

Why would anyone give Kacy a scholarship based on a meeting on a sidewalk?

Kacy didn't trust the offer either. Yet the man had left them with money—enough for her mother to pay the rent and buy some food. He also left his card. A card that Mama wouldn't touch, as if by touching it she would accept the deal. A deal she was convinced came from the devil.

The following morning, the bruises on Kacy's body had blossomed, and even worse, outside the window, she and Mama could see the boys waiting for her to come out.

As for her brothers, they didn't come home.

The cowards.

The cops wouldn't get involved. No one would get involved.

Despite Kacy's assertion that she would be fine, with a sigh, Mama picked up the phone and dialed.

Later that day, after her first plane ride, Kacy was ushered into a room at the academy. Her own room. With a door. And a lock. She could call her mama every night. She got food three times a day. A snack whenever she wanted one, and an allowance to use on the weekends.

But all that paled in comparison to what they taught her.

They gave Kacy a new life, a better life, and while they tried to convince her to leave her old one behind, on that, she remained firm. While she wanted nothing to do with her brothers, she wouldn't abandon her mother. Mama didn't deserve to lose her baby girl.

And her savior, the man who saved her that day?

A younger Harry. Now her boss and the owner of Bad Boy Inc., specialists in international realty. And the man she owed everything to.

During her time at the Secundus Academy—a top-secret place that took students by special invitation only —Harry had checked in on her. He'd become like a father to her, and it became important that she show him her appreciation by doing well at the academy, a school that drove her hard. So hard, that, at times, she wanted to quit.

But she didn't. Kacy persevered, excelled in many areas, and graduated. Harry could lie all he wanted about the dust in the air. She saw the tears of pride shining in his eyes when she'd gotten her diploma.

Pride wasn't the only reason she worked hard, though. She wanted something better for herself.

The school didn't just save her life. It gave her a future that didn't involve slopping food in a restaurant, hoping INS didn't deport her. It prevented her from being sold on the streets or having to date a guy in a gang just for protection. With the academy's help, she'd not only gotten skills that got her hired by Bad Boy Inc., she'd also become a legal citizen, as had her mother.

She owed everything to the academy and Harry. Maybe, someday, she'd write a book about it. Except when she did put it into words, she might omit the part about her being nervous for a simple bodyguard job.

The flight itself to Miami didn't bother her. Harry booked her in business class, so she had legroom and used the time to nap. The hotel room the company reserved for her was nice. Nicer than she would have booked if left to her own devices. Why did she need a suite when just a room with a bed would do?

She spent that first day on the ground, maintaining her cover by visiting city hall to pull surveys and information on the history of the property she'd supposedly come to check out. A property owned by the city and left derelict. No one wanted it, not even the homeless. She poked around the dusty building that stood one step away from being condemned, on a piece of land in the middle of nowhere, and had to wonder why anyone would want it.

Bad Boy Inc. certainly didn't. So she felt no qualms about sending them a report about the unsuitability of it just before she showered for her blind date.

Date.

Ha. When was the last time she'd gone on one of those? She didn't have the time, or patience, to deal with the small talk and dance that went with getting to know a man.

It explained why she spent most of her evenings alone.

The butterflies didn't start until she had to slide on one of those slick new dresses, which she then immediately took off.

It's too fancy.

Yet, what else could she wear? Sherry had told her to dress up. Apparently, the restaurant where she'd meet her client—ahem, her fake date—was high-end. That meant a dress code that probably didn't include ragged jeans.

Suck it up, bambina. What was wrong with her that she feared wearing a dress? She had ragged shorts at home that showed off more of her ass when she gardened.

With a sigh, she wiggled back into the little cocktail dress—tight on the top but loose on the bottom—but she drew the line at the handful of skimpy panties in her suitcase, opting instead for some boy-short under-pants. New ones, she might add. They would keep her papaya covered in case she had to do things ladies shouldn't do in short skirts. She couldn't ditch the dress shoes, but she derived some satisfaction in knowing that the thick heels held some gadgets in case she ran into a situation.

Her holster sat high on her thigh, the material specially made so as not to chafe, but it took some adjusting to walk naturally with it. Thankfully, the skirt had enough material and pleats to hide it. Her slim knife in its sheath was slid between her breasts and clipped to the plunging v-neckline of her bodice so that it appeared she wore a glittery broach. A present from Harry.

Her small purse held the necessities: a slim wallet with ID and cash, a compact, lip gloss, cell phone, and a charging cube with a green light. The hairclip pinning up her hair to the side—one that could disassemble in a moment into a set of lock picks—completed the ensemble.

For her makeup, she kept it simple, using a dark shadow to give her eyes a smoky effect, a light blush to the cheeks, and bright red for her lips. She chose to keep her long hair loose and mostly down, the clip being the only thing she used. The final piece to her look was giant hoop earrings. The only truly girly thing that Kacy allowed herself day-to-day, and the one item in her reper-toire that didn't turn into a tool of the trade or a weapon.

During the cab ride to the restaurant, she worried that her makeup would melt off her face as she sweated from the humidity and nerves. So stupid, especially since if she was given a mission involving face paint, a swamp, and an assassination, Kacy could handle it without a qualm. Send her on a fake date at some fancy-pants restaurant, and she was ready to turn tail and run.

I don't know if this job is worth the price.

Led to her table by a snooty dude in a suit, Kacy felt like an imposter in the fancy restaurant. White linen draped the tables. Candles, fat ones sitting in glass votive holders, flickered. The waiters held themselves straight and seemed aloof. Even snobbier clientele pretended to not see the staff that refilled wineglasses and removed empty plates.

This place is snooty central. And she was the pretender amidst them.

Seeing the tiny portions of foods being served on small plates, she had to wonder if it would be any good. Harry had explained during his briefing that the restaurant where she'd meet the client had some kind of Michelin star. She wasn't sure what tires had to do with food, but her boss had sounded impressed. Kacy, on the other hand, wanted to fidget and check to make sure her skirt wasn't tucked into her underpants.

When it came to places such as this, girls like Kacy usually worked in the kitchen or as waitstaff. A Latina from the wrong part of town certainly didn't sit in the dining room as a patron—unless she was paid to do so. There was a name for those kinds of girls.

Did the patrons look at her and assume she was a whore? Probably. The things she did for work. Like wearing a damned bra. Horribly confining thing.

Kacy tried not to scowl too much as she followed the dude who insisted on guiding her to her table. Harry would ream her out if she busted her cover before she even began. *Stupid sexist mission.* Posing as some rich *hombre's* girlfriend because he was scared of getting his pansy ass shot off.

Other than the man's name, Harry refused to tell her much about the guy, claiming their meeting and getting to know each other had to look authentic to anyone watching. Hence the blind date setup.

The whole thing stank, except for her. She'd showered and deodorized. She'd also shaved her legs, but she drew the line at getting a Brazilian. There was no man, client or not, that was getting a peek at those goods.

Seated, she waited, drumming the table with her fingertips, painted a seashell pink because Sherry had insisted—they matched her toes. Although, as Kacy had told Sherry just because she knew it would make her laugh, "Ain't no man going to see them if I put them around his ears."

A deep voice rumbled at her back. "You must be Kacy."

It took her by surprise because she was seated at the rear of the restaurant and had been watching the front.

Bloody client had decided to pop in from the rear. Sly.

Standing, she turned and beheld a chest. A really wide chest covered in a snowy white shirt. She had to look up, even in her heels, and she noted a craggy face, piercing eyes, and lips pulled taut in displeasure.

"Yeah, I'm Kacy."

"You're awfully small," was the first mistake he made. The second was to loom even closer, crowding Kacy.

A man who liked to intimidate? She'd known her fair share and knew how to handle them, too.

Kacy pressed into him and smiled—as her hand tucked between their bodies and squeezed his balls in a vise. "Call me small again, and I'll make sure you sing soprano for life."

Because this pint-sized killer didn't take shit from nobody.

CHAPTER THREE

"I DON'T SUPPOSE YOU'D MIND LETTING GO OF Marcus?" Darren stepped around him and smiled at the tiny Latina.

Obviously, his boss wasn't the one getting his nuts crushed into a pulp.

"You're lucky I don't hit girls," Marcus grumbled.

"No, you're lucky my boss said to play nice." She released him and patted Marcus on the cheek before turning to Darren. "Next time, don't be a dick." She turned a smile on his boss. "You must be Darren. So nice to meet you."

"And you." Darren clasped her hand and widened his grin.

Marcus wanted to hit something. Especially since his nuts still throbbed, and from a girl who didn't even reach his chin.

This is who they sent to protect Darren? He remained less than impressed.

About a lot of things.

This whole blind date idea didn't sit well. Grown men, especially successful ones, didn't go on blind dates, even if set up by a trusted friend. Yet, what other cover could be used for Darren to meet this girl who would act as his girlfriend slash bodyguard until the threat was eliminated?

The fact that Darren even wanted someone else to help do his job pissed Marcus off. Sharing his responsibility with a girl he could tuck under one arm really stuck in his craw.

And, yeah, he didn't care how fucking sexist that sounded. In his life, he'd only met a few women who could handle themselves when shit hit the fan. His own mother couldn't even handle raising a kid, claimed caring for Marcus was the reason she'd turned to drugs and alcohol.

Weak. She was weak and irresponsible. But Marcus knew that didn't describe all women. Back in his Army days, Jess had used to muck around in the dirt and kick ass as hard as any boy. She was also six-foot and built like a brick wall.

This little thing in front of him? Sure, she could squeeze a man below the belt, but what else could she do?

Bat her thick and dark eyelashes. Pout with those full lips. *And this is who the boss wants me to partner with?*

At least the girl was cute because Marcus's retort on the way over to the restaurant of, "What if she's dog ugly?" was met by Darren's calmly stated, "Harry wouldn't send me someone unsuitable."

No, instead, he'd sent a munchkin-sized Latina with attitude. And a firm grip. His aching balls could attest to that.

While Darren and the lady exchanged banalities, Marcus scanned the restaurant's occupants, looking for anyone spending an inordinate amount of time eyeballing Darren.

The place chosen for this meeting, the Hidden Cuisine, would serve their purpose well. For one thing, guests enjoyed their fine dining in booths with high backs and thick padding. Low music piped through the restaurant aided the privacy, along with the dim lighting.

Cell phones found it hard to get reception inside—unless a person knew the owner and had a special network key. It wasn't the walls of the building that blocked signals but rather a dampener kept in the basement.

Welcome to the restaurant for the rich and private.

It no longer surprised Marcus that the maître d' knew Darren by name and face, not that he ever presumed to use it or stare overlong. Despite their arrival via the back entrance, the maître d', elegantly dressed in a suit, had been there to lead him and Darren to their table.

A table that already had an occupant.

A woman they knew little about. Just her name—Kacy—and the fact that she was academy trained.

As part of the charade, Harry had told them on the phone, in a voice too jovial, "You have got to meet Kacy.

She's been working here for years, and she's going to be in your neck of the woods doing some recon on a property for me."

And that was how the fake blind date had gotten arranged.

Given his height advantage, Marcus had been able to see the booth and the top of the head of the woman who appeared to study the weave of the tablecloth on the table. A wineglass sat by her hand. The picture of relaxation and someone waiting for her date. A sham, he realized.

As she'd taken a sip from her glass, her eyes did a quick scan before she dropped her gaze again. She'd watched the front of the restaurant. But their surprise approach hadn't daunted her in the least.

His size hadn't caused her to flinch.

She touched me.

What a pity she'd touched him only to hurt because, as a man, he couldn't help but notice how well she filled out her dress.

Shoot me now.

The mention of his name drew Marcus's attention. "...my full-time bodyguard. I hope you don't mind."

"Goodness. Do you have enemies?" Kacy batted her lashes, and Marcus held in a smirk because he could see the fakeness of her gushy query.

Darren hastened to reassure. "No danger with Marcus here to guard me."

He might have grunted in reply.

Darren gestured to the table, and Kacy slid in first,

perching herself on the left. Darren slid in and moved to the opposite side, and then Marcus pushed in beside him, forcing Darren over until Marcus sat across from his date.

Kacy cocked her head. "Is it normal for your bodyguard to join you for dinner? Shouldn't he be sitting with the help?"

"Someone's got to keep an eye on you to make sure you don't stab my boss with a steak knife."

"Well, if I do, I'll make sure to wait until dessert. I'm famished."

Flummoxed described Marcus's state of mind. The more he stared at the woman and listened to her flighty talk and husky laughter, the more he wondered if Harry fucked with them.

How could this vibrant woman possibly have the skills needed to protect?

Look at her, tasting off the boss's plate. Sipping from his glass, claiming it was good luck on a first date.

Let her try and touch the yummy things on his. He'd jab her with his fork. Marcus didn't share his food. But he eschewed the wine. On the job meant staying clear-headed, especially since the woman obviously wouldn't be much help.

Look at her tossing back the wine from the bottle she'd special-ordered before their arrival. Smiling brightly. Surely no one believed her fake chatter about the property she'd supposedly inspected. This woman with her fancy dress and big earrings clearly lied about crawling around in a basement with rats.

And he said so. "Do you scream and climb a chair when you see rodents?"

"Actually, I bring a gun with me when I go into derelict buildings. Never know what vermin you'll find." She smiled at him, and in her gaze, he saw a challenge.

It sparked something in him—below the belt.

Oh, hell no. He would not lust after her.

He shoveled more food into his mouth, but that didn't entirely quell his semi-erection.

A good thing he wouldn't act on it. Marcus had only a few rules in life when it came to women. No sisters of guys he knew. No staff. And nobody who dated his friends. Even fake dates.

Still, though, as the dinner progressed and Kacy revealed little bits of herself, nothing truly revealing but enough for him to grasp a less-than-stellar childhood, he couldn't help but wonder how it would feel if some of that fake smile was aimed his way.

What would it take for a genuine grin?

And why the fuck did she keep kicking him under the table?

CHAPTER FOUR

Right about the time the dessert arrived, Kacy had had enough of the bodyguard. Apparently, he couldn't take a hint; either that, or he didn't mind bruised shins.

She leaned close to Darren, whispering in his ear. "He's going to wreck our cover if he doesn't stop staring."

Turning to her so that his lips almost touched her ear, he muttered back, "You don't have to whisper. No one can hear us."

"How can you be sure?" she asked.

"It's a safe place. You can speak freely."

"Very well. Your bodyguard is going to blow this operation if he doesn't stop ogling me."

"Can you blame him? You're attractive."

Somehow, she doubted that was why he stared. She got the distinct impression that he didn't like her.

Marcus proved it a moment later. "You're passable.

And where else would I look? You're sitting right across from me."

"Which brings me to my second point. Won't people think it's weird he's hanging with us? We're supposed to be on a date."

"Indeed, we are." Darren reached over and held her hand, the hand of a man who'd never done true manual labor. The pads were too soft for that. She resisted an urge to yank her palm back. "Ignore him. I do."

"You do realize I'm sitting right here," Marcus rumbled.

"Exactly the problem. If I'm going to make people believe your boss and me are an item, then it would stand to reason we'd want privacy. Unless..." She turned a suspicious look Darren's way. "Are you the type of freak who gets off on people watching him? Not that I care. But Harry'd better have made it clear that I am not here to fulfill any perverted fantasies."

"I assure you, my desires are normal and containable. While you are an attractive young lady, I have no interest in you."

Kacy relaxed a little. "In the future, I would suggest your bodyguard stand apart, that is if you expect this to work."

"I'm sorry, would you like me to stand three feet behind and become mute? That can be arranged, princess pint."

Tossing his napkin on the table, the big guy slid out of the booth and stood about a pace away, back to them, shoulders and back rigid.

"Now you've done it," Darren murmured.

"If meathead can't stand the truth, then maybe he's in the wrong business." She glared at his back.

"You'll have to cut him some slack. While he's been my bodyguard for years, the most he's had to do up until now is rough up the paparazzi and cock block the mothers looking to marry their daughters to me."

Great. A bodyguard with no actual experience killing or protecting against a real threat. It now made the second part of her mission much clearer. "You're both going to have to make some adjustments." She held her tongue as the waiter stepped around Marcus to ask them if they required anything else.

They were done, which was why, a few minutes later, with Kacy once again pretending to be a vapid Latina out on a hot date, they weaved their way through the restaurant to the front.

Stepping outside, she tried to keep from gritting her teeth as Darren placed his hand in the middle of her back to guide her. Ladies didn't need help walking, but tell that to the man who insisted on taking this pretense to a gentlemanly level that she'd never seen outside the movies. In her world, the men let the girls work, and even fight, without interfering.

"Would you care to join me for a nightcap at my place?" he asked.

Real Kacy, the one who went on a first date and insisted on paying her own way, would have said a very emphatic, "No." Despite what people thought, Latina girls, especially this one, weren't easy. But this was a mission, not real life, and in order to make her mission look real, she had to pretend.

Just like she'd pretended at dinner that she actually cared that Darren enjoyed horseback riding, playing squash, and romantic comedies.

Blech.

"A drink at your place sounds"—awesome, cool, um—"lovely," she finally spat out.

From behind, she could have sworn she heard the big guy laugh. If they weren't on the street, she'd have punched him. Below the belt. And then claimed it was his fault for being too tall for her fist.

As they waited off to the side for the valet to bring the car around, Kacy smiled mirthlessly at Darren, who, for his part, seemed stuck between wry amusement and discomfort.

He wasn't what she'd expected. Far from the spoiled and pampered, soft, rich *hombre*, he appeared to have a hard quality to him and intelligence in those eyes.

Were he not a client, and out of her league, she might have found him attractive.

Much more attractive than the walking tree, who—

A sharp crack split the air, the muffler of a car letting go, and yet, the meathead jumped as if gang bangers were opening fire, his arm sweeping her into Darren. Darren himself was shoved against the wall, pinning Kacy between the men.

It meant her face was smooshed into Darren's chest, and the big guy was plastered against her back, using himself as a shield. At least he had good reflexes, even if the action was worthless. Seriously, bullets would have ripped through him like butter and killed those he protected anyway.

"I think we're safe," she mumbled against the fabric of the shirt she face planted. "Unless you're worried the fumes from that muffler are gonna kill us."

"A thank you would have sufficed," Marcus rumbled, still pressing into her, making her all too aware of how large he truly was once again.

"Thank you for trying to make me the salami in your manwich." She couldn't help herself. It was doubtful anyone could hear her mumbled words, and Harry had only told her to be nice to the rich dude, not his lackey.

"Manwich?" Darren sounded choked.

"See if I cover you next time," snapped Marcus.

"Next time, try looking before acting," she retorted. Amateur.

"The car is here." Marcus moved away from them, and she paused a moment before following, mostly because Darren held her for a moment and whispered, "Be nice. He's not used to sharing me."

Was that a hint that things were a little more personal than Harry had suspected?

"Don't worry," she said in a low voice. "I promise not to walk in if I hear the springs bouncing."

"Wait, that's not what I meant."

A genuine smile curving her lips, Kacy turned away from Darren and caught the big guy staring at her. His brow creased as he held open the door to a luxury town car.

Her smile widened. With a saucy swish of her hips, she entered the car and sat primly with her hands on her lap.

Perhaps she'd find a way to make this job fun, after all.

But first, she needed to lay down some ground rules.

CHAPTER FIVE

WHAT'S UP WITH THAT SMIRK?

It curved her lips and brought a mischievousness quality to her face, an expression completely at odds with her acerbic tone. Marcus only wished her body matched her attitude, yet while her tongue might be rapier sharp, her body was smoking.

But Marcus had ignored hot chicks before.

Settling himself into the driver's seat, he started the car and had his hand on the shifter when she said, "Do you mind not driving yet."

Yeah, he minded. But acting like a dick and pulling away wouldn't solve shit. "Are we waiting for something?"

"Does your driver always question his orders?"

He did when they came from a pint-sized little dictator, who didn't explain why. Worse, his boss expected him to obey. "Hold off for a minute, Marcus."

The command caused him to simmer, mostly because Darren had deferred to Kacy. A newcomer and a woman.

Not even on the job a day and already she's pissing me off.

Everything about Kacy irritated Marcus, from her diminutive size—*I could do arm curls with her, using just one hand*—to her sassy attitude—*doesn't she know ladies are gracious?*—to her curvy body. Hello, bodyguards weren't supposed to be attractive. She should cover it up.

Yes, cover up, because she was distracting the fuck out of him.

She'd caught him staring in the restaurant. Dammit, what else could he do? The way she looked, dressed, smelled...everything drew the eye and attention.

Yet, oddly enough, Darren didn't seem affected.

So why did she plague *him*?

Acting as chauffeur meant Marcus got to sit behind the wheel, tapping his fingers on it, wondering about the hold-up. What was the girl doing back there? Why did they wait? He peeked into the rearview mirror.

"Are you seriously making us wait so you can do your makeup?" Marcus snapped.

Ignoring him, she held up her compact and lipstick, angling this way and that before snapping it shut and tucking the items into her purse.

"We're clear," she announced.

"Clear of what? A mishap with your mascara?"

Her gaze met his in the mirror. "Clear of any listening or recording devices."

The reply caused him to laugh. "Do you seriously think someone bugged the car while we were eating?"

"Yes, and you should have thought of it, too," she said in clear chastisement. "Any operative worth his or her salt who is targeting someone would plant bugs anywhere they could. Car, house, even the restaurant if they knew of your reservation ahead of time."

"The car was secured. No one tampered with it."

"Says you. But you're still going to drive really slow, take your first right, and stop at the next street over."

"What for?" Marcus asked, putting the car in gear and moving it away from the curb slowly, obeying her, but mostly because taking off in a scream of tires would seem childish. He was still tempted, though.

"We need to stop because you're going to get out and use this"—she leaned forward and held something out —"to check for bombs."

"Bombs?" The word expelled from him, and yet Marcus no sooner turned onto the next block than he screeched the car to a halt. "Listen, little pint, this isn't some third world country where terrorists are blowing shit up left and right."

"You're right. This is America, where criminal elements have access to extremely sophisticated gadgetry for spying and devices that can create a spark in the gas tank to blow us up."

"Are you going to sit there listening to this crazy shit?" Marcus asked his boss.

"She doesn't know that the gas tank on this car is almost impenetrable," Darren replied. "But she is right.

While the parking lot for the restaurant is enclosed and guarded, a determined assassin could get in and place a bomb."

"If you're so worried about a bomb, then why did you get in the car before checking?" Marcus said with heavy sarcasm.

"Because a bomb tied to the ignition would have gone off once the valet started the engine. Those types of devices tend to be used mostly on vehicles parked in unsecured driveways, not secured valet locations."

"I still don't get why we moved instead of checking it out first if you're so paranoid."

"For one thing, I needed to ensure that the car wasn't bugged. Unlike you, I am trying to stay undercover."

"No one bugged the car."

"Yet. As for pulling away, if you got out in view of someone watching and they had the device set on a remote, they would have activated it."

"Who says they won't do it now that we're out of sight?" Marcus arched a brow.

Darren jumped in. "Actually, remote-activated bombs are going out of style. Too many things can jam the signal."

"Your boss is correct." She smiled at Darren and ignored Marcus's scowl. "GPS and timed devices are the preferred methods these days."

"What do you mean by GPS?" Marcus asked.

"GPS activated means the bomb will only go off when you hit a certain specified location. Popular areas for this would be small bridges or roads bordering ravines. The hope is that the car will veer off the road and that the subsequent crash will obliterate any evidence."

Marcus gaped at her. "You're fucking nuts. No one planted a bomb."

She kept going as if he hadn't spoken. "If it was a timer bomb, then you're wasting time arguing with me instead of checking. The clock could be ticking." She waggled her hand. "Use this to scan the car."

"You want me to use a USB charger?"

"That's the disguise. In actuality, this little box will detect any electronics that don't belong to this make and model of vehicle. Just like my compact and lipstick scanned for signs of any listening devices or cameras."

He wanted to tell her to shove her gadget and her conspiracy theory, and yet...Darren didn't say a word. Not for the first time, Marcus realized just how different his training in the Army had been compared to someone who'd gone to Darren's special academy.

Unlike other boys his age, Marcus had spent his high school years working two jobs because his mom kept flaking out on him and his grandpa. When he'd graduated, there was no money for college, so it was off to the military he went, serving for years before matters at home called him back for an early retirement.

A military career didn't exactly prepare him for high-end bodyguarding. Marcus didn't know how assassins worked or thought.

Kacy did. Kacy had the training Marcus lacked.

Fuck. He couldn't let pride get in the way of doing his job.

Snatching the gadget, Marcus exited the town car, luxury on four wheels. Bulletproof and armored like a tank, the only thing it lacked was missile launchers. Darren wouldn't let Marcus get any, claiming they were illegal in the USA.

Spoilsport.

Walking around the vehicle, Marcus aimed the small box at the top, sides, hood, and trunk. Then he crouched to point it at the undercarriage. It might stick in his craw that the girl had more training in some areas than he did, but...*I'd still beat her in an arm wrestle.*

Although, if it came down to naked wrestling, he might just let her get on top.

Better not let his mind veer there.

Given the green light on the device never wavered, Marcus felt pretty confident getting back in and declaring, "All clear." He went to hand the device back, but Kacy shook her head.

"Keep it for next time. It's not like I can use it while I'm pretending to be some airhead who thinks your boss is funny."

"What do you mean pretend? I am funny," Darren protested.

"You keep telling yourself that, *cariño.*" Her placating tone made Darren frown, but Marcus laughed.

"Anything else you want me to check, little pint?" Marcus asked.

"What did I say about calling me little pint, meathead?"

"Listen, you want me to stay in character, then that means me calling you little pint."

"Is this how he treats all your girlfriends?" she asked Darren.

"Actually, that's one of his nicer names. I had one a few years ago that he called barracuda."

"And you didn't fire him?" she asked.

"Fire him for telling the truth?" Darren shrugged. "The woman was as vicious as they come, but she had something I wanted so—"

"You used her." Kacy's nose wrinkled.

"Sometimes, a man has to do ugly things to get a job done." In that case, Darren had taken one for the team. Marcus would have shot the blonde bitch point-blank.

"What a revolting thing to say." Her indignity showed, but only because she'd never met the other woman.

"Listen, little pint, you're going to have to trust us when we say barracuda was ugly."

"Not entirely true," Darren interjected. "On the outside, she was drop-dead gorgeous. Model perfect. But on the inside..." Darren tapered off, so Marcus finished the sentence.

"Bitch would have sold her own mother for a profit."

"What happened to her when you got what you needed?" What the tone clearly said was, exactly what kind of man was she protecting?

It made Marcus bristle. How dare she question Darren's integrity?

Darren didn't take offense. "The lovely lady is now

doing jail time. It seems she was involved in a scam that involved funneling children's charity money into an offshore account. Someone tipped off the IRS, who, in turn, reported her to the authorities."

At that, Kacy's lip flattened. "She was a crook."

"Of the most heinous kind."

"I still say we should have shot her," Marcus grumbled.

"On that, we can agree," Kacy muttered. "Getting back on track, a few questions. Do you have a current girlfriend?"

Darren shook his head.

"What about a booty call? Anyone that might cast my role into doubt?"

"Nope. I'm in between relationships right now."

Understatement. Marcus knew for a fact that Darren hadn't really been into anyone since the blowup with Francesca.

"Are you and your bodyguard intimately involved?"

"No!" The vehemence emerged from them both, and Marcus gripped the wheel tightly, glowering, while Darren laughed.

"Despite our close friendship, we are not, and never will be, romantically involved. Although Marcus has been known to get drunk and confess his undying love to me."

"As a bro," Marcus muttered through gritted teeth.

"What will your staff think of you bringing a girl home?"

Again, Darren's shoulder lifted and fell. "They won't

say a word. I don't do it often if that's what you're asking, but at the same time, they are paid well to do their jobs and keep their mouths shut."

"How do you know they're not talking about you?"

"I don't, but nothing embarrassing has ever been leaked to the tabloids, and no sex videos have emerged."

"Only because I'm holding out for the right time to release that moment you had with that pot roast," Marcus added. "You should have seen it, little pint. Someone smoked a joint for stress relief, and next thing you know, he's in that fridge, cradling the leftover roast like it's his best friend. Crooning sweet nothings."

"In my defense, it was a really good roast."

Kacy's lips quirked. She fought the smile, but it won. "I hope you at least paid it homage by eating it with some cold gravy."

"I did. And Marcus hasn't forgiven me yet for not sharing."

"I was high, too. And hungry." He said it with a smile, and yet that brought a frown to her face.

"Do you guys make a habit of getting high or intoxicated?"

"If you mean am I neglecting my duties, then the answer is no. That was a one-time deal. For me, at least."

Her gaze veered to Darren.

"I do it sometimes for stress relief and to help me sleep. It's easier to wake up from than the pills the doctor prescribed. I sometimes suffer from insomnia."

Again, mostly after the incident with a certain ex-girlfriend.

"Given the danger to Darren at this time, I'll expect meathead to completely abstain, and as for you..." She eyed Marcus's boss. "If you must indulge, only do so if we're safe or it can't be avoided in a social setting."

"Yes, ma'am." Darren saluted.

"That's priceless coming from the girl downing glasses of wine at dinner," Marcus retorted.

"It was water, you idiot. Made to look like wine. Harry told me what to order. Apparently, he knows the place and said if I ordered a 1980 white chardonnay they would understand that I meant water in a wine bottle."

Now he felt like a moron, especially since Marcus had never heard of that option. "Anything else you'd like to know or you need to forbid?" Marcus asked, unable to hide his annoyance, as she kept smacking him down at every turn. His poor balls kept reaping the abuse.

"There is one more thing you forgot." Kacy pulled a gun out of nowhere and pointed it at Darren's head.

Marcus knew he was too big to lunge over the seat and grab her, but he did growl. "What the fuck are you doing?"

"I am now displaying your ineptitude at not ensuring I was who I said I was. Neither of you did anything to check me. How do you know I really am Kacy? What if I killed her and took her place?"

Despite the gun pointed at his head, Darren didn't flinch and calmly said, "I read your file and knew what you looked like."

At that, Marcus frowned. Darren had never showed the file to him.

"I'll wager the pictures you saw of me were without makeup or my hair styled. Given the advancement of cosmetic arts, it's not hard to change someone's features enough to pass as them. Especially if you've never met before."

"Is this your way of saying I should have asked for identification? That seems rather harsh for a first date," Darren added.

"Not you, but meathead should have."

"What good would that have done?" Marcus stated. "Identification is easily faked."

"True. And yet, you should have made an attempt. You sat down with a total stranger."

"So what should I have done? Carded you and run your prints against a database? Frisked my boss's date?" Give him a second chance, and he'd skim his hands over her curves.

"Yes, you should have. You're his bodyguard. It's expected you'll keep him safe."

A frown creased Marcus's forehead. "You would have slapped me for laying hands on you."

A hint of a smile lurked around her lips as she nodded. "Probably, and then I would have complained loudly about your treatment. To which Darren would have excused you and explained the precaution. But you didn't, and now..." She cocked the hammer. "I've got a gun against your boss's head, which you never even knew I carried, and you can't do a thing before I shoot."

The rebuke stung. Especially since Marcus knew part of the reason he hadn't frisked the girl was because of misogyny. For all that he was a modern man, it irritated him to realize he'd assumed her petite and cute stature relegated her to non-threat status. It stung to have those blinders yanked away.

After his time spent in the Middle East, he should have learned that the fairer sex didn't always play fair. How many bombs had he seen the burkha-clad ladies set off?

Properly put in his place, only a moron would keep arguing. "You've made your point. I fucked up."

"Good. Don't let it happen again. And consider this another lesson."

"What do you mean lesson?"

She smiled. "Didn't your boss tell you? I'm not just guarding his ass. I'm going to be teaching you some academy secrets."

That earned Darren a mighty glare. The bastard just smiled. "I offered to send you to the academy so you could learn some of this shit. You said you didn't want to train with kids. So, instead, I got you some private tutoring. You can thank me later."

Marcus would thank Darren all right, with a foot up his ass.

CHAPTER SIX

EVEN THOUGH HE FACED FORWARD, WATCHING THE road, Kacy could see that the big guy simmered. She almost felt sorry for him. After all, he seemed to have some decent instincts and, even more importantly, he genuinely cared about his employer. That last thing could make a huge difference because those who guarded needed to actually want to save their bosses if shit hit the fan.

But her respect for his passion didn't extend to his skills or lack thereof. He needed to learn, and learn quickly, if they were to make an effective protective detail.

Kacy turned to the man she was designated to protect. "How long of a drive to your place?"

"We've less than five minutes left. Why?"

"Because I need some information, and given I know this car is secure for the moment, I want to make the most of it."

"My home is secure."

"Not from what I hear."

Darren frowned. "We're working on ensuring that an incident like the other night doesn't happen again."

"Even if you plug that particular breach, your adversaries will be looking for a new one."

"Let them try. I'll take care of them."

Her hair swung as she shook her head. "And, see, it's that kind of macho attitude you need to work on. Both of you. Most assassinations aren't bold attacks. The majority opt for subtle kills."

"I would say a guy climbing a balcony in the middle of the night and bypassing security is kind of bold."

"In that instance, yes, I'd agree because he came in person. There were numerous obstacles to overcome, any of which could have raised an alarm. He made it through and ultimately failed. The chances of someone trying that again are slim. My guess is the attacks we'll have to watch for will be more subtle. That's not to say someone won't try and sniper you from afar. That's always a possibility. As are explosive devices. We already discussed if they attempt to bomb the car. Which means, from now on, before we go anywhere, meathead, you need to secure the vehicle and check it for tampering."

"Would it help if we randomly changed up the cars each time we went out?" Marcus asked.

"Actually, that would be great because that will make it harder for them to infiltrate your garage and choose a vehicle to tamper with. Another thing we'll have to deal with are your phones."

"They're encrypted," Darren stated.

"Great. But they're still beacons to the right hacker. Might as well hang out a sign and say, 'here I am.'"

Her client's features turned stubborn. "I need my phone for business."

Boys and their toys. "You can have it on when you're in the house, but as soon as you walk out of those doors, then you and meathead are to place them in this holder." She pulled a pair of slim black sleeves from the lining of her purse. "These will block any signals trying to ping your devices."

"It means people won't be able to contact me."

"They can call, but you won't get it right away. They'll have to leave a message. By having the signal unavailable for long periods of time, it will force an assassin to rely on old-fashioned visual staking out." Forcing someone to follow closely meant more chances for her to spot them and mount a counter-attack.

"Fine. We'll put our phones in the special pouches when we leave the house."

"Phone condoms," Marcus coughed in the front.

"Isn't that like a man to have a problem with safety," Kacy retorted.

Darren smirked. "Anything else?"

"Leaving the house. As of now, you don't go anywhere without me."

"Or me," Marcus grumbled.

"Until I know the level of your skills, I will take point with the client's protection."

"Nothing wrong with my skills." The big guy turned his gaze from the road long enough to shoot her a glare.

She remained unimpressed. "Don't let your giant ego get in the way of protecting the client. You might be large and intimidating, which is great with in-person confrontations, but when it comes to the more subtle attempts, size means shit."

"We'll see about that," was his mumbled reply.

"I draw the line at either of you following me into the bathroom," Darren declared. "A man likes to do his business in peace."

"A man had better learn to leave the door unlocked then and carry his panic button in case he's attacked while doing his number two."

"Panic button?" Marcus queried.

"Don't tell me your boss doesn't have one?" She turned an incredulous look on Darren. "What is the point of having a bodyguard if he doesn't know when you need help?"

"I can handle myself," Darren replied, finally showing some annoyance. "I'm not completely useless."

"That button would have helped the other night when that guy broke in." Marcus looked in the rearview mirror and sought her gaze. "Where do we get one?"

"I know where to get it." Looking disgruntled, Darren nonetheless seemed amenable to the things she suggested. "I'll order a package of toys from a supplier I know. It will probably take a day or so to arrive."

"Anything else we should do?" Marcus asked. While still not exactly happy about things, she could see that he was at least willing to listen. Good, because the moment he wasn't, she'd have to teach him a lesson. One in humility.

"I think that covers the basics for now. Harry said something about a trip?"

"We leave in two days. Long enough for us to fake falling madly in lust and me insisting you join me."

"Do you have the plane ticket already?"

"It's a chartered flight, arranged by the hosts of the meeting. None of us attending have any idea where we're going."

"You're kidding, right?"

"Would it help if I mentioned we need to pack warm-weather clothing?"

Sighing, Kacy leaned against the supple leather upholstery. "I'm going to fucking kill Harry. How am I supposed to protect you if I don't know all the facts?"

"If Harry has faith in you, then so do I," Darren noted. "We're almost home."

She took a moment to peek outside and noted the measures they had to go through to get into his property. Metal gates stretched between a high stone wall. An electronic panel required Marcus placing his hand on it. It flashed green, and the gates swung open.

"How many people have access to the property?" she asked.

"Only staff, me, and Marcus. Anyone else has to get permission from the security detail at the house."

"Is it a live biometric unit or just a basic fingerprint scanner?" she asked.

"Live. I've seen the movies, too, where the bad guys chop off hands to use them."

"Good. Finally, something you did right."

Darren might have looked affronted, but the meat-head snickered.

Misery loved company.

The long driveway was lit by lampposts. She remarked on them. "Electric or solar?"

"Solar with an electric backup. They are also independently wired, so cutting the juice to one light doesn't affect the others."

"How many guards on the grounds?"

"Four at all times. Plus a pair of trained dogs. They are swapped out at alternating times, so there's never a gap in the security."

"How did they miss the intruder the other night?"

Darren's lips flattened. "It's a big place."

"We relied too much on the cameras. That's part of the hole we're fixing now," Marcus added.

"Does that stone wall run the entire perimeter?"

"Three-quarters. The back end is pure marsh. Too soggy to build a wall but also too muddy for boats to traverse."

"But someone could come through that way?"

"They could, but they wouldn't make it far. Gators," Marcus stated. "There're also some vipers in there, and a few other traps for those who try."

"Really?" She couldn't help but brighten at the news. "You'll have to show me."

At that, Darren laughed. "Sure, impress the girl with

your overgrown lizards."

"Not my fault girls like big beasts," Marcus said before slowing the car to a stop.

For some reason, his words made Kacy think of Marcus not just as a guy who needed training but a man.

A big man. Did that extend everywhere?

I can't even believe I'm thinking about it.

Unable to stay inside the close confines of the car, she spilled out and then, conscious that people might be watching, did her best to look awestruck by the place.

It wasn't really an act.

She stood before a freaking mansion. Like, seriously huge. As in she could have fit her whole family, plus a few relatives big.

Under the guise of taking it in, she spun around, her eyes scanning the illuminated area, the solar-powered globes planted along the low-lying garden beds, the bushes too low to hide in. The same glowing bulbs lined the roundabout for the driveway, only changing into the taller lampposts as they marched down its winding expanse. She'd yet to see any signs of guards or dogs, and yet she'd been watching since their arrival through the heavy, metal gates as she chatted with her temporary boss.

Chatted.

Ugh.

The loquaciousness she'd had to pretend at dinner couldn't even be blamed on the wine since she'd abstained and stuck to water. At least she'd managed to stick to work chatter for the drive.

Amazing how little thought Darren and Marcus had put into Darren's protection. Much as she might hate this assignment, there was no doubt they needed her.

Pivoting back to the car, she noticed that Marcus stood beside it, also paying close attention to their surroundings. He spoke into his watch, the quiet murmurs too low for her to hear.

Kacy couldn't ask the questions she wanted, so she hid them amongst banal ones. "This place is huge. You must have an army to take care of it." It also had innumerable hiding spots where a sniper could be concealed. A vest might be a good idea to ensure some protection for Darren when he went outside.

A smile lifting his lips, Darren again put a hand in the middle of her back and guided her toward the house. "Almost an army. I have a housekeeper, who is a live-in, but her staff of cleaners only comes in at set times. The grounds are also maintained by a live-in fellow; he's got a place in the far corner. Then there's the security detail. I've got four people at all times patrolling the grounds, as well as a pair of trained dogs."

"Wow, you must never get a minute alone."

"Eyes are always watching," he agreed. "So why don't we adjourn to my room where we can be alone."

By alone, he meant Marcus would follow them every step of the way.

After the shit she'd given him in the car about not leaving Darren alone, she couldn't fault him for it, though.

Apparently, Darren had been raised with some old-fashioned manners that treated women as if they couldn't figure out where to go on their own. Kacy allowed the hand in the middle of her back even if, under other circumstances, she might have grabbed it and twisted it. Until she went over this house with her detector, she wouldn't trust they weren't being watched. Darren might have had some academy training and have access to tools of their trade, but better shit was always coming along. Nothing remained infallible.

Even if the place appeared clean, she had to remember that his staff would be watching. Any one of them could find themselves tempted for the right price. Bribery could tempt even the most loyal, and when that didn't work, threats often did.

The sweeping staircase belonged in *Lifestyles of the Rich and Never Going to be in My Future* magazine. Polished wood, wrought iron railings leading up to a balcony area that looked down over the entrance. A princess in a ball gown wouldn't have been out of place.

A short Latina dressed in a slutty cocktail dress, wearing too much makeup and big hoop earrings did not belong.

Harry should have sent someone else. I don't fit in.

While Darren led her from the back, Marcus kept ahead, meaning she got to watch the movement of his ass in his slacks. They were loosely fitted but expensive, obviously tailored to his size. She wondered if the bulk came from fat or muscle. The face indicated the latter, as did his thick neck and defined chin.

Not her type at all. Kacy usually went for guys her

size, maybe an inch or so taller. Men she could lay flat on their backs and control.

Not giant meatheads who thought a woman's place was probably in the kitchen and under him.

Flesh to flesh ...

His body pressing into hers—

She wrenched her gaze away and concentrated on the details of the house.

At the top of the stairs, polished white marble with an intricate inlay met them along with two corridors on either side. Smack-dab between them, opposite the balcony, was a massive window. Kacy shifted to put herself between Darren and that glass and said aloud, "Wow, that's the biggest window ever. Aren't you afraid of people looking in?"

"It's mirrored so, no matter the time of day, we can see out, but no one can see in." Then Darren winked as he added, "You can streak naked past it and only have to worry about the inside staff."

"Streaking is a thing boys do."

"Usually, because they're chasing a girl," Marcus muttered, to which Darren laughed.

No surprise that at the end of the long hall stood a pair of massive, white-paneled doors. Marcus flung them open with a flourish, announcing, "The master suite."

"And where's your room?" she asked Marcus with a pointed look. He waved a hand at the door to their left. "Right in here. I'll leave you two then, I guess."

Marcus saluted her and spun to enter his room.

Amateur. No wonder Darren had hired her. She shut

the doors behind them, clicked the deadbolt on it, and pulled out her compact.

Darren shook his head. "This room is clean."

"Says you," she muttered. A quick whirl with her compact, which acted as a mini radar for electronics emitting a wireless signal, and she was satisfied there was no one watching remotely.

With the realization that there were no cameras she could detect, she dropped all pretense. The high-heeled shoes got kicked off, the gun came out of the holster strapped to her thigh, and she ignored Darren as she inched around the place. The antechamber they'd entered acted as a mini living room with a couch and chair. A wall separated it from the bedroom area, the opening wide enough for a pair of pocket doors.

Slipping into the main sleeping area, she disliked on sight the gap under the giant king-sized bed that could hide a body, and the fact that the suite had too many doors. Walk-in closet being one of them. A mini office in another.

She peeked through them both, the bathroom, too—a room the size of her apartment with a shower that could have bathed everyone on her street with room to spare—before she returned to the antechamber to find the men sitting on the couch.

"How did he get in here?" She'd heard the door click as she locked it. From the outside, she'd noted no keyhole.

Marcus pointed to a hole in the wall that she previously would have sworn was paneled. "Secret entrance."

"Do you have any more in this room?" she asked.

Darren nodded. "One behind the fireplace. It leads to a shaft with a ladder that goes down below the level of the house to a tunnel that emerges on the pool deck by the guest house."

"Is that your only escape route?"

He shook his head. "I have another one in my office on the main floor."

"Does the fireplace work?"

"Yes. It runs on natural gas via a switch, so it looks perfectly legit from the outside."

"Show me how it works." It was Marcus who sprang to his feet to trip the latch. He also stood back as she peered down the hole. Satisfied it was empty for the moment, she closed the secret escape and then grabbed a vase to put over the trap door in the fireplace.

"Most people burn wood," the big guy remarked.

"But a vase will make noise if knocked over," she sassed back. She checked all the nooks and corners, peeked out at the balcony, too, but she drew the line at entering Marcus's room.

If an intruder hid in there, then maybe they'd kill the meathead.

Tucking her gun back into its holster, she announced, "The place is clear."

"I know," Marcus stated.

"How would you know since you sat your fat ass down on that couch? No wonder your boss needs a real bodyguard."

"You can lose the attitude. I knew the room was clear

because I had one of our security team check it out as we were coming up the drive."

"And how do you know he wasn't compromised?"

"Do you see a conspiracy everywhere you look?" Marcus snapped.

"Yes. And so should you."

"Listen, little pint—"

"Call me little again, and you'll be talking in a soprano voice the rest of your life." The attitude on this man, and the fact that he kept diminishing her with the name, made her snap.

"Going to hit me below the belt again?" he admonished. "Is that the only way you can win a fight?"

"Get off your lazy ass, and I'll show you just how well I can fight." She held up her fists, knowing Harry would rebuke her, realizing she shouldn't let Marcus get to her, but something about the man set her off.

"I don't know who put the stick up your ass, but you're going to have to loosen it."

"That stick is what will probably end up saving your boss's life."

"Now, children, no need to fight over me." The placating tone from the client veered her attention.

Kacy's glare met a smile. Darren found this amusing.

"Listen, *cariño*, I was hired to protect your ass. You might be rich, but don't think that makes you special. And don't think because you've got some fancy toys and hired security that you are invulnerable. I've only been here a few minutes, and I already see all kinds of holes in your defenses."

"Of course there are holes," Marcus interjected, "because he wants to live like a real person and not a prisoner in his own home."

"Yeah, well, his home is going to get him killed if the price on his head is high enough."

"I've got a state-of-the-art system," Darren noted.

"I heard you were attacked in bed. How did that system work for you?"

"That was a mistake that's been corrected."

"How many more mistakes around here?" She waved a hand around. "Windows all over. Balconies. A huge property with a stone wall, which won't stop even a child from climbing."

"What do you suggest, then?" Marcus asked. "Put him in a cement box and hope he doesn't suffocate?"

"For starters, how about not assuming his room was safe before going into yours?"

"Because that would have looked suspicious, little pint. Weren't you the one advocating I not blow your cover? Do you know a lot of bodyguards who hone in on their boss when he's about to get lucky?"

"You had no problem interfering at dinner."

"Only because I like their pasta."

The reply took her aback. "Excuse me?"

He shrugged, and the first genuine smile lit his craggy features. "They make the best linguine topped with cream sauce and scallops."

"So you get some for takeout. You don't sit in on a first date."

"Weren't you the one telling me I should have frisked

my boss's date? And now you're going to be pissed I stuck around for dinner to ensure you didn't stab him with a fork?"

She planted her hands on her hips. "Don't you dare turn this back on me, meathead. You're just pissed because I'm showing you the holes in your training."

"Holes? Maybe, instead of flapping your pie hole, you should do something constructive."

"Let me guess, make you a sandwich?"

"What, don't you have a special recipe for a taco?"

"You did not just say that!" she screeched.

"What's wrong? Can't take it? Funny, because you seem able to dish it."

"You're a xenophobic, misogynistic pig!"

"At least I'm not a pint-sized shrew with a chip on her shoulder that makes her think she can just insult people."

Darren stood from the couch. "Ahem, well, since the two of you seem determined to get to know each other, I think I'll go to bed."

"I'll be there shortly. Keep your clothes on," she snapped. "And don't you dare go out on that balcony for any reason."

"Would you like him to leave the door open when he uses the bathroom so he can yell if he needs help wiping his ass?" Marcus asked rather sarcastically.

"I'll leave the cleaning-up-shit part to you since that's all you're qualified for."

"Why you little—"

"Don't say it!" Darren tapped his man on the arm.

"The two of you need to work together. So get whatever it is you've got against each other out of your systems. Now. But try not to get any blood on the floor," Darren admonished before disappearing into the bedroom part of his suite.

Only once the door closed—something she allowed for the moment—did she jab the big guy in the chest. "Listen here, meathead. Just because your feelings are hurt that your boss needed a real pro to guard him isn't a reason to be an asshole."

"Hate to break it to you, little pint, but this is me all the time. And before you think you're so fucking special, the only reason you were hired is because the boss has some business shit coming up where bodyguards aren't welcome but the flavor of the week is."

"What's wrong, meathead? Were you too big of a man to put on a pink shirt and call him 'honey?' Couldn't muster up the courage to kiss him on the lips, grab him by the ass, and goose him?"

A chuckle rumbled out of him. "I'm not afraid to wear pink or a kilt. I even offered. He turned me down. It was the boss's idea to get a girl because, for one thing, he's never been into guys and, second, he didn't want to ruin any future prospects with the ladies. But if I'd known his buddy would send the smallest gal he had, one who seems to think bitchiness is an acceptable trait, I would have put on a fucking dress and a bra and called myself Daisy."

"Daisy?" She eyed him up and down. "You look more like a Bernice."

"And you don't look anything at all like the ladies he usually dates."

"Let me guess, petite blondes who gush and bat their eyes every time he talks." She snorted. "Yeah, I can see that. Too fucking bad. We were all out of blonde bimbos with rifle nipples in their fake boobs."

"Is that really a thing?" he asked.

"No!" At least she'd yet to come across some, but then again, given today's technology, she wouldn't be surprised.

"Listen, I get that we didn't get off on the right foot. However, we need to be able to work together," the big guy said. "Even if I don't like it."

"You don't have to like it to be professional." But... only a real bitch would ignore the olive branch he extended. "You're right. We do need to learn to deal with each other if this is going to succeed. Truce?" She held out her hand.

He looked at her hand then her. "By truce, does that mean you're going to stop shitting on everything I do and don't do?"

"Nope. By truce, it means I will teach you what to do and not do, and not kill you in the process."

"You really think you can take me?" His smile was all male, all arrogance, and it killed Kacy—fucking killed her —when her body actually reacted. She crossed her arms over her chest lest he notice her tightening nipples.

"You let me know when you want to be schooled, big boy. And I'll make sure someone is taping it."

"Deal." He held out his hand, and she took it, noting

the massive size of his paw engulfing hers, feeling the calluses, unlike the soft hand of his boss, who pushed paper for a living. This man had obviously done some work in his life before he took up bodyguarding.

Not that she cared. Marcus wasn't the focus of her mission. And yet, he seemed determined to play a part in her dreams.

At least the dreams she had when she finally managed to fall asleep. Her new client rivaled a freight train with the noises that came out of his mouth.

At about three a.m., she wondered how much the bounty on his head was worth as she held a pillow over his face.

CHAPTER SEVEN

THAT NIGHT, MARCUS SLEPT IN HIS BED, BUT HE left the secret panel open.

While he hated to admit it, the damned woman had a point, several actually, that he should heed and not let his pride get in the way.

Truth was, his bodyguarding skills could use some improvement. The defense that Marcus never had to guard much against actual harm before didn't excuse complacency. Laxity could get Darren killed, and Marcus couldn't allow that to happen. He owed too much to the man. Way too much.

Darren saved my life. He'd found Marcus right when he'd reached the end of his rope.

Today, he looked back on that dark time and couldn't believe he'd ever contemplated suicide. But when people talked of the swallowing darkness, the hole inside them that wouldn't let them crawl out, Marcus understood.

I've been in that hole.

As to how he'd gotten to that point? His sob story resembled so many others. Marcus had lost his father at a young age to a car crash. It had hurt the little boy to lose his dad, but it had crushed his mother. She couldn't cope, and so she'd turned to things that she thought would help her. Booze, drugs, and a mixture of pain meds. Yet, nothing could take the hollow shell-shocked look from her eyes; nothing could make her snap out of her own misery enough to notice the little boy still in need of his mother. Given her issues, they'd moved around a lot, following some path only she could see that she thought would fix things.

Running couldn't fix sadness. But she never did learn that lesson. As his mother struggled with her addiction, the necessities of life were ignored—things like ensuring Marcus had clean clothes, a bed, even food to eat. Children's services stepped in, claiming his mother unfit. They placed him with his paternal grandfather, a man Marcus barely knew because his mother had moved them across the country. A man restricted to a wheelchair, having lost his legs to shrapnel while in the Army.

But the surprise of becoming someone's guardian and the disability didn't prevent the grizzled old man from loving his grandson, even if he was tough about it. Their apartment was small but clean, the food plain, but Marcus got a meal three times a day. Specials treats were for when he did something great such as an *A* on a test or making the football team.

Some local charities offered to help, but pride meant Granddad wouldn't accept any handouts, and neither would Marcus. A man took care of his problems, took care of his family.

When Marcus entered his teen years, he repaid some of that kindness to his granddad by working two jobs while going to school, trying to offer not only himself but also his grandfather a better life.

Shortly before his graduation, Marcus's mother passed of an overdose. He flew out west to attend the funeral, a small event that left Marcus dry-eyed. The woman who'd died bore no resemblance to the one he'd known when his dad was alive.

Going back home, he returned to his life, going through the motions, and only realized when the time to apply to colleges had passed that he didn't have it in him to do more studying. With his grandfather's blessing, Marcus had joined the Army. Enjoyed it, too. There was a certain serenity to having rules that governed his every moment.

A big man at this point, Marcus enjoyed the physical aspects of it. Loved the shooting drills. He didn't even mind the tours they sent him on overseas. He rose in the ranks, a long career ahead of him.

That all changed the day he got the message that his grandfather was dying.

He didn't hesitate to go home. Not that it did any good.

Cancer. Such an ugly thing, especially what it did to a person who'd always been so strong, shriveling them into a pale shell of their former self. Marcus didn't care about all that. His grandfather had always been there for Marcus, and now, Marcus would do the same.

It was a lonely and emotionally wrenching time. The friends Marcus had made in the military tried to keep in touch, but Marcus more or less ignored them. Adjusting to civilian life after almost ten years in the military proved hard. He missed the rules, the missions, the friendships that developed.

When his granddad died, Marcus found himself adrift, alone. He didn't have his job with the Army anymore and had no interest in reapplying.

Why bother? Who would he send his checks to? Who did he have to impress?

No one.

Who would notice if Marcus left this world?

Marcus still remembered the conviction that he had nothing left to offer as he stood on the edge of the bridge and stared at the water swirling below. It would take only one step, one tiny forward movement into nothingness to end it all.

And then, Darren had appeared beside him. Annoying—God fucking bless him—Darren with his questions. "Hey, you, in the Army coat, kind of cold for a swim."

"Fuck off."

"I usually get better results when I fuck on, or in."

Marcus ignored him. The man would leave. Everyone left.

"I don't suppose you're looking for a job."

"Nope." Why work when he had no one to support?

"Want to grab a coffee?"

"I hate coffee."

"Me too. But a nice, cold beer..." Darren made a humming sound. "Love beer. Want to grab one?"

Yes. But instead, Marcus said, "No."

"I don't suppose you're any good with a gun?"

"If I had one, I'd shoot you. Can't you fucking see I'm busy?"

But Darren wouldn't leave. "Can you kill yourself later? I've got this man I've got to meet in a shitty part of town. I could use a behemoth with a scowl to make sure I get out of there in one piece."

"Are you asking me to bodyguard you?"

"Yeah."

The deal was sealed when Marcus asked, "Will there be a chance to hit something?"

"How about I make sure there is?"

It turned out they'd both needed to fight their way out that night. A night that had turned into a few days as Darren kept asking him to do this and that for him. Next thing Marcus knew, he worked for the guy and killing himself seemed like the stupidest idea ever.

And now, he finally had a real chance to pay back that debt. To actually save Darren.

But only if his ignorance didn't get in the way.

Slipping through the secret door, he noted the couch torn apart, the reason being the cushions were piled by the bedroom doors, which were mostly shut.

A form lay huddled under a blanket.

From the bedroom, he could hear the snoring and grinned.

"How was your night, little pint?"

Eyes rimmed in dark circles appeared. Her lips turned down. "Fuck off."

"Aren't you just a ray of sunshine." He couldn't help but smile wider. "What happened to sleeping with the boss?"

"Sleep? Who can sleep with a man who snores like a freight train?" She waved at the door. "It's not right."

"He's a little noisy."

"A little?" She arched a brow. "I was tempted to kill him myself."

"I heard that," Darren shouted from the room, the snoring having stopped as they conversed.

"You have a problem," she yelled back.

"He does," Marcus agreed, "which is why I told him he should go as Darth Vader last Halloween."

"You're an asshole," Darren announced, sliding the doors open wide and glaring.

"Hey, don't get mad at me. I'm not the one complaining about your raucous snoring habit."

"You look like shit," Darren remarked, finally glancing down at Kacy.

"Thanks. I feel so much better knowing that," she sassed. As she crawled out of the blankets, Marcus noted she'd changed into one of Darren's shirts. For some reason, that bothered him.

"I was going to hit the gym. Want to join me?" Marcus asked his boss.

"Sounds like a plan."

"I don't have the right clothes," Kacy grumbled.

"Isn't that just like a woman to complain about her wardrobe?" Marcus remarked. He totally deserved the kick to his shin before she popped out of her makeshift bed.

"I finally know what it's like to be attacked by a munchkin," Marcus remarked, crossing his arms and looking down at her. "It tickles."

"I'll fucking show you a tickle," she snapped. "Where is this gym?"

"While I would greatly love seeing you school Marcus, by the looks of you, you need some sleep," Darren interjected.

"I'll be fine," she snapped.

"I'm sure you will be, but what's one of the rules they teach at the academy?"

"What do you know of the academy?" she asked suspiciously.

"Enough to know that you're supposed to get sleep whenever you get a chance because a tired operative—"

"Is a sloppy operative." Her lips turned down. "I'll skip the gym then to grab a nap."

A shame. Marcus would love to see Kacy put her hands on him. "Yeah, pint-sized princess, better get some beauty rest. Maybe you'll wake up in a better mood."

"You know what would make me happy? Carving off your testicles."

Darren stepped between them and cleared his throat.

"I can see it's going to take some adjustment before you can work together."

"He's an ass," Kacy stated.

"And you're someone who can dish it but not take it," Marcus retorted, peering at her around his boss.

"Enough. From both of you," Darren added, giving them both a fierce glare. "Kacy, you are going to grab a few more z's while I work out with Marcus." Before she could protest, he held up his hand. "The gym is secure. It doesn't have windows, and unless someone's found a way to put a bomb inside my weights, then I'm pretty sure nothing's going to try and kill me."

"Don't be so sure of that." Marcus cracked his knuckles.

Kacy bounced her gaze between them. "You won't go outside?"

"Not even to smell the roses," Marcus offered.

"You'll keep him away from windows, meathead?"

A nod to agree.

She bit her lip. He would have offered to bite it for her, but she'd probably slap him.

A finger jabbed Darren. "No food unless you peel it yourself. Check it first for punctures, too."

"Poison?" Marcus wrinkled his nose.

"It's a possibility. Why do you think I was tasting his food last night?"

"Seems kind of risky."

"Exactly. Everything we do to ensure the client's safety carries a risk. And if something were to happen, my mascara hides an EpiPen, and my perfume atomizer in my purse is a multi-function antidote."

"Dude, you need to get me some of her toys," Marcus said to Darren.

"Be a good boy, and you'll get some for Christmas."

"If you live that long," was Kacy's ominous addition. "Remember what I've said."

Marcus clapped Darren on the shoulder. "I love you, bro, but I am not chewing your food and spitting it into your mouth after."

"You can forget a raise then," Darren joked.

"I'll settle for schooling your ass in the gym."

"Give me a minute to put on some athletic gear." Darren returned to his room, leaving them alone.

Good news, Kacy didn't seem inclined to hit Marcus, but she probably hid a gun under that shirt somewhere, so a gunshot remained possible.

I wonder what she'd say if I frisked her now...

Probably keep good on her promise to remove his balls.

She bent over and gathered the blanket to toss it on the chair. The shirt rode up, but not enough to reveal if she wore panties or what kind. "I'll need to go to the hotel at some point today to grab my things."

"We can also send someone to fetch them for you. Unless you're worried they'll see something." Or keep something, say like a pair of panties.

Perhaps I should oversee this job myself.

Again, she worried at her lower lip. "Nothing overt is out and about, if that's what you mean, but I did leave things strewn about, trying to make it seem as if I planned a longer stay at the hotel. My more covert stuff is well hidden in the lining of the case."

"You mean there are more toys?"

A genuine smile lit her face. "You haven't seen anything yet."

More and more, Marcus was beginning to realize that. Even better, the discovery of what she had hidden excited him.

She excited him.

"Tell you what, you get some sleep, and when you get up, we'll swap places while I grab your stuff."

"Agreeing to be an errand boy? That seems out of character." The suspicious look had returned to her face.

"More like saving myself the boredom of watching Darren work. Maybe you like overseeing someone do paperwork for hours on end. Me, I'd rather riffle through your panties." He winked.

She slugged him in the diaphragm—hard—with a jab of her little fist before turning to face Darren who'd reappeared. "Don't leave the house," she admonished before slipping into his room.

Marcus meanwhile tried to breathe. Little pint had good aim.

"Shall we?" Darren led the way.

Fucking right, they would. Marcus had some frustration to mete out and a point to prove. Bigger was better.

And yet, something about the little woman upstairs scared the fuck out of him.

CHAPTER EIGHT

The phone rang, and rang, an annoying ditty that kept screaming, "it's your mother," louder and louder until she finally scrambled from the bed and dug the phone out of her purse. At times, she wished she believed in voicemail.

Such as now, when her mother exclaimed, "How did your date go?"

Fuck. Kacy had forgotten she'd lied to her mother about her fake outing. "Great, Mama. Just lovely."

"Are you going to see him again?"

Considering that she stood in his bedroom wearing his shirt, most definitely, but she wasn't about to tell her mother that. "We're meeting later for lunch."

The excited squeal had Kacy's ears ringing. She held the phone away and waited for the excitement to die down.

"Be a good girl. And, remember, don't order the most expensive thing on the menu. Men don't like that."

"I don't think he'll mind, Mama. He can afford it."

"You're seeing a rich man?" Kacy could just picture her mother's rounded eyes.

"Listen, Mama, did that guy looking for Tito come back?"

"No, but Harry did stop in. Such a nice man. I sent him home with *churros* for the *bambinos*."

"Did you tell him about the *hombre* bothering you?"

"Yes. He told me not to worry."

If her boss said it, then Kacy knew it would be handled. Mama had become a sort of honorary grandmother to his children. Harry would take care of it.

"Be careful. I've got to get ready for my date"—ugh—"now."

Another squeal preceded some I love yous before she hung up. Her poor mother. Kacy felt bad about misleading her. Darren most definitely wasn't dating material. However, the white lie at least gave her mother hope that perhaps, one day, her baby girl would settle down.

Never.

Still wearing Darren's shirt, which Kacy had found in the closet, paired with a pair of boxers, that required her knotting them so they wouldn't fall down, she exited his room. Her nap lasted long enough to leave her feeling, if not entirely rested, at least not suffering from gritty eyes and a slow brain.

She couldn't entirely blame Darren for her lack of sleep. The man did snore something fierce, but she'd grown up in a house that constantly had noise. Part of what had kept her awake was the job itself.

More specifically, her partner.

Marcus, the giant-sized bodyguard, who was obviously was more for window dressing than true protection. He didn't know the first thing about how to prevent actual harm to his client, other than standing in front of Darren acting as a wall. To be fair, in most cases, his bulky presence would be enough to stop most attacks. But it wouldn't stop a dedicated assassin.

However, his lack of skill wasn't what disturbed her most. Marcus, as a man, bothered her. Somehow, without meaning to, his very existence teased her at every turn. He grumbled at having to work with Kacy, a woman, and at the same time, despite his clear chauvinist attitude, there was something hot about him, something alpha that called to the woman in her.

Since when do I want a man who is domineering? A better question, since when did it turn her on to be treated submissively?

Whatever the answer, Marcus was a distraction she couldn't afford.

Leaving the bedroom, Kacy encountered a few of Darren's staff and knew how it must look. Slutty girl who came home with the boss running around in his clothes with wild hair.

They'd draw the right conclusion, and if they were the type to gossip, her stay would circulate past the boundaries of this home.

Good.

Let people think Darren and Kacy were an item. They had to make this believable and fast if he was to arrange to bring her with him on this business trip. A trip to an unknown location.

Fucking Harry. He just had to give her a challenge. Bless his heart. She'd show him he'd chosen right.

Wandering into the kitchen, she noted a man preparing fruits and arranging them on a platter with pastries.

"Hi there."

He shot her a brief glance.

When he didn't speak, she did, asking, "Where can I find Darren?" Then to cement her presence as a guest, she snagged a goodie from the tray, totally messing up the arrangement.

The chef didn't stab her with his knife, but he did point with it. "Boss is in the basement gym."

Must be nice to have a real workout space. Kacy eschewed a membership to one. Why pay to exercise when she could do it for free? Jogging up three flights of stairs to her apartment a dozen times a day when she came home kept her cardio active. Carrying a twenty-pound bag of rice in each hand, lifting them in curls, worked her arms. Sit-ups took care of her abs. As for keeping her skills in good practice? Every so often, she entered the local fights, face masked, body covered in spandex. Her code name? *Ardilla Rabiosa*. The Rabid Squirrel. Not exactly the most distinguished name, but she usually made those who laughed at it cry, so...she kept it.

When it came to her code name within Bad Boy, she used *parum cattus*, little cat, because of her ability to slink in and out of places. And to the guy at the academy who'd dared to change it to pussy... He'd spent six months in the hospital.

The stairs to the lower level proved well lit, each riser having its own LED light. At the bottom, she had two choices. The left-most door required a handprint for access. Pressing her ear against the portal, she heard the hum of equipment. Probably a utility room. The door across from it had no type of lock at all, so she pulled it open and immediately heard the soft thumps and grunts of people sparring.

Black mats lined the floor, providing a soft cushion. Around the edges of the room, weight-lifting equipment from standard barbells to pulley systems and a bench were lined up. In the middle of the room was the main attraction, two men dressed only in athletic pants, their shirts tossed to the side, revealing muscular upper bodies covered in sheens of sweat.

As physical states went, they both appeared in tremendous shape, both of them without fat, their muscles clearly delineated, but where Darren possessed a slim build, Marcus was thick. Thick all over from his broad shoulders and his wide chest to his tree-trunk arms.

He caught her watching and smiled, a smile that Darren took advantage of, his fist whapping Marcus, a good blow that only slightly tilted his jaw.

Without turning to look at his boss, Marcus lunged

his leg sideways, shot out an arm, and sent Darren tumbling to the mat.

Her new boss sprang to his feet. "Fucker. I thought we were only using our fists."

"Pay attention," Marcus rumbled. "Your enemies won't always play fair."

"Your bodyguard is right," Kacy said, moving farther into the room. "You fight as if your opponent will give you time to breathe. That's not always the case."

"How much do you know about fighting?" Marcus asked, taking time to grab a white towel hanging off a bar to wipe his face.

"I know enough. Is this your way of asking to see my skills? I'm more than happy to demonstrate."

"I wouldn't want to hurt you."

Such a predictable male answer, and one that had Darren chuckling. "Oh, fuck, now you've done it, bro. She is going to school your ass."

Marcus shot a look at his boss and then Kacy. He shook his head. "Even if she had the maddest skills, size will always beat her."

"Is that so?" Kacy shook her head as she grabbed hold of the large button-down shirt and knotted it so it wouldn't get in her way.

"You can't seriously expect me to fight you? I could kill you with one punch."

"If you managed to land it."

"I won't hit a girl."

"Are you sure? Because I have no problem hitting a guy." She noted how he watched her hips as she got close, his distraction too obvious. He couldn't help but look at her as a woman. That had to stop, because every time he did, she couldn't help but see him as a man.

She stopped within two feet of him, close enough to smell the masculine musk of a man who'd exerted himself. Close enough to feel the heat radiating off his body.

Peering up at him, way up because he was stupidly tall, she met his gaze. "Please don't cry when I hurt you. I hate it when boys cry."

"I won't—"

Whack. Her first blow hit him on the side, the soft spot not protected by a wall of muscle. People often made the mistake of hitting right in the middle. Amateurs. Why go after the most protected organs when the liver was open for blows?

Whap. She hit him again in the same spot before he shifted and blocked her third blow, but that meant he wasn't watching her feet. She stomped his bare foot and didn't expect him to hop around screaming like in a cartoon, but it had to hurt. He barely flinched. But he did look warier as she danced away from him.

She talked as she bounced on the balls of her feet. "The most common error people make is underestimating their opponent. In your case, because I'm small and a girl, you think you can beat me."

"I could sit on you, and the game would be over," he grumbled, and yet, he kept pace with her, turning to keep her within sight.

"You are heavier, yes, that is your advantage. You'll

have great force behind your blows. No denying it. But..." She moved, lightning quick, ducking under his arms and popping up behind him, her foot landing against his ass, the kick barely causing him to stumble, but she'd proved her point. "Little is oftentimes faster."

"I'm fast, too." He whirled around and lunged, his fingers brushing the fabric of her shirt.

Close.

"You missed." She grinned. "Gonna have to try harder, meathead."

Again, she rushed him, her feint to the left hiding her true intent. She dropped and rolled to hit him behind the knee. His leg buckled, but he quickly righted himself as she sprang to her feet.

He no longer smiled.

Good. However, she, on the other hand, was a tad impressed. He was a tough bastard and not so slow. He provided more challenge than she'd expected for a guy his size. Most big guys thought bulk alone could make up for skill. Marcus had some skill.

But she had more tricks up her sleeve.

She flipped away from him, a backflip that turned into several, and he watched, pivoting and turning to keep an eye on her. She bounced upright and ran at him, straight at him, and he crouched, ready for her. Instead of running into him full tilt, she leaped, forcing him to catch her.

For a moment, his eyes lit with masculine pleasure as his hands gripped her by the ass and her thighs locked around his upper body.

He thought he'd won.

"Gotcha!" he exclaimed.

"Think again." She clapped his ears.

He grunted at the pain of it but held on. So she did it again, and his hands loosened their grip. She pushed away from him. He recovered too quickly and held on, but he couldn't remain standing, not with the force she put into escaping. They went down onto the mat, him turning enough that he took the brunt of the fall.

How can he still be so gentle when I keep hurting him?

She didn't understand it. Yet being gentle didn't stop him from trying to gain the advantage.

He quickly rolled with her, trying to trap her under him, but she pulled her legs so that they were bent between their bodies. Then she pushed enough that she could gain some room to turn and squirm.

Their sweat made them slippery, something she counted on, that and the fact that he didn't want to really hurt her.

Oddly enough, she didn't want to hurt him too badly either.

He grabbed hold of her shirt as she pulled away. She heard it tearing, and he growled, "Admit it. I've got you beat."

Beat because he held on to her shirt? Did he not know the rules of winning?

Winning had no modesty.

She yanked away, hearing the tearing of fabric, feeling the air of the gym kissing her bare skin. She immediately whirled around and noted Marcus's eyes on her chest.

Her breasts. Breasts with nipples that peaked into tight buds as he stared, held him mesmerized enough that when she hit him in the gut, he wasn't expecting it. And when he huffed out his breath and bent over, she scissored his legs and toppled him.

Not wasting time, she pinned him to the mat, held her elbow over his throat, and said, "If this were a real fight, you'd be dead."

Lying on the ground, huffing, Marcus smiled.

Smiled, goddamn him.

And said, "You're tougher than you look."

Meaner, too. But as she vaulted off his big—oh so big and solid—body, she couldn't bring herself to slam an elbow into his groin. She also thanked God Darren clapped and said bravo, reminding her that they had an audience because she had this crazy urge to pounce on Marcus and kiss him better.

Instead, she shoved those feelings down and aimed her fingers at him pistol style and said, "Next time, don't underestimate your opponent."

"Next time, I promise you won't be on top."

Now why did those words bring a shudder—of pleasure?

CHAPTER NINE

SHE'D WON. WON BY PLAYING DIRTY, SO DIRTY, AND Darren thought Marcus was pissed because little pint had laid him out.

Partially correct. The tiny woman had gotten the better of him. She had some mad fighting skills in that tempting body.

Yet the bigger reason for his ire was something a lot more inexplicable. Something he would have never expected and only rarely experienced.

Jealousy.

When Kacy tore away from him, sacrificing her shirt, she'd bared herself, not just to his lusty, admiring gaze, but Darren's, too.

Darren had gotten an eyeful, and it bothered the hell out of Marcus.

It made no sense. He'd known the girl for like a day. Not even. She annoyed the piss out of him, and yet Marcus couldn't deny that his first impulse, once he picked his jaw up off the floor, was a desire to beat the hell out of Darren because the man had noted Kacy's assets. Then Marcus wanted to beat the hell out of him again, for once again loaning little pint his shirt.

I need to get laid. In a bad way because lusting after a girl who'd done nothing but demean him at every turn, who embarrassed him as a man, made no sense. He'd obviously not dipped his wick in a while and thus lusted after anything with two legs and a hole in the middle.

Speaking of hole in the middle, he'd have to remember to get some donuts on the way back from Kacy's hotel because if he couldn't have one sweet treat, then he'd placate himself with another.

Given his ignoble—and titillating—defeat, he'd welcomed the escape from the house, especially since he couldn't stand watching Kacy fake her interest in Darren over the breakfast table. Giggling at his every word, patting his hand, looking, for all intents and purposes, like his paramour.

It didn't matter that Marcus knew of the fakeness behind the actions; it still bothered him. But why? Marcus understood envy and jealousy. It was what a young boy felt when mothers volunteered at school in the classroom, but his was at home passed out drunk. It was seeing fathers in the stands cheering on their sons while he had no one because it was too hard for his grandfather to get around. It was hearing about big family gatherings with lots of food and cheer, and all they had was frozen dinners on the couch.

Don't get Marcus wrong. His guardian had loved

him, but his granddad didn't go out much or do much. Most of their family time was spent in that little apartment. According to his grandfather, holidays were a marketing ploy to swindle people out of their hard-earned money.

Was it any wonder the boy sometimes envied the life he could have had if his dad had lived?

What Marcus couldn't understand was, why now? Why the jealousy with Kacy? Darren had women in his life. A steady parade of them for the most part. Until recently. His ex, Francesca, had really done a number on him. But even when it was a revolving door of females, Marcus had never lusted after any of them. Not even a twitch.

And yet, get one fiery Latina who mocked his skills and intentionally set out to humiliate him, and he craved her something fierce.

Maybe he'd taken one too many shots to the head.

I'll have to schedule an MRI.

Arriving at the hotel, he parked the car himself in the visitor lot in front of the entrance. He wouldn't be here long. The keycard she'd given him allowed easy access to her room on the fourth floor.

Upon entering, his nose wrinkled. Did he smell cigarette smoke? Not fresh, more like the lingering scent left behind from someone with an intense nicotine habit.

Yet Kacy didn't smoke. Perhaps someone from housekeeping?

Looking around the room, he noted no signs of anything out of place. The beds were still made, the drawers all shut. The only mess appeared caused by Kacy herself.

It didn't take long for him to place the clothing strewn on the bed into the suitcase. The outfits he handled felt crisp and new. None of them carried her scent. Had she bought a new wardrobe for this job?

What did Kacy usually wear?

Unable to stem his curiosity, his hands dug into her luggage and encountered more of the silks and stiff linen, except for at the bottom. His hands touched buttery soft denim. Tugging it free, he noted the worn, smooth texture of the fibers, evidence that this denim had seen better days. An item well worn. Holding the jeans up to his nose, he noticed they smelled clean but were definitely not new.

Was this the real Kacy? Jeans and the T-shirt he found in the bottom, as well?

It would better match her personality thus far. Just like the cotton boy shorts seemed more in character than the lacy thongs.

He needed to quit acting like a weirdo. Sniffing a woman's garments, getting jealous for no reason. He had to begin thinking of Kacy as one of the guys, a soldier he served with. They had a mission to complete, and that mission didn't involve ways of getting his dick inside her.

Reminding himself of his idiocy helped him to shake off whatever plagued him as he stuffed the clothes he'd played with back into the suitcase, along with the cosmetics and toiletries from the bathroom. Somehow, though, he couldn't get it all to fit.

What the fuck? He saw no other bag, so it all should have fit inside. He'd not even touched the boots tucked at the bottom.

He tried again. He folded stuff. He crammed it. Sat on the case. It didn't work, so grumbling about the evil ways women had to pack, he yanked a few things out of the suitcase—the jeans, some silky stuff that could have been a shirt or a dress and some toiletries—and crammed them into a laundry bag he pulled from the closet.

Exiting the hotel with her suitcase and the bag tucked under his arm, his phone pinged. Darren sending him a text.

Grab some donuts, would you?

Despite the fact that Marcus had already planned to get some, he wrote back, **No, your ass is too fat.** He tossed the suitcase in the trunk and shut it before he realized he still held the bag. He tossed it in the front seat as Darren replied. **Take a look in the mirror.**

Marcus chuckled. He'd get the fucking donuts, but he'd eat Darren's favorite one before he got back.

Just because.

Arriving at the house a while later, he parked out front instead of in the garage and grabbed the box of donuts and the bag sitting on the passenger seat before heading into the house.

He ran into Kacy at the door, wearing her dress from the night before, her hair pulled back in a ponytail. She remained barefoot, but he noticed her shoes just inside the door.

He shoved the bag at her. "Here's some of your shit."

"Where's the suitcase?" she asked.

"In the car."

Her brow wrinkled. "Why is some of it in a bag then?"

"I couldn't fit all your stuff back in."

"What do you mean it wouldn't fit?" She rolled her eyes. "Did you think of maybe trying to fold the stuff?"

"I did almost ten years in the military, little pint. Of course I folded it. And sat on it. Not my fault women have some weird knack for packing that no man can replicate."

"So you shoved some stuff into a bag? Even my hair-spray?" She held up the bag and shook it at him. "Are you a moron? What if it leaked onto my clothes?"

"You know, a simple thank you would have sufficed," he snapped.

"Thank you for trying to wreck my shit. And thank you for not bringing in my actual suitcase."

"Don't get your panties in a twist. I'll grab it in a second. The boss asked for donuts, so I brought donuts." He held up the box.

"Glad to see where your priorities are."

"Playing servant to your bossy ass isn't high on my list, little pint."

"Wait until I tell Darren that you were mean to me," she huffed.

For a second, he almost told her to can the girly act, and then he realized that someone watched them. A house servant who'd been around for at least the last few months, but still. They had to maintain appearances.

"I'll get your bag."

"Don't bother. I'll do it myself." She went to head out the door, but he body checked her.

"I said, I'll get it. Why don't you make yourself useful and hold the donuts." Handing off the box to her, Marcus headed down the stairs.

"I still don't get how you didn't fit it all," she muttered from behind him.

"Maybe if you hadn't brought those boots with you."

"Boots? What boots?"

"The ones tucked in the bottom of your suitcase with your jeans."

"Are you on drugs? I didn't bring any—"

Boom!

CHAPTER TEN

THE TRUNK OF THE CAR BUCKLED, BUT THE TOUGH alloy used to build the frame of the vehicle held in the majority of the blast.

I am such a fucking idiot. Kacy could have slapped herself. The mention of boots threw her off, and yet as soon as the explosion happened, she clued in.

Someone had planted a bomb in her stuff.

And someone else didn't catch it.

Given they were outside, out of hearing range of anyone in the house, she skipped down the steps until she stood by the big guy.

Arms folded, Kacy glared at Marcus. To his credit, he hung his head.

"You didn't do a bomb check." Stated not asked.

"How was I supposed to know someone tagged your luggage?"

"How?" she hissed. "Because I told you to check everything."

"I'm sorry."

"You're sorry?" She jabbed him in the chest. "If it hadn't been for you and those stupid donuts, that suitcase would have been in the house. And what do you think would have happened then?"

"You don't have to berate me. I get it."

"Do you?" she asked, doing her best to keep her voice low in case anyone tried to listen. "I told you this job was serious. You are not dealing with paparazzi or marriage-minded gold diggers anymore. This is deadly."

"I understand, okay? You think I wanted this to happen? I owe everything to Darren. Everything."

"Then put your ego aside and start doing something about it."

"Do something about what?" Darren asked, stepping from the house before exclaiming, "What the fuck happened to the car?"

"This idiot somehow managed to blow up my suitcase," she exclaimed. "I thought I told you to be careful with my cans of aerosol. Do you know how expensive beauty products are nowadays?" She tossed her hair before sashaying back into the house.

Darren followed, which meant Marcus brought up the rear.

"Don't worry, baby, I'll buy you some new stuff."

Was it her, or did Marcus gag behind her?

"Maybe I should just go home." Kacy sighed loudly. "I mean, all I've got is this." She held up the bag containing the mishmash of clothes.

"No way, baby. We're just getting to know each other and starting to have fun. Stay with me awhile."

"What about your trip?" Kacy whined. "I thought you had to leave in a day or so on business."

"I do, but I don't want to be apart from you."

"Oh, *cariño*, I feel the same way." She batted her eyelashes and saw Marcus make a moue of distaste. She wondered if Marcus understood they were playacting. Would he know to play his part? Did he finally understand that it wasn't just paranoia that made Kacy do and say the things she did? Hopefully, the fact that someone was willing to slip a bomb into her luggage—*ruining all my shit, the fuckers*—would finally smarten him up.

"Gag me with a spoon," Marcus said.

"I was talking to Darren, not you, meathead." She glared at him, hands on her hips.

"Now, baby." Darren put an arm around her waist, and she fought not to recoil. She didn't like people in her space. "Be nice to Marcus. He's just doing his job."

"His job should be acting nicer to me." Nice, like how he'd taken the brunt of the fall on the mat and then allowed himself to become vulnerable because he couldn't stop staring at her tits?

"My job is to guard his ass, not yours." Marcus glared at her.

"See what I mean?" Her lower lip jutted, and she wanted to gag herself for acting like such a petulant brat.

"Ignore him. He's always grumpy. I know what will make you smile. The invitation I got for my trip said I could bring a guest."

"Are you asking me?" She presented a coy smile, fully aware that one of the staff was just off the front hall, probably listening.

"Come with me."

"But I have nothing to wear." The classic reply of any woman.

"I have a friend. I'll have her deliver some stuff this afternoon."

"Why can't we go shopping ourselves?" She already knew why, because going out at this point would be too dangerous.

Darren waggled his brows. "Because I've got other plans for you."

She couldn't help but note the grimace on Marcus's face. Did this fake act bother him, too? She knew he didn't like her. Did he worry that somehow Darren would fall for her?

He needn't fear. Darren didn't appeal to her at all. His bodyguard, though...

With a giggle, she left Marcus behind, skipping up the stairs, squealing as Darren chased her right into his bedroom. Only once the door was shut and she'd done a quick check with her compact did the smile drop from her lips.

"While you're calling for a new wardrobe, I need to call Harry."

"You going to report what happened?"

"Yeah, and I need to put in an order for some more supplies." Because shit had just gotten serious. Blow up her luggage with her favorite t-shirt, would they?

Time for her to get her hands on some bigger guns. Now, it was personal.

CHAPTER ELEVEN

As Kacy acted like a young woman in lust, bouncing and giggling, Marcus gagged for real. The simpering woman he'd just had to endure wasn't the real Kacy. Funny how this version of her didn't attract him at all.

Shoot me now. I like it better when she's acting mean toward me.

He preferred it when she stood toe to toe and harangued him.

I think I'm a sadomasochist. Because, apparently, he enjoyed abuse.

Kacy and Darren ran out of sight, yet Marcus didn't immediately follow. The rational part of him realized they were going to his room so they could discuss more of the plan. But the jealous part of him...

Yeah, that part wanted to punch Darren out.

Rather than do or say something unfortunate, he remained on the main floor so that he could take care of the now ruined car. Getting it fixed wouldn't be a problem. After his years of service with Darren, Marcus knew people, the kind who didn't ask questions—and would install a rocket launcher if only Darren would agree.

Maybe now that the car had blown up, Darren would understand the importance of decking out the car superhero style.

Once that was taken care of, Marcus spent the rest of the day roaming the house, noting things he'd never thought of before, such as how the French doors to the patio were rarely locked.

Added to a list of entries that needed better security.

The fridge didn't have a lock. Anyone could access the food inside.

Perhaps he should have a mini bar stocked upstairs just in case.

There was more staff milling about inside than seemed necessary. Hadn't they just vacuumed that hall the day before? Surely, Darren and Marcus didn't create that much dirt.

Suddenly paranoid, he sent the cleaning staff home. Told them to take a week's vacation, paid. It made a handful fewer people in the house.

Yet, still, Marcus couldn't help seeing danger everywhere.

A truck arrived to deliver food to the kitchen. A guy Marcus had never met or vetted carried in the crates of groceries. Who'd packed them? Who drove? How had he not realized just how many ways an assassin could enter the property?

Yet wasn't I the one who said Darren couldn't live in a concrete box?

He began to wonder if perhaps that wasn't a better plan.

Given the fridge appeared fully stocked, Marcus also told the cooks, both the daytime and nighttime ones, to take a week's break. They'd manage. Even Marcus could figure out a sandwich.

By midafternoon, the only staff left was the guards. He'd sent everyone else home.

The paranoia now infecting him made him eye the aluminum foil in the kitchen and wonder if he should tape it on the windows to block any signals beaming in.

That was probably a tad crazy. Still, just to be safe, he disconnected their internal network from the worldwide web. No more Internet coming into the house and possibly infiltrating their security.

Late afternoon, Marcus ran into Kacy as she left the suite wearing the jeans he'd stuffed into the bag, along with an oversized T-shirt. Still not his.

Grrr.

Seeing her, his heart rate quickened, and for a moment, her lips curved into a welcoming smile. It quickly turned into a frown.

"There you are. Darren needs to talk to you about his trip."

Only once she'd dragged him into the room did he notice Darren was nowhere to be seen.

"Your boss is in his office." She mentioned with a

wave of her hand. "I just couldn't stand it anymore. All that reading and typing."

"I told you it was boring. So, listen"—his shoulders hunched as he looked for the right words—"I want to apologize for not listening more closely to you. I should have checked your suitcase before loading it in the car."

"Yeah, you should have. But, if it makes you feel any better, I wouldn't have thought to check it either."

"Really?"

She shrugged. "The fact that they bombed my case and set it on a delayed GPS timer was pretty fucking slick."

"It was, and..." Marcus decided to mention the thing bothering him most. "The only way they could have known about you and the fact that we were grabbing the stuff was if—"

"There's a mole." She nodded. "I know. I realized that, too. It's why we've been up here all afternoon going over employee files."

"Did anyone jump out?"

"No."

"I sent the staff home, all but the guards."

"Good idea. Although I am wondering if we should get rid of them, too."

"They've been vetted."

"Doesn't mean shit," she said. "Everyone has a price."

"I don't."

At his declaration, she stared at him. "Are you sure of that?"

"I don't give a shit about money. I've lived without

before. I could do it again. Although, I probably wouldn't have to. Darren pays me well."

"Money isn't the only bribery factor. What if they threatened the right person?"

He shook his head. "I have no one. Only Darren. I would die for the man in a heartbeat."

"Surely you have some family..."

He kept shaking his head. "No siblings. Parents dead. My granddad, too. No girlfriend. No kids. Not even a pet."

At his admission, she stared at him, long enough that he shifted uncomfortably.

"Go ahead. Mock me. Call me a big fucking loser or a socially inept dummy. As you've noticed, I'm not the most approachable person."

"Me either." Her lips quirked. "My mother is convinced I'll end up a spinster because I scare off all the men who show an interest."

"If they can't handle your feisty side, then they're morons."

"Feisty?" She arched a brow. "Why that's almost a compliment, meathead."

"Almost. You're also bossy and mean. But then again"—his turn to smile—"so am I."

At that, she laughed, a genuine chortle that warmed him to the toes.

"I like you, meathead. When you're not being a chauvinistic pig, you're actually decent."

"Quick, someone call poison control. I think you've been infected."

"Ha. Ha. Very funny." Heavily sarcastic and yet she still smiled.

"So I've told you about my lack of life outside of work. What about you?"

"None of your business."

"That doesn't seem fair, little pint. Sharing is caring."

"All I care about is getting the job done." And that ended their moment.

The rest of that day was spent going over plans as the mystery trip was set for the day after next. According to a message Darren had received, a car would pick them up at eight a.m. The ass-crack of dawn, or so his boss, Darren, had declared. He tended to gravitate more to nighttime activities, whereas Marcus, after years in the military, found his body rebelling against sleeping half the day away.

The evening passed quietly, with Darren staying away from windows and dealing with as much business as he could before their upcoming trip.

Wandering up from the kitchen, hands laden with food, Marcus stopped just outside the master bedroom suite and unabashedly eavesdropped on a conversation between Kacy and her mom.

"Lunch was good, Mama." A pause as she listened to a reply. "No, he hasn't kissed me." Another moment of silence, then, "He's asked me to go away with him for a few days."

Even hidden outside the door, which was only ajar a few inches, Marcus heard the squeal and smiled.

"Mama!"

He couldn't hear what the comment was, but Kacy's tone appeared rather shocked.

"Has that man come back to harass you?"

What man?

"Love you, too, Mama." Then, "I know you're spying, meathead."

He pushed open the door with his foot and grinned. "Was that really your mother you were talking to or your handler?"

Kacy flopped onto the couch and sighed. "Real mother. Who thinks I am really dating your boss."

"Why lie to her?"

She shrugged. "Because it makes her happy to think I'm not all alone."

"Are you? Alone?"

"Is this your way of finding out if I'm hitting the sheets with a guy?"

Yes. "Are you dating anyone?"

"No." Her lips turned down. "I don't have time to date."

"Don't have time and can't connect with people," Marcus admitted. He immediately wanted to punch himself for sounding like a fucking pussy.

But she didn't disparage him. "It's hard to find someone who understands what I do. Most guys are like... they see a tiny Latina, and they assume I'm some useless bimbo."

"And then you punch them," he said before biting into a sandwich he'd made.

For a moment, she gaped at him and then smiled, a

genuine grin that lit her features. "Yes, I do punch them for being fucking assholes."

"Sorry I was one of those assholes."

"You can't help yourself. It's a genetic predisposition."

"To be chauvinistic?"

"I was going to say stupid, but that also works."

Verbal sparring filled their evening until Darren went to bed.

Kacy then left him watching so she could take a peek around the grounds.

Marcus didn't see her much the next day. When she wasn't personally watching over Darren, Marcus was while she went scouting.

He didn't really get to connect with her until dinner, when they all ended up in the kitchen, with Kacy making them...

"Burgers?" Marcus said, noting the patties on the grill part of the stovetop.

"If you say you wanted tacos, I'll throat punch you," she growled.

"I was going to say tamales." He laughed as he ducked the spatula she sent his way.

Meanwhile, Darren shook his head. "What happened to getting along?"

"This is getting along. Isn't it, little pint?"

She glared at him, but it wasn't a mean one, and when he got close to grab some plates for them to use, she didn't hit him. Not even a nudge.

He kind of missed it.

After their meal, Darren once again closeted himself in his office, leaving Marcus alone with Kacy.

"So, how old are you?" he asked.

"Why do you want to know? Gonna claim I'm too young to do this job?"

He rolled his eyes. "It's called conversation. I'm twenty-nine."

"Twenty-seven. Which, according to my mother, means my prime childbearing years are almost over."

"Do you want kids?" he asked.

"How about we not talk about personal shit and we, instead, stick to the mission. When we get to wherever we're going, we might not have chances to exchange information."

"Should we develop a special hand signal?"

Her brow knit. "That might be a plan. Except it's got to be something no one would suspect. Remember, once we get there, you are the employee, and I'm your boss's bratty girlfriend."

"So no putting you over my knee for a spanking?"

"That means no innuendos at all."

"Way to suck all the fun out of it."

Her gaze turned serious. "This isn't a game, meat-head. The stakes are very real. How we perform could mean life or death."

Way to give a man anxiety. Just thinking about the fact that he might fuck up kept him awake.

Did Kacy manage to sleep knowing just how much rode on their skills?

Later that night, he lay awake in his bed, listening,

the secret panel between the rooms once again open. He couldn't have said why he couldn't sleep. The security system was armed. All four guards with the dogs patrolled. Even if someone got past them, they'd have a hard time gaining entrance without making a racket, seeing as how Kacy had booby-trapped all the windows with as many tippy vases and glasses as she could find.

Crazy, but he had to admit, clever too.

With the entrances secured, he should sleep, tomorrow would be a busy day, and yet his mind whirred.

It spun, wondering if he was up to the task.

If he peeked through the door, would he see her once again burrowed into a nest of pillows on the floor? Did she sleep alongside Darren, wearing something like the filmy pajamas that had arrived that afternoon, along with the other replacement clothes for the trip?

He'd seen it when she'd pulled it from one of the bags embossed in gold with the name of a posh shop.

The soft silk would barely cover her curves. It would slide so easily against her skin, leaving her exposed. The king-sized bed might seem large, but perhaps she would seek another body in her slumber. Something warm to cuddle.

The more he wondered, the more his irritation grew.

The more he had to know.

Forget explaining his irrational jealousy.

Sliding from his bed, he remained barefoot and padded into the other room, and as he neared the break in the wall leading to the bedroom section, he noticed an odd scent.

Rotten eggs. It took him a half second to clue in to what it meant.

He swept into the bedroom, noting Darren on the bed and Kacy draped on the half-back divan, her phone clutched in her hand. Neither of them stirred at his entry. He could hear a slight hiss, and the smell of eggs grew stronger. A gas leak. But how?

He headed to the fireplace and noted the switch in the off position, yet gas hissed. A crouch down showed the pilot flame missing.

Not good. Opening the doors to the balcony, he let in some fresh air, but he needed to do more than that. Everyone needed to clear this room.

He hesitated between Kacy and Darren.

As the more petite person, gas would affect Kacy more. But he could hear her harangue now. *How dare you rescue me before your boss.*

Sigh. He'd have to hope the influx of fresh air would counter some of the gas. Going to the bed, he grabbed Darren, whose snores had slowed to a soft rumble. The man barely reacted, managing only a slurred, "Go away. I'm sleeping."

"Too bad." Marcus heaved Darren across his shoulders, fireman style. He couldn't help but take a breath between the bed and the door, the pungent gas making him grimace. At the bedroom door leading to the hall, he thumbed the lock and then turned the handle. It moved, but the door didn't budge.

Seriously?

If this were a normal door, he would have kicked it in,

but Darren had more paranoia than you'd expect. The bedroom could double as a panic room, which meant the doors were made of reinforced steel set in a solid steel frame. A simple kick wouldn't do it.

No matter. He'd get out through his room. Except, his door also appeared blocked from the outside.

Someone had infiltrated the premises and blocked them in.

Mother humping fuckers.

Grumbling about nervy little bastards that wanted to get him in trouble—because he was sure Kacy would flip when she found out—he carried Darren back to the room and right out to the balcony, where he dumped him on the floor. The cold tile against his face did more to revive Darren, and he mumbled, "Fuck me, how much did I drink?"

Speaking of drink, Marcus could use one, but his job wasn't done. He headed inside and found Kacy, his head spinning at the gas he'd now inhaled too much of. He heaved her into his arms, princess-style. Her head lolled to the side, but she managed a mumbled, "Go away. I don't want to like you."

Like who? Me, or someone else? He dearly wanted to know.

Returning to the balcony, he stepped outside and, just as he knelt, heard a sharp crack. A sound he knew all too well from his years in the military.

A shot whistled past where his head had been just a moment ago and shattered the stone beside the balcony.

"Are you fucking kidding me?" he griped. Someone

was shooting at them? What the hell had happened to their supposed security?

Ping. Pow. Crack.

The shots pinged off the stone balustrade ringing the balcony, but he knew it was only a matter of time before a shot got lucky. He peered back inside, to where the gas awaited, or out here where bullet holes did.

Rock, meet hard place. Fuck.

He needed another exit.

"Don't move," he said to the pair still lying comatose on the marble floor. He crept back into the room, holding his breath. The fresh air had helped combat some of his earlier dizziness. He waddled to the fireplace, hearing the occasional crack of gunfire.

Then the more reassuring baying of dogs. However, he couldn't know how long it would take them to find the intruder.

A pity he didn't have a sniper rifle. He could have solved the problem of the shooter himself. Mental note to self—get one.

His fingers fumbled for the latch on the fireplace, swinging it open on its hinges, revealing the secret escape hatch. He just didn't know how he'd go down the narrow ladder with two of them at once. In a stroke of good luck finally, he did find the gas valve, which he quickly turned. It wouldn't clear the tainted air, but it would at least stop new gas from escaping.

Leaving the escape route open, he returned to find them both stirring but remaining flat.

"What happened?" Kacy slurred, her gaze cross-eyed as she struggled to open her lids.

"Gas leak in the fireplace and someone is taking potshots."

That widened her eyes, and her lips muttered a curse as another bullet shattered stone. "How the fuck did that happen? We were in the room almost the entire day."

Except for dinner.

More evidence of a mole. Maybe even more than one.

Pow. A shower of more stone as the missile shattered the façade.

Darren pulled himself toward Marcus. "We have to get out of here."

"The bedroom door is barricaded. We'll have to use the fireplace exit. I've already got it open. Get yourself moving. I'll distract our shooter." Because Marcus had snared the gun in Darren's nightstand on the way back. It wasn't the rifle and scope he'd used in the military, but when he stood and aimed it— *pop, pop, pop*—it gave the other shooter pause.

He ducked down and peered back to see Kacy and Darren crawling across the bedroom, one of them making retching noises.

Crack. A shot hit stone, and shrapnel peppered Marcus, a sliver of it slicing his arm.

A mere scratch that he ignored. He directed the barrel between the stone pillars, not aiming at anything in particular, just shooting wild to give them more time to escape.

When he looked back, Darren appeared to be gone,

and Kacy was crouched by the entrance to the fireplace. He tucked the gun into the waistband of his track pants and scuttled after them.

Noticing him approaching, Kacy slid down the hole.

The smell of gas still lingered in a cloying manner. Marcus peeked down the hidden shaft in the fireplace and noted them climbing, not as quickly as he'd like, the poison they'd inhaled still affecting them. They were in no condition to confront anyone.

So...taking a page out of Kacy's book, Marcus decided to set the stage and divert attention. Popping down the hole, he held on to the ladder as he hit a switch on the inside. As the trap to the fireplace swung shut, he pulled his gun and fired through the narrowing crack at the nightstand, shattering the bulb of the lamp. It caused a small spark, enough to ignite the gas.

Whoosh!

CHAPTER TWELVE

THE HOUSE SHOOK OVERHEAD, AND KACY HELD ON AS she realized what Marcus had done.

He'd bought them time.

Unfortunately, the client didn't exactly see it that way.

"You blew up my house!" Darren yelled, the sound bouncing around the interior of the shaft.

"I only blew up your bedroom. And the proper reply is, 'thank you,'" Marcus replied.

"Thank you? Did that gas kill off what brains cells you had?"

"Because of Marcus, we're all alive," Kacy interjected. "Surely that's worth the cost of a little renovation, so say thank you and get moving."

"But if I say thank you, do you know how conceited he'll get?" Darren glowered upwards, and a peek above her showed Marcus looked smug.

"I saved your life," the big man sang. "And now we're even."

He'd saved Kacy's, too, because she'd missed the tampering on the fireplace.

How? There was no smell of gas when she'd gone into the room. She would have noticed it. The natural gas companies used a product called mercaptan to give a sulfuric smell to the gas to warn of leaks.

She'd passed out breathing it, judging by the phone still clutched in her hand. But Marcus had caught it.

"Good job," she said as she waited for Darren to move so she could continue the climb down.

The compliment brought a smile to his rugged face. "You're welcome," he hollered down to Darren. "See, she knows I'm the man, so suck it up, buttercup. I'm finally ahead of you."

"Not for long," Darren replied rather ominously.

Men and their need to constantly one-up each other.

"We need to plan our next move," Kacy noted.

"How about we worry about getting out of this tunnel alive first? I'm pretty sure the explosion didn't hurt the sniper outside. He might still be around."

Good point, and she didn't think of it. Stupid gas addling her brain. "How long before the fire trucks arrive?"

"Not long. By now the sprinkler system on the top floor will have engaged, and once that happens, they are automatically called."

"What about the local law enforcement?" Most cases

of fire saw at least one car dispatched in case there was arson suspected.

"I expect they'll show up not long after."

Reaching the bottom of the shaft and a narrow, stone-block tunnel, Darren paused, mostly because Kacy grabbed hold of him. "Hold on a second. How much farther?"

"The tunnel's exit is about thirty yards ahead. There's a flagstone at the far end of the pool deck that lifts."

"I'll go ahead and make sure it's clear." Marcus squeezed past, his big body brushing against hers, and she was glad she'd fallen asleep fully dressed because he hadn't, and the bare flesh of his chest rubbing against the fabric of her shirt was enough to make her nipples harden.

She bit her lip as Marcus squished past Darren. It almost didn't work; the space wasn't very large.

Marcus went ahead, pulling a gun from his waist-band, barely visible. Which made her frown. "How come we can see in here?" She hadn't noticed any obvious light sources.

"A bioluminescent paint. It reacts to the presence of carbon dioxide and provides a faint light. It's expensive but more reliable than running electricity or banking on bulbs."

Very cool. She'd have to mention it to Harry. "Stay behind me." Kacy slid past Darren and couldn't help but note that her body didn't react at all. Not a bit. Her attraction really was for only one man.

A big man, who moved quickly ahead of her.

She increased her pace to catch up but didn't run. Let Marcus exit first. If someone waited, better Marcus find out than their client.

The faint sound of sirens filled the tunnel as, ahead, Marcus opened the trap door to the outside. She could see his lower body on the ladder, and then heard the more ominous pop of a gun being fired—not by Marcus.

She sprinted, cursing as Marcus's legs disappeared and all outside sound was cut off. He'd closed the door.

Hitting the ladder, she climbed, only to quickly find herself confronted by the concrete slab on huge hydraulic hinges.

Where was the catch to open it?

Darren must have read her mind because he arrived and said, "To your left."

Fingers fumbling in the dim light, she found the recessed lever and yanked. Without a sound, the lid lifted, and the noise of fire engine sirens filled the air. But aside from that, she didn't hear a thing—no Marcus and no gunman.

"Stay down there," she ordered Darren before slithering out of the hole. A tug on the lip of stone brought it back down where it clicked into place.

For a moment, she lay flat on her stomach, listening. Then she heard it, even amidst the sirens. *Pop.*

Pop.

Close by and yet not aimed at her. Where was Marcus?

Jumping to her feet, she ran, heading for the pool

house, only to realize as she looked up that she'd found the gunman. Perched on the rooftop of the cabana house, he lay flat and took aim at the water slide made of cement and shaped to look like natural rock.

The shooter had yet to notice her.

Crack.

The single shot fired from the slide confirmed her guess as to Marcus's location. While he kept the shooter occupied, she ran for the cabana and leaped, grabbing at the lip of the roof.

The wailing fire engines kept anyone from hearing her scrabble for purchase. She dug the tips of her fingers into the terra cotta tile and swung her legs. Climbing things was easy for her. First in her class when it came to getting into places at the academy.

Keeping herself crouched low on the roof, she padded across the stone layers, sneaking up behind the gunman. But he must have heard or sensed something because he rolled and shot at her!

She lunged to the side, hitting the roof hard, but immediately crawled toward him before he could take aim again. Diving onto the gunman, Kacy grabbed for his gun, pushing it away, but not before he fired another shot.

Kacy wrestled with the guy. He was a slender fellow with a wiry strength.

But she played dirty.

Her knee found the nice, soft, squishy underside of his balls. Before he'd had time to gasp in pain, she kneed him again, and his grip loosened on the gun enough for her to yank it from his hands and toss it. That left her

132 · EVE LANGLAIS

hands free to grab him by the dark hood covering his head and smash it against the roof. It took only a few hard blows before he went limp.

Good.

But she couldn't stay here on the cabana with him forever. Red lights lit the sky. The firemen had arrived.

Wrapping her fingers in the fabric of his hoodie, she tugged him to the edge of the roof and rolled him off.

Crunch.

That didn't sound good. She hoped she hadn't killed him, though not because of any kindness on her part. Dead people were hard to question.

As she went to lower herself from the roof, arms wrapped around her legs, but she held off kicking when Marcus rumbled, "I got you, little pint."

Normal Kacy would have told him to fuck off, that she didn't need his help. New Kacy, the one who didn't understand her burgeoning attraction to the giant meat-head, let herself slide down into his capable grip. And he took full advantage, letting her feel every hard ridge of his body as he slowly lowered her to the ground.

"Nice job," he stated.

"I'm surprised you didn't take care of him yourself."

He shrugged, and his white teeth gleamed in the shadowy yard as he claimed, "I don't climb."

Kacy, on the other hand, did, and Marcus was tall enough she could totally use him as a tree.

Naked came to mind.

Now was not the time, though.

"I'll get the client." She ordered. "You stash the body for later."

They needed to present themselves to the arriving fire crew before anyone noticed anything amiss.

She led Darren out of the hidden tunnel and had him seated on a reclining chair by the pool, hunched over, pretending he was sick when the first fireman rounded the corner of the house.

If the guy dressed in full gear thought it odd that Marcus suddenly appeared a few minutes later, he didn't remark on it. Then again, Kacy kept him plenty distracted by exclaiming in a mixture of English and Spanish about how scared she was. And how sick the gas made her feel. Oh, and could she have more of that oxygen? Was he single? She had a cousin.

Babbling wasn't her thing, but in this case, she had to remain in character. In character meant a girl terrified and yet excited by what had happened. Not a cold-blooded operative itching to get back to the cabana to question their captive.

The firemen and the policemen who showed up didn't question them too much. Marcus stuck to the truth, more or less. He told them he'd been checking on his boss and his boss's girlfriend when he smelled gas. He'd gotten them out of there just before something ignited everything.

The officials seemed satisfied, although one of the cops did say, "We also got a report about gunfire. Did you hear anything?"

"No idea what you're talking about, officer. But with

the swamp nearby, it's not uncommon for poachers to try and net some of the gators at night." Darren remained composed, despite the attempt on his life.

If money greased any palms, Kacy didn't see it. What she did know was as soon as the fire was controlled—thanks to sprinkler systems in the house and fire-retardant walls—and Darren had reassured them that they would stay the night in the cabana out back until the premises could be inspected, the fire trucks and cops left.

About time.

The moment they found themselves alone, standing on the front step of the house, Darren muttered, "Where are all the guards?"

Marcus cursed. "I heard the dogs earlier when the shooting started."

Nothing since. Entering the house, the front foyer damp and dirty from the firemen, Marcus made a beeline for the nearest security panel and began pressing the surface. Nothing happened, the power having been cut off to the house.

Marcus cursed as he stomped barefoot and disheveled to the small command center inside. The screens were blank, the chair empty, but he was after the handheld set on the desk. It worked off batteries and crackled when he depressed the tab on the side. "Calling unit one." Nothing. "Calling unit two." More silence. "Fuck."

"Do you think they're all dead?" Darren asked.

"If they're not dead, then they're either out of

commission or were the ones who betrayed you." Kacy didn't pussyfoot around the truth.

"Probably dead. The guy I stashed in the cabana was on duty tonight as the fourth unit," Marcus revealed.

Betrayal from within.

"What do you say we go ask him some questions?" Kacy had some anger issues that needed to be worked out. She'd almost died tonight. And not in a blaze of glory. She'd almost succumbed to poison.

Before heading out back, she had Marcus arm her. The man at least had the common sense to keep weapons stashed around the house. A gun in hand made her feel better. Fuck anyone who might be watching.

Right now, keeping Darren safe was the only important thing. That and finding out who was behind the attempted hits.

Answers wouldn't be forthcoming, though. Entering the cabana, Marcus cursed. "Where the fuck is he? I had him tied to that chair."

A chair that still held traces of the curtain ties that Marcus had used to bind the fellow, but the guard-turned-traitor was gone.

"Now what?" Darren asked.

"I think it's time we consider getting you into a safe house. This place is compromised." Kacy hated to admit defeat, and yet, she'd come close to losing her client.

"Like hell," Darren snapped.

"She might be right," Marcus rumbled. "Whoever is after you went all out tonight."

"And?"

"And I think we need to put you somewhere where you can lie low until we figure out who's behind it."

"I'll make some phone calls." Harry would help Kacy find a place for Darren. She just hated to admit that she'd failed.

"You'll have to cancel your trip," Marcus stated.

"Like fuck am I hiding or canceling anything." Darren paced the living room of the cabana—which she should note was not only much more luxurious than her apartment, but bigger, too. "I am not letting these assassination attempts control my actions. Besides, where the hell else are we going to go?"

Anywhere but here would work. Kacy could think of innumerable options to keep a client safe. But Darren seemed determined to ignore common sense.

"How are you going to travel? In case you hadn't noticed, we have nothing to pack. Our bedrooms blew up with all our shit," Marcus noted.

"First off, our bags were already packed and by the front door. So long as they didn't get soaked or trampled, we're good to go. And if we're missing shit, then we can buy new stuff. Again."

Rich people and their money. They really thought nothing of dropping a few hundred, or in this case, thousands of dollars on clothing. Darren had already bought a new wardrobe for Kacy the previous day, having packages delivered with all kinds of expensive garments in her size—which she'd warned him she wasn't paying for.

She wagged a finger at him. "Clothes are easy to replace, but the gadgets I had to keep you safe, the things that blew up in the car yesterday, plus some of the stuff I had upstairs, are gone. If we go on this trip, then we'll be going in at a disadvantage." She'd lost her favorite gun to the explosion. Her knife, however, was in the pre-packed suitcase, along with her compact and lipstick combo, her shoes and her hair comb/lock pick. But the other toys she'd counted on—the listening devices, the poison pen, and other cool things Harry had sent her with wouldn't be easily replaced.

"You seem to forget I have connections. We might not have those items for the trip itself, but we'll manage until Harry can get us some new equipment. And if he can't, then we'll make do."

"Why are you so keen on taking this trip?" she asked.

Darren rolled his shoulders. "Because."

Marcus snorted. "Tell her the real reason."

Darren's lips flattened.

"Well?" Marcus sighed. "What he won't admit is he's curious. The whole thing has this big air of mystery around it, and he's intrigued."

"So what if I am? Whoever we're dealing with has money. And they know things. I'd be stupid to turn down an opportunity to see what they want."

"He has a death wish, doesn't he?" she asked Marcus.

"I am very much interested in living, but I'm also not going to become a paranoid shut-in."

"If you die, I'm blaming you," Kacy muttered. "It's going on my report that you ignored good advice."

"If I live, expect a bonus. Because we are going on this trip. Oh, and just to make it more tempting for you..."

Darren smiled. "Apparently, the person who's behind the assassination attempts will be there."

She paused by the window, keeping watch outside. "How do you know that?"

"I have my sources."

"From who?" she asked as she whirled to face him.

The only reply was an enigmatic smile as her client shut himself in the bedroom.

"He can't do that." She glared at the closed door. "He has to tell me."

"Darren will tell you when he's ready. And he's not going to change his mind about this trip."

"He'll find it hard to go if I break both his legs."

Marcus laughed. "He's never let that stop him before. He had me wheeling his ass around at the Super Bowl a few years ago rather than give up his boxed seats after a skiing incident."

"How does he think he can make this trip work?" She pointed to her dirty garments. "We look like refugees. No pilot worth his salt, even a privately chartered one, will let us on board like this."

"Nothing a shower and a change of clothes won't fix. I brought the suitcases in from the house." He waved to them. "Easy enough to clean up and get changed."

"Easy for you to say, those are your things. None of the shit in that case is mine, though."

"Then keep your dirty jeans."

"I can't do that."

"Why not? I think you look rather nice."

He what? The compliment took her off guard, and

she blamed her lack of sleep on the blush igniting her cheeks. "I look like a street thug." Whereas Marcus looked...big, bold, sexy. His bottoms rode low on his hips, but ignoring that vee angling down from his waist meant noticing the wide expanse of his chest.

"I've never wanted to kiss a thug before."

She couldn't have said who was more shocked. Him, because the red in his cheeks showed he'd not meant to say it, or her, because she wanted him to prove it.

"We can't get involved. The safety of the client comes first."

"I know. I shouldn't have said that." He dropped his gaze.

And she couldn't help an odd disappointment at his retraction.

"Ah, fuck it." He moved so fast, she didn't have time to react, his arms wrapping around her and lifting her off her feet.

Before she could exclaim, "What are you doing?" he showed her.

More like he kissed her. He slanted his hard mouth across hers with a sizzling need that ignited her own passion—an arousal that had simmered below the surface since they'd met. Was it only days ago? Because it felt longer.

Felt right.

For a moment, she allowed herself to relax and enjoy the embrace. She opened her mouth against the persistent probe of his tongue. Sighed against his mouth as he let his tongue twine intimately with hers.

Felt red-cheeked embarrassment as the client opened his door and said, "Our ride will be here at eight, which only gives us a few hours to rest. Carry on."

No, they wouldn't *carry on*. Because it shouldn't have happened.

She pushed against Marcus's wide chest, and for a moment, his hold on her tightened before loosening.

He set her on the floor.

To avoid temptation, she took a step back. Inhaled a deep breath. And then slugged him.

"Don't ever do that again."

Because she wasn't sure she had the willpower to say no if he did.

CHAPTER THIRTEEN

Kacy still wouldn't talk to him.

Or look at him.

Little pint tried to pretend she didn't notice him at all.

It stroked Marcus's ego to know she was very aware of him.

It scared the fuck out of him that he was only too aware of her, as well.

Currently, he sat behind the wheel of the car that had shown up at the house right at eight o'clock on the dot. A car that drove itself.

Marcus didn't trust it, hence his spot behind the wheel, and yet, he quickly learned that whatever controlled it wouldn't let him override. He could only hope they didn't crash.

Kacy sat in the back with his boss. Clean and dressed in clothes they'd found in the car. The packages neatly labeled with each of their names. The sizes inside perfect. The clothes... Well, that turned out to be interesting.

Marcus got a black T-shirt labeled *Security* with black khakis and boots. There was even underwear and socks for him, plus all his favorite toiletries.

For Darren, a casual suit in a crisp gray linen—no tie —also perfectly fitted and of quality fabric. It didn't come off any rack.

As for Kacy, hers came with a girly dress in a bright floral pattern, strappy heels, no bra, and... "A fucking G-string?" She held up the dental floss and twirled it on her finger, her expression aghast.

Marcus couldn't help but murmur for her ears only, "You don't have to wear it. I'm going commando."

Totally worth the red in her cheeks.

As to why they wore the clothing, it came with a typed note.

Shame about the fire. Please accept this token as a gift. We look forward to seeing you.

Darren thought it might be rude to refuse the present. Kacy didn't trust it and insisted on running her fingers along every seam, looking for anything out of place.

But the clothes appeared safe enough, and so they dressed in their new clothes, completely mystified as to how the person knew they needed them and had managed to get such a perfect fit in such a short time.

As soon as they got into the car, the doors locked, starting a mild panic from the passengers, especially once the vehicle started moving. Okay,

Marcus and Kacy panicked; Darren sat back with a cool smile.

"Chill. Let's see where it takes us."

The Zen attitude brought scowls to little pint's and Marcus's faces but...what other choice did they have? Shooting out the windows could backfire if they were bulletproof and the shot ricocheted.

The car purred, the electric engine a low hum as the car sped along the roads, keeping to within one mile of the speed limit, avoiding obstacles and even passing slow-moving traffic.

They were now on their way to... Well, they didn't actually know where they were going yet. The assumption was an airfield, but given the subterfuge thus far, it was anyone's guess at this point.

Of more interest, the car appeared to have no listening devices. Despite her bitching, Kacy hadn't lost all her toys after all. Her purse had survived the chaos, the explosion that blew out the doors having tossed the leather handbag out into the hall.

Kacy had clutched it to her chest when Marcus presented it to her.

Upon seeing the car, she'd immediately scanned it for electronics. However, other than the onboard navigation system that drove the car, she could find so sign of anyone looking or listening.

And even if they were, it was becoming more and more evident that whoever planned this secret trip knew things about them all, including Kacy's role in it because, amongst her toiletries was a holster and a new handgun.

"Tell me everything you know about this person who contacted you about this trip." As the car took them to destinations unknown, Kacy questioned Darren.

"They're rich. They know about me. And I am not the only one they invited."

"How do you know that?"

"I'm not at liberty to say." Darren bestowed the same enigmatic words and smile on Kacy that he had on Marcus when he'd first informed him of the trip.

"You do realize this could be a trap."

"Seems like an awful lot of trouble to arrange this kind of transportation just for a simple kill."

"Then maybe they want you for ransom."

"Who would pay it?" Darren shrugged. "Certainly not my company. If I die, the company will be split up among the shareholders. Any assets outside it will be donated to charity."

"Then what do you have that this person wants?"

He shrugged. "That's what I intend to find out."

"If you don't think they want you dead, then why the hit on your life? Surely you know of some reason someone would want you dead. A business adversary? Ex-lover? Someone you cut off in traffic?"

"I thought we'd ascertained already it was academy related."

"But why? You're not an academy graduate."

"How much did Harry tell you about me?"

"Not much." Her tone expressed her displeasure. "All I really know is that you're Harry's friend, and he thinks you're some kind of important shit. Important enough that he wanted me to guard your ass."

"Important shit." Darren's lips twitched. "You could say that."

"What does your company do that's so important?"

He grinned as he replied. "This and that."

She gave him the eye, the evil eye, the look all women seemed to know. Marcus had rarely experienced it, but he could feel the power from where he sat.

Under its force, Darren caved. "I'm part of Thorne Enterprises."

"*The* Thorne Enterprises?" She arched a brow. "Big name. Big company. What's your job with them?"

Marcus snorted. "Try king of it all."

"You own Thorne?"

He shrugged. "Yes, but I doubt that's why someone placed a contract on my life."

"Have you seen the contract? What are the terms?"

"Why bother asking now?" Marcus turned around in his seat, even if it felt wrong with the car in motion.

"Because now I want the full details. What happened last night..." She shook her head. "That was more than just an assassination attempt. Whoever wants Darren dead is willing to kill other people who get in their way. Willing to make a mess. That's not usual."

"What *is* usual?" Marcus asked.

"Sniper shots. Poison. A bomb. Even the natural gas poisoning would be in character. But having a gunman on the premises? Plus, the elimination of other employees?" Employees that Marcus had found—dead of gunshot wounds—and disposed of in the swamp. "That's taking a hit pretty damned far."

"Marcus, do you still have a screenshot of the offer?" Darren asked with good reason since the original post had disappeared from the Dark Web. Which didn't mean the original buyer had pulled the deal. More than likely, they'd gotten enough offers that someone would get the job done.

Marcus shook his wrist and, a moment later, handed his watch over the seat. She grabbed it and growled when it wouldn't unlock.

He reached between the seats and pressed his finger against the screen.

"It's in the gallery," he offered, withdrawing his hand.

She stroked the screen as she flipped to it. It didn't take her long to read the short post and frown. "It's a general call asking for the death of someone called Dominus." She looked over at Darren. "That's you?"

"Yes. It's my code name."

Realization dawned on her face. "You're academy trained?"

He nodded.

"You don't look it."

Marcus almost snickered at the disparagement inherent in the statement.

"Because I only did a partial training."

"Flunked out." Her smirk couldn't be hidden.

He shook his head. "Not exactly. My academy lessons only had a small focus on the physical. I had other pressing matters that I needed to be taught."

"Like?"

"I can't tell. Academy secrets." Darren shrugged. "Suffice it to say, I know of the academy and the fact that you and Harry and countless others were trained there."

"Marcus, too?"

Sitting in the front but listening in, Marcus shook his head. "No. I am the product of our military program."

"That explains a lot," she muttered. To Darren, she said, "Why would they come after you? You said it yourself, you're not the usual kind of graduate."

"Because I'm something more. What do you know of the Secundus Academy and its founders?"

She shrugged. "Not much other than some rich dude created it. Perhaps they taught its history at school, but I had this habit of sleeping through classes that bored me."

"That sounds familiar." Marcus had done the same thing. "When my teacher gave me detention and asked me why I had no interest in our past, I told him dead people couldn't affect the future."

At that, Kacy snickered. "Mine said the past repeated itself, and I told him I disagreed. People are the ones who keep fucking up over and over. As far as I can tell, history doesn't teach anyone any lessons."

"Two peas in a fucking pod," Darren remarked. "And you both might be right, but in this case, the history of the academy is important, especially since not many people know the story. Let me ask, if you had to guess, why do you think the academy was created?"

"To have an army of specialists so the founder of it could rule the world."

"Ruling the world sounds like a lot of work," Marcus remarked from the front.

"You've got that right." Darren laughed. "And no, the school wasn't created for such an enormous purpose. The original founder of the school was rich, that much is true, but it might surprise you to learn that he was the most non-violent man you could ever meet. Perhaps he ran his businesses with a bit of a strict fist, but he was fair with his employees. Rewarded hard work. People respected him. But, as with anyone who makes money, there are some who envy it. Who don't want to put in the hard work. Who think the world owes them. Who think they own the world."

"I've met those kinds of people." Her lips turned down, and Marcus wondered whom Darren's description had made her think of. "Someone shook down the rich dude."

"Indeed. They demanded money. A lot of it. Claimed if he wanted to stay in business, then he needed to pay up...or else. Being a man of principle, the man said no. The gang vandalized his place of business, so he went to the police. The police, bribed and scared of the gang, said 'sorry we can't help you. Pay up.'"

"But he didn't want to pay."

Kacy took the words right out of Marcus's brain. Because people with morals couldn't understand people who didn't have any. They didn't realize that being right wasn't enough.

"He refused to pay them. Told them they could

vandalize as much as they wanted but he would rebuild and never give in. So the gang killed his wife."

"So he built the academy to create an army to protect him."

Darren shook his head. "Not exactly. Initially, he wanted revenge. In his grief, he wanted to make someone pay. Despite the obvious murder of his wife, the cops would do nothing. The law wouldn't help him, and so he decided to take care of it himself, a man who'd never fired a gun in his life. He went after the gang with a revolver he'd bought."

"And he killed them? I find that hard to believe. Only in the movies do inexperienced good guys beat the bad ones."

Actually, not entirely true. Marcus had seen it happen overseas. Just not often.

"Not a single one of those killers died. Instead, they beat the ever loving shit out of the man. But they didn't kill him. They left him alive and told him to pay up, or they'd start killing his children. However, the man became angry at the threat to his children's lives. He didn't want to bow down to crooks. To give in to blackmail. He realized that it would never stop. So he went out and hired his own gang. Gave them twice as much money as the gang demanded."

"Because it was never about money. He just wanted revenge."

"He did, and then the same people he hired tried to blackmail him. Because, you see, career thieves and killers have no loyalty to anyone but themselves. And the man thought, 'this isn't right. How can we fight against this?' He found the answer in the strangest place. In a bar where he got drunk and met a man named Kringle."

"Kringle. As in Sergeant Kringle?" Kacy's expression brightened.

"The very same."

"He trained me at the academy. He's a tough old bastard."

"He is. As you know, Kringle used to be a military sniper. He killed so many people, and yet he didn't sink into the darkness that seduces many. The man asked him, 'why did you stop?'"

"You stop because a true soldier doesn't kill for no reason." Marcus uttered the answer, and she tossed him a sharp look. He'd learned that lesson in the military. Those who didn't got discharged or sent to serve on the front lines.

"Marcus nailed it. The difference between thugs who kill for a reason and those who don't is a matter of discipline. Order. Soldiers don't want to kill. Soldiers kill because it's their job. When the job is over, they stop. So the man asked the retired soldier if he would work for him. And Kringle killed all the scum who had turned on the man. When it was done, the man asked him, 'how can we make more of you?' Because, see, the man knew he wasn't the only one who needed help. All around the world, injustice kept happening."

"Injustice will always happen," Marcus said softly. "Because there will always be greed."

"And laziness," she added. "Not everyone wants to

work hard. Some people just want to take."

"Exactly," said Darren. "And the founder was tired of the imbalance. So he asked Kringle what they could do. The sergeant told him that to fight injustice, you needed people of honor, people not hamstrung by laws or morals but with the skills and the mental fortitude to do what has to be done. People who will do what they're ordered and nothing more."

"For a price."

"Yes, a price, because without payment, without a set mission, the people have no guidance. How do they decide who lives and dies? How do they, in turn, live with their choices?"

"Someone makes the choices for them, and it becomes a job." Kacy peered at Darren. "You seem to know an awful lot about the academy and its founding. Why?"

"The woman in the story, the woman who was killed, she was my mother."

At that, Kacy snapped her mouth shut.

"Is your dad still running the academy?" she asked after a moment.

"I made him retire to a nice island in the Pacific a few years ago. I run the academy now, along with a few other people I trust, like my brother, and a cousin. The reasoning being that this kind of endeavor should never be in the hands of just one person."

"Just in case he turns into Dr. Evil and wants to rule the world," Marcus interjected.

"Can you imagine the paperwork?" Darren rolled his

eyes and laughed. "Anyhow, that was close to thirty years ago. Now, there are several academies in the world. Each of them unaware of the others, all the graduates abiding by the code."

A lengthy code that was drilled into them but that boiled down to a few basic rules. Break them only if you had a last will and testament because the academy didn't fuck around. It also had a strict code of silence. Marcus might not have gone to the academy, but he knew enough about it.

"He's not an academy graduate." She jerked her head toward Marcus.

"No. But not for lack of trying. Were you young when you were recruited?"

"Fifteen," she admitted. No point in hiding it. Darren could probably pull the file on any student he wanted. "I graduated at twenty and immediately went to work for Harry."

"Harry was your sponsor."

She gave him a sharp look. "You read my file."

"Darned right I did. You didn't seriously think I'd let just anyone close to me?"

"He wouldn't let me read it." Disgruntlement colored Marcus's words. Damned academy secrets.

"Kacy's training and past are no one's business."

"But you know." Her lips flattened.

"I do, but I promise not to tell. If you don't mind, let me ask you since I don't often get a chance being the man behind the scenes, what do you think of the academy?"

She slanted a look at Darren and then Marcus. He could see the indecision in her face.

"Tell him," Marcus urged softly. "He deserves to know if he's made a difference." Because Darren certainly had with Marcus.

For a moment, Marcus expected her to shut down and tell them both to fuck off, but her shoulders slumped.

"When I was fifteen, I was attacked by some boys I knew."

The car bucked as Marcus punched the steering wheel.

"Pothole," Marcus mumbled.

Her gaze narrowed.

Darren cleared his throat. "Continue."

She shrugged. "What can I say other than if Harry hadn't come to my rescue, I'd have probably ended up gang-raped before being sold on the street to cover my brother's debts."

"Fucking kill them." Again mumbled by Marcus, who stared intently at the road ahead because if he looked at her, if he saw any hint of pain, he'd have to hurt something. Someone.

But ignoring her wasn't in him. He found his gaze watching her in the rearview mirror.

Head bowed, she stared at her hands. It killed him. She fidgeted, probably feeling the combined weight of his and Darren's stares.

"Even if they hadn't attacked me, I was looking at a shitty future, one that would have resulted in me either being a street whore or hooking up with an *hombre* for protection and popping out babies for welfare checks."

"You could have run away," Marcus snapped. How could this strong and vibrant woman ever for a moment have allowed this shit to happen? The Kacy he knew would never have stood for it. But the Kacy he knew now was probably a far cry from the one at fifteen, facing shit no girl should ever face.

"Running doesn't solve problems."

Gently, Darren prodded her. Marcus wanted to tell him to stop. Couldn't he see how uncomfortable it made Kacy? Yet, at the same time, he wanted to know the whole story because it explained so much.

"Harry saved you and brought you to the academy. Do you miss your family?"

"No." She squirmed in her seat. "I didn't abandon them. I couldn't. How could I leave my mother alone to deal with my brothers? To suffer the pain of losing her only daughter?"

"I thought one of the academy rules was you had to cut all ties to your former life," Marcus said turning his head, showing he followed the story.

"Exceptions can be made," Darren replied. "Keep in mind, most academy students come from broken homes and foster care where there are few ties to sever. But it's not recommended that students keep in touch. Especially those who will eventually have to work undercover."

"They told me all this when I joined, but I wouldn't budge. And when I told Harry I'd rather stay home with my mother than lose her forever, he made a deal with me."

"What was the deal?"

"If I promised to work my ass off, then the academy would take care of my mother, but my brothers were on their own."

Which made Marcus wonder just how bad her brothers were.

"According to your file, you graduated second in your class."

A moue of annoyance creased her features. "Only because the number one guy outweighed me and took me down to the mat each time."

"Size matters, little pint." Marcus grinned, especially since he could see the red staining her cheeks in the mirror. "I think we're here."

The car had pulled to a stop before Darren got her to divulge any more secrets.

"Don't get out of the car," she warned Darren. She pulled the gun free from the holster hidden under the skirt of her dress. "Marcus. Take a look around."

A look around at what? He stepped out of the car, pulling free his own weapon, his shades preventing him from squinting in the bright glare of the sun.

The car that had driven itself had stopped on the gravel shoulder of a road that wound along the coast. Eroding wooden posts kept traffic from veering onto the low-lying shoreline, a barren stretch that had only a few sparse people enjoying the sun and waves. The other side of the road was bordered by a steep cliff, atop which sat expansive homes and towering condominiums, places with money to burn and epic views. What he didn't see was a plane or a reason for them to be here.

With one arm braced on the car, he leaned down and poked his head in. "I don't see anything, but then again, I don't know what I'm looking for."

Kacy leaned forward to speak to him through the seats. "If they're planning a hit, then they're probably up on the cliffs. And don't be fooled by the folks on the beach."

Yet they seemed so mundane. The guy with the flapping shirt wearing the wide-brimmed hat and sweeping the sand with a metal detector didn't seem harmful, and neither did the mother in the one-piece suit chasing after a little boy who squealed as he ran through the waves. The traffic didn't stop moving, with cars sweeping past in a constant stream.

Closing the door to the car, Marcus leaned against it and tried to keep an eye on everything, but the space was too vast. There was so much to distract, including the helicopter flying low overhead.

Lower.

The fucking thing kept dropping, causing the mother to screech and sweep her child close while the guy looking for treasure raised an arm over his eyes and shouted something that was lost in the wind and noise of the rotor blades.

The helicopter alit on the sand and waited. The passenger door of the car opened, and Darren stepped out, despite Kacy yelling, "Get your ass back in here. We don't know if it's safe." Probably not, but that didn't stop Darren. He held out his hand for Kacy, who emerged from the car with a scowl. "Keep ignoring me, and I'll collect the bounty myself," she snapped.

"I already said, if they wanted me dead, they could have done so by now."

"Your optimism makes me wonder if you have a brain tumor," she griped as Marcus grabbed their luggage and walked with them to the chopper. Darren kept his hand on her waist to prevent her from helping.

"Assuming the worst doesn't accomplish anything. A million things could kill me. Does that mean I should never leave the house, walk down some stairs, eat a grape?"

"No, but there's nothing wrong with caution, like wearing a bulletproof vest when you leave the house, holding the railing when you go down the stairs, and cutting those grapes into smaller pieces."

"And miss out on that sweet crunch when you bite down on a whole one?" Darren grinned. "Lighten up."

"I'll lighten up when we survive this trip."

"There's the spirit," Darren said as he walked her to the helicopter. "Shall we see what adventure awaits us?"

"Fine, but you'd better hope it's not death," she said, clambering into the chopper's small cabin.

Famous last words that later proved prophetic when the pilot jumped out mid-flight and the helicopter began to plummet.

CHAPTER FOURTEEN

THERE WERE ONLY A FEW THINGS THAT FREAKED Kacy out.

The underwear currently flossing her cheeks.

Not having a weapon handy.

And helicopters whose pilots suddenly shoved open a door while crossing an ocean and dove out. The fucker even had a parachute that he popped open so he could drift down slowly, aiming for the motorboat keeping pace with them below.

"The academy didn't train me for this," Kacy muttered.

Hot-wire a car? She could do it in under a minute. Even the newer models were no match for her.

Ride a motorcycle? She could even pop a wheelie if the bike wasn't too heavy.

She could absolutely drive a speedboat and had once managed to time her wave jumping so well, she landed on top of her suspect and his slower piece of shit.

But things that flew?

Ah, hell no.

"Motherfucker screwed us," Marcus muttered before unbuckling and popping out of his seat. He'd chosen to sit in the front with the asshole but hadn't been quick enough to grab the pilot before he jumped. Then again, who would suspect a pilot with a jovial smile who told them to, "Look at the dolphins jumping," to be a kamikaze asshole who didn't mind jumping out of a moving aircraft hundreds of feet in the air?

Marcus leaned over the pilot's seat and grabbed hold of an oh-shit bar. He leaned partially out and aimed his gun.

Pop.

A peek out her window showed Marcus hadn't missed. The parachute spun and flopped around, plummeting fast and hard before hitting the water with a splash.

And sinking.

"He's dead," Marcus announced.

Lovely, however, the fact that there was no pilot meant—

"We're going to crash!" She might have screamed like a girl.

"No, we're not." Marcus shifted himself in the front of the cab, which caused the helicopter to wobble because, oh yeah...

There was no fucking pilot!

Who was that whimpering?

Marcus settled himself into the vacated seat and grabbed hold of the controls.

It somewhat put her mind at ease. "You know how to fly a 'copter?" She shouldn't have been so surprised. He'd probably trained in the military. He certainly had good aim under pressure. That wasn't an easy shot he'd made, especially with a revolver.

"Not really. But I did participate in some flight simulation programs while in the Army."

"That's better than nothing." She tried to sound more reassured than she felt.

He completely squashed it with his next words. "If you say so. I flunked out of flight training because I crashed each time."

The panic returned. She dug her nails into her seat, gouging the fabric and not caring.

Darren saw her panic and patted her thigh. "Don't worry. I'm sure Marcus will figure it out."

A brash man, Marcus boasted, "Of course I will. How hard can it be? It's got a motor. I'm a man. It should come naturally."

If she weren't afraid of tipping them, she might have lunged forward to throttle him. She settled for yelling, "Are you fucking kidding me?"

"If anyone can do this, Marcus can," soothed Darren. "Especially if you promise him a kiss."

"I am not promising him anything."

The helicopter dipped. She squeaked and clenched her eyes tight.

"Are you sure you don't want to give him an incentive?" Darren prodded.

"Fine. He can have a kiss. A whole bunch of them. But only if we don't die."

"Prepare to pucker those lips, little pint."

The helicopter shuddered.

She ducked her head and began to pray in Spanish.

The 'copter wobbled.

Her jaw locked so tight, her teeth verged on cracking.

The flight evened out. Not even a slight tremble rocked them.

She dared to peek out of an eye. When she noticed they weren't plunging to a watery death, she pried open the other.

"We're not crashing?"

"Nope." Marcus sounded so smugly pleased. "You owe me a kiss."

She noticed something perturbing. "Hold on a second. Why aren't your hands on the controls?"

He waggled them in the air. "Funny thing happened. While I was trying to figure it out, I lost all control. Something took over. Turns out there's some kind of autopilot on this thing, too."

"Why you lying bastard. I am not kissing you."

"Are you welshing already?"

"You're not flying."

"You never said I had to fly this thing, only that we weren't to die. I'm holding up my end of the bargain. Are you going to honor yours?"

"Yes." Spoken through gritted teeth. Yet, it wasn't

really anger driving her. Okay, a little bit of ire because both men had conned her into agreeing, but more annoyance from the fact that she would have promised a lot more than a kiss if asked. "You'll get your bloody kiss."

"Keep it. With that kind of enthusiasm, you can forget you owe me." Marcus appeared annoyed at her for some reason.

"I said I'd do it."

"Well, now I don't want you to," he barked back. "I'd rather kiss someone who doesn't act as if I'm asking her to do something repulsive. There are plenty of women who don't mind kissing me. I'll find one of those instead."

Find someone else? For a moment, a red film descended over her, one with a hint of green. "Why, you—"

Darren interrupted. "I think we're heading to that island."

The observation had them all peeking out the windows of the craft and noticing a lush, green mass of land. The 'copter appeared to be aiming for a massive dock that projected from the shore of the island, a long, narrow strip that ended in a wide platform. The massive square bore a giant, painted X contained inside a circle.

As the craft dipped—nice time to remember that no one actually flew this thing—Kacy's fingers once again dug into her seat. Give her a wall to climb, or even a building to scale, and she wouldn't hesitate. But flying... If God had meant mankind to fly, he'd have given them wings.

The 'copter landed lightly on the dock, and the

engines powered down, but it still took a moment for Kacy to uncurl her fingers.

"Safe and sound while another assassin bites the dust. I am expecting a big bottle of booze as my bonus for Christmas this year," Marcus joked before he swung out of the chopper. A moment later, he opened the door and helped Darren out, who then turned around to give Kacy a hand.

All these stupid manners, treating her like a girl when she could have just jumped out by herself.

When Darren slid his arm around her waist, she remembered to paste a smile on her face. Now that they'd arrived on this mystery island, the show would begin. Staying in character would now be of utmost importance.

Since ladies expected men to guide them—because without the arm around their waist they'd surely get lost —she forewent twisting Darren's arm and sending him to his knees.

Being a lady also meant no whirling around to punch Marcus, even though she heard him snicker.

There was no one on the fat part of the dock to meet them, but on the shore, she could see someone in a white pantsuit waiting. Her heels clicked on the boards as they moved. With a smile pasted on her face, she pretended idle chatter with Darren.

"We're going to have to wing it from here on out. Whatever you do, stick close to Marcus or me. Don't eat anything unless I've had a chance to check it out first."

"Am I allowed to bathe?"

"Only if I've checked the bathroom first for poisonous critters."

"Ocean swims?"

"Do you have a death wish?"

"You're sucking all the fun out of this tropical paradise already," Darren muttered. "Anything else?"

"Don't get killed."

"I'll do my best."

"No, he won't," muttered Marcus.

Any reply she might have had literally blew away as a strong ocean gust lifted her skirt at the back, high enough that she felt the breeze brushing her bare cheeks. Head held high, she tried to pretend she'd not just flashed Marcus her ass.

He, on the other hand, didn't seem inclined to ignore it because, as they approached the end of the pier, he brushed past her saying, "Nice cheeks."

Red cheeks was more apt.

Leaning close to Darren, she asked, "Is the guy in the suit who arranged for you to come?"

"Doubtful. Take a look at what he's carrying."

Probably weren't too many rich *hombres* who stood waiting like a servant with a towel folded over an arm and a tray of drinks.

She didn't get to observe much because Marcus stood in front of them, looking every inch the big and burly guard. Staring at his broad back, she couldn't help but wonder if he'd truly meant what he said about kissing other girls.

Let him.

She didn't care.

Although, if he let any women get in the way of him doing his job—and if they pissed her off—they were on an island surrounded by water. It wouldn't be hard to get rid of a body.

"Welcome, Mr. Thorne, and, of course, your lovely guest." She bit her lip lest she snicker when the servant bowed. "The master couldn't be on hand to greet you but wishes you welcome."

"Welcome to where?" Darren asked.

"Paradise."

Kacy had to admit, the name fit the location, as Gerard—such a proper butler name—led them along stone paths on foot. They'd eschewed the offer of a golf cart. After the incident with the helicopter, they all preferred to be in control of where their bodies went.

The lush island boasted numerous wide paths comprised of crushed seashells that meandered through a vegetative jungle bright with blooms and redolent with flowery perfume. While Kacy didn't spot any bugs, she noticed brightly colored birds dipping in and out of the foliage. A closer glance showed feeders where they could alight and feast. The owner of the isle might have eliminated the bug population, but had ensured that the feathery ones stayed fed, or so Gerard explained as he pointed out the island's attributes.

The manservant didn't just keep a steady dialogue going. He also answered almost all of their questions.

"How many people are there on the island?" Darren asked.

"Quite a few if you include staff. And given that our master has invited so many guests, we've had to bring in extra."

Playing the part of arm candy—blech—Kacy asked, "What kind of amenities do you have?"

"Three pools interconnected by a lazy river that goes around the entire island. You can hop into it from any of the guest cabanas on the isle. Foam noodles and other flotation devices are available upon request."

"A blow-up ring would be nice," Kacy remarked. "Marcus has enough hot air to inflate it no problem."

Gerard didn't even crack a smile. "There is a tennis court on the east side of the island. A fully equipped gymnasium is attached to the main house. Meals will be served on the grand terrace if the weather is cooperative. In the great room if it's not. But you can also choose to have room service. Simply use the intercom system to place your request with staff."

"Intercoms? What about a phone? And Wi-Fi? I seem to be having a problem getting a signal." Darren held up his phone. A new one since his old one had gotten blown up. Apparently, he kept spares stashed around his house because he had a habit of losing them.

"Unfortunately, there is no service on the island, but should you require contact with the mainland, there is a satellite phone option in the main house."

How convenient.

Not.

What she didn't mention was that her cell phone in her purse already worked off a satellite. What surprised her was that Darren's supposedly didn't. Or was he stringing Gerard along...?

"Here is the guest house you'll be using during your stay. Unfortunately, it doesn't have two bedrooms like some of the others, so we had to make other accommodations for your security detail."

"I'm sure whatever you have will be fine. Marcus is used to roughing it." Darren clapped his bodyguard on the back. Marcus, for his part, looked big and mean.

As Gerard explained the attributes of the cabana, Kacy looked around. The outside appeared to be made of planking, painted a pastel pink with bright yellow shutters and a thickly thatched roof that rose into a peak. The windows set in the walls of the building were round and obviously custom with their wooden frames painted white.

Stepping inside, she noted that the luxurious guesthouse boasted a simple living area and, closed off from it with sliding, wicker doors, a large bedroom and a decadent bathroom. The height of opulent island living.

For Kacy and Darren, at least. As for Marcus, he got the utility room that could only be entered from the outside around the side of the house. A tight space with a few rough shelves holding empty jars, and on one wall, an electrical panel that hummed. Wires ran thickly out of it into the house. Whatever tools had used to reside in the space had been removed, and the floor swept to allow the addition of a cot.

Marcus glared at the space and then looked at his boss. "They can't seriously expect me to sleep in here."

"You could always try the couch," Darren offered.

"Me and wicker furniture don't get along. I'll move this bed inside."

"And give our host the impression we don't trust their security and accommodations?"

Kacy jumped in to help Marcus. "Considering the helicopter pilot they hired jumped out and wanted us to crash, I'm sure they'll forgive any precautions we take."

Besides, having Marcus nearby would reassure her. The cabana assigned to them was a nightmare from a security standpoint. None of the windows actually locked. The doors either. Anyone could walk in with the least bit of effort. And a thatched roof? All it would take was one flaming arrow to set the place on fire.

Which, she would note, she'd never actually heard of or seen happen, but given the lengths the assassins kept going to, she wouldn't put it past them.

Exiting Marcus's solitary cell—try sneaking a girl in there, snicker—they returned to the pink cabana, and Kacy pursed her lips, looking around. She'd thought to grab her purse from the helicopter when they hopped out, and she rummaged through it as Darren spoke.

"This place is amazing. According to Gerard, we have about two hours before the gathering of the guests for the evening reception. I say we get ready now so we can go exploring. I wouldn't mind checking out the lazy river thing."

"If I'm going to do my face, then don't expect me to go into the water," Kacy sassed, using that opening to pull out her compact and pretend to reapply her lip gloss.

"You don't need makeup, baby."

Snapping the compact shut, Kacy uttered a false laugh. "Says the man who wakes up looking like a chiseled god. Is it me, or is it dark in here?" She walked over to a lamp and casually grabbed the nodule sitting on it. She dropped it into the glass of wine they'd arrived with. Then, signaling Darren to keep talking, she kept roving.

"If you don't want to go for a swim, then how about a walk?" Darren said. "I wouldn't mind checking out the tennis court. It's been a while since..."

As he continued to speak, she snared the listening device on the windowsill. It met a watery death.

Heading into the bedroom again, she knew what to look for and snared a third bug from the lamp, and yet another from in the bathroom. Checking again with her compact, she was finally satisfied that they were clear, or as clear as could be expected.

Given the gun in their special package of replacement items, whoever had brought them here obviously already knew or suspected what Kacy was. But that didn't mean their host had planted the bugs. The assassins had obviously infiltrated Darren's plans to come here, and Gerard had said they'd brought in extra folk to work. Anyone could be an assassin.

Fun. But only if the boys listened.

Adopting a more businesslike persona, Kacy snapped out orders. "Marcus, you go and check out this place. Figure out how many people are on the island."

"A lot."

"Smartass. I want a more specific number than just *a*

lot. See if you can get the name of our host, too. Also, keep an eye out for a way off this island. Helicopter, obviously, but what about boats? You"—she pointed to Darren—"are going to see who you recognize when we go out and mingle. If you don't know them, get a name so we can run a check."

"Without a phone or Internet access?" Marcus raised a brow in doubt.

"I have my ways." Hopefully, she wouldn't get caught using her specialized methods because that would cause a bit of a dilemma. Touch her phone, and someone might die.

Darren laughed. "I feel like I'm on an episode of *Mission: Impossible.*"

"More like the *A-Team,*" Marcus grumbled.

"Only if I get to be Mr. T," she quipped. "He had the best lines."

With their roles set, Marcus left while she and Darren prepped for their evening. They took turns bathing, her guarding the door by sitting on the vanity while he showered first, making exaggerated groans of pleasure and a few, "Oh yeah, baby," exclamations that had her rolling her eyes. But she could hardly bitch him out for trying to act in character just in case someone listened outside. The high windows wouldn't allow anyone to peek in, but someone could lurk outside, spying.

When he stepped out of the shower, it was her turn to drop her clothes on the floor—only after she made a gesture that clearly indicated she'd rip his eyes from his head if he peeked. With his back turned to her, Darren kept up his crazy vocal byplay of their fake lovemaking to the point that she felt she had to contribute with an exaggerated, "*Dios*, you're soooo big."

Then she had to hide her giggles in the pouring spray while Darren's shoulders shook.

Interesting how she could joke about sex with Darren, and yet Marcus, whom she'd known just as long, would have probably disquieted her.

Me, tongue-tied and flustered because of a man. If her mother knew, she'd be calling her pastor and setting a date.

Mama still had dreams of her only daughter getting married.

Shutting off the shower, she wrapped her hair in a towel and another around her body. Darren wore his around his hips, leaving his upper body bare. It looked good. Real good. She didn't feel a thing.

Emerging in towels, she noted their luggage in the room. Had Marcus brought it in or someone else?

Did it matter? She couldn't exactly raise a stink about it. She pulled out her knife and its holster from the suitcase and strapped it to her thigh. She shook her head at the clothes Darren had bought to replace her previous wardrobe. She hated it all on sight.

"What is wrong with a pair of comfy denim cutoffs?" she moaned. Everything in the suitcase required hanging and ironing. It was also a lot more feminine than she liked. The bikini would probably never get any use, mostly because the little triangles just wouldn't cover enough. She preferred a one-piece to swim in. It tended to stay on when diving off high places.

She dressed while still grumbling, and when they emerged from the bedroom, they found a tray of snacks and a sweating pitcher of water in the bedroom. Kacy hated that the staff came and went as they pleased, but she couldn't make a stink about it, not unless she wanted to draw attention.

Rich folk expected staff to wait on them hand and foot. Most of the wealthy didn't even notice them scurrying about doing their chores.

Kacy did, though. She remained all too conscious of the fact that the staff appeared comprised of a mix of Jamaicans, their dark skin and bright smiles along with their French accent giving their heritage away and, on the other end of the spectrum, the tanned, dark-haired servants with their rapid-fire Spanish.

Kacy looked more like the staff than a guest, a fact she felt became glaringly obvious once they made it to the main house to mingle. The fine clothes she wore didn't detract from the fact that she felt out of place. With her tanned skin and obvious Latin heritage, she should have been one of the people serving drinks, not sipping them.

Darren slid an arm around her waist, and she was so proud of herself. She didn't flinch or break his hand.

He whispered, "What's wrong?"

"They'll know I'm a fraud."

"Only because you're scowling."

"A smile won't hide the fact that they'll just see a girl from the *barrio*."

"Only if you tell them. As of this moment, consider yourself a Spanish heiress, whose father made a fortune in shawls."

"Shawls?" she quipped.

"Fancy ones."

"That's dumb."

"Then think of something better. That shouldn't be hard. You're academy trained. Act like it."

The rebuke served as a reminder that her past and her doubts didn't have any bearing on the here and now. If she wanted people to believe she belonged here, she had to act as if she did.

Chin up. Shoulders back. Time to stop letting the obvious wealth in this place intimidate. These people weren't any better than she. They peed the same, and some probably farted, too. Except for the lady in the tight, silver-sequined gown. She'd probably pop a stitch if she let one rip.

After that, the smile proved easier to paste on her face, the act not so onerous. And that was all it was, an act.

But people bought it. Kacy mingled and chatted and did all the things rich people did, including eating little bite-sized pieces of food—no wonder they were all so skinny—and drinking copious amounts of wine. At least, *they* drank the wine. Kacy found ways to dispose of hers so it looked as if she imbibed more than she did.

All the time, she observed. She noted there appeared to be seven different couples. Six of them with men in their forties or older. But the women varied in age from young enough to be their partner's daughter to probably married thirty-plus years. The seventh couple was a Mrs. Robinson combination, with a gorgeous woman in her fifties, perhaps even older, accompanied by a boy toy who looked yummy in a suit. He didn't talk much, just smiled and kept his arm around his date.

It seemed everyone had brought a partner. At least two she figured were security, and she told that to Darren, whispering in his ear. "The redhead with the British fellow is security. She's wearing a gun." Kacy recognized the walk that female operatives adopted when wearing a thigh piece. "And the Asian woman. Her date is also a bodyguard, I'd wager."

"Are you sure? He seems kind of old," Darren murmured back. "I saw them kissing earlier."

"They might be screwing, but he's also wearing a piece."

Which surprised her. She would have thought their host would have disarmed them all. Then again, how comfortable would these people be if they felt as if they were at the mercy of their unknown host?

Although introductions were made, most neglected to offer last names. Those who did a full introduction were folks that Darren claimed were public figures. In other words, their faces were known, so there was no point in hiding.

As the owner of Thorne Enterprises, Darren was one of those people who didn't conceal his identity. Smart— because each time he shook a hand and said his name, she could watch for a flicker of something in the other person's eyes—but dumb, as well. He appeared determined to paint a bull's-eye on himself.

Being rich, none of them came out and asked why they were here or speculated aloud about their mysterious host. It was enough to drive Kacy batty.

Pretending to kiss Darren, pulling his head down and keeping them tilted sideways so her hair shielded their lips, she whispered, "Why is everyone acting like this is some kind of beachside holiday?"

Darren chuckled. "Because no one wants to be the first to admit their curiosity. Nobody wants to admit that they know nothing."

"Pride? But for all they know, this is a trap."

"Yes. And those who feared for their lives probably turned down the invitation. Those who couldn't stand the curiosity accepted."

"Money won't save you from a bullet."

"No, but money does mean that whoever our host is needs to tread carefully. I might not know each of these people by name or face, but there is enough combined power on this island to draw considerable attention should something untoward happen to us."

His belief proved a cold comfort as she spent another hour pretending to smile and exchange the most inane chitchat.

Only a brief moment with the redhead who asked, "What agency are you with?" proved that Kacy wasn't the only one who found this whole affair surreal—and dangerous.

The evening wound down as the stars made an

appearance with couples drifting off in the directions of their cabins.

Pretending to toss back one last glass of champagne, which Kacy actually poured out in a sleight of hand that the academy Magician—the code name he replied to—would applaud, she declared herself ready for bed. Wink. Wink.

Darren grinned. "Bed sounds like a great idea."

In keeping with her drunken persona, she adopted a stumble and giggle for their walk back to their cabana. Her erratic swaying and occasional giddy spins allowed her to peer into pockets of shadow and look for danger behind them.

Arriving at their abode, she noticed the door to the utility shed stood open, the cot inside visible and empty. Marcus hadn't moved his bed after all, and she didn't spot any sign of him.

I am not worried. Nope, that nagging feeling in her gut had more to do with the tiny bites of food she'd eaten. It wouldn't be a bullet that killed her, but starvation.

Following Darren into the bedroom, she danced around, keeping up the pretense as she held up her lipstick and bobbled, trying to find her mouth.

The room still appeared clean.

She stopped the act. "What's your first impression?"

"Of the island or the people?"

"Everything. You recognized a couple."

"I recognized a few of them, and I'd bet if I had a computer, I'd quickly figure out the others."

"Any clue as to what you all have in common?"

His brow arched. "Other than the obvious wealth?"

"Are your business interests aligned?"

"Not in the least. Madame Bouvier, the lady with the younger companion, deals in lingerie and sexual enhancements for older women."

Kacy's nose wrinkled. "That doesn't seem to have anything in common with that guy from Australia, who is a cattleman."

"I'm going to guess there is something else that binds us together."

She planned to discover that reason. "Get ready for bed and don't leave this room." She slipped off her high-heeled shoes and laid them in front of the bathroom door. The windows were high and narrow; however, that wouldn't stop someone wily and of slim build. "I'll leave you my gun."

"Why? Where are you going?"

"I'm going to find Marcus and see if he has any news for us." Because she didn't like the fact that he hadn't met them at the door.

Still not worried about him. He's a big boy. But he wasn't academy trained.

Leaving the client alone was not an approved academy strategy; however, she didn't plan to go far, and she ensured she'd hear if something happened. Working quickly, she strung items across the sliding door to their deck that led down to the beach. She layered more things on the windowsill. If anyone tried to come in, they'd make enough noise. She hoped.

"Will you hear this over your snoring?" Kacy asked.

"I do have some sense of preservation," he retorted.

"Not really, because if you did, we'd have never come here."

"Where would the fun be in that? I thought the academy trained its operatives to take chances."

"Operatives, yes. Clients, no."

"You're no fun." Said with a smile as Darren laced his hands behind his head.

She was okay with that. "Here. Keep this handy in case you need it." This being her gun. She chose to tuck a knife into the sheath on her thigh because only dumb girls went out unarmed.

Leaving Darren, she strung more items across the threshold of the bedroom door. A vase, a few seashells. The knickknacks in this place proved plenty.

Emerging from the cabana, she noted the shed door still stood open, and the strand of Christmas lights strung along the path provided only faint illumination.

She didn't have the slightest idea where to start looking for Marcus. Calling out for him probably wasn't the brightest idea either.

To anyone watching, she had to appear as if she had a purpose, so she muttered, "Where does a girl find some wine in this place?"

She didn't expect a reply, and most definitely didn't anticipate the hand that slapped over her mouth.

So she bit it.

Hard.

CHAPTER FIFTEEN

"Ow! Why are you biting me?" Marcus couldn't help but yelp as Kacy's sharp teeth nipped him.

He removed his hand from her mouth but kept her tucked against him in the shadows, mostly because he liked the feel of her. She didn't thrash or elbow him in the nuts, yet, so he enjoyed the cheap thrill of holding her while he could.

"If you don't want to get bitten, then don't grab me without warning."

"If I warned you, then I'd never get my hands on you."

"I should have Darren fire you." Said in an indignant huff.

"You can drop the act, little pint."

"Who says it's an act?"

"We both know you like me."

"In your dreams, meathead."

He laughed, a low, husky sound. "You wouldn't believe what you do in those."

Whirling in his grip, she pulled her arm back, but he tensed to absorb the punch.

"How's my acting now?" she snarled.

"Wasted since no one is watching. I took a page from your book and found the hidden cameras out here. Three to be exact, plus a microphone."

"People could be watching in person," she said, pulling out of his grip and putting space between them.

"They could, but they'd have a hard time. Whoever designed the foliage in this place did so brilliantly. There is no real place for anyone to hide."

"You hid."

"In the only spot available. Anyone else wouldn't be able to get close without me noticing."

"From this side perhaps, but what about on the beach side?"

He shrugged. "Not much I can do about that. Anyone with scuba or snorkeling gear could technically swim right up to our beach. The good news is we'd see them coming."

"If we're watching, which we're not."

"I can't be in two places at once, little pint."

"You should try harder."

Harder? He'd never been so hard in his life.

"If you're so worried about Darren, then why are you outside?"

"I was looking for you." A grudging admission.

"Why, little pint, I'm touched. You were worried about me."

"Was not," she hotly retorted.

"Is it because you were thinking about the kiss you owe me?" He wanted to punch himself for saying it, and yet, his query had an effect.

She inhaled sharply, and her cheeks bore a bright spot of color. "I owe you nothing."

"I didn't take you for a welsher of bets."

She scowled—and still managed to look sexy. "Let's go inside. Before we attract attention."

"Yes, kissing out in the open might blow your cover."

"I was thinking more along the lines of whipping your ass."

"Anything involving your hands on my body is okay with me."

With a growl of annoyance—or lust, maybe a combination of both—Kacy stalked back into the cabana.

Following her in, he noted that, while she'd ditched the shoes, she still wore the dress, a summery frock that skimmed her body in ways that enhanced her curves.

Curves he really shouldn't notice. But...he was a man. A man whose balls ached. Whose cock refused to be tamed in her presence.

And she kept torturing him.

Perched on a chair, Kacy tucked her legs under her, nothing lady-like about her pose, and yet he'd never seen anything more sexy and feminine.

She turned all business. "Did you find anything?"

Ah, yes, the job. "Shouldn't Darren hear this?"

"You can report to him in the morning. Let him get some sleep. You'll have the breakfast shift with him while I grab some extra z's."

"You trust me to guard him?"

"I don't have a choice." Then, more grudgingly, "You aren't completely useless."

He grabbed his heart. "Ack. I think I must be dying because that wasn't an insult."

She threw a flowered pillow at him. "Don't be a meathead."

"Why? You going to beat me up again?" *Please do.*

She shook her head and sighed, but he could see the smile hovering. "Tell me what you found."

It wasn't as much as he would have liked. There were eight guest cabanas in total, ringing the island, far enough apart to give each one privacy. All were occupied by couples, and most, like Darren, had also brought a security person.

The main house didn't appear to have anyone staying in it, although it was harder to figure out, given none of the staff spoke English, and he didn't want to push too hard.

"I'll see if I can subtly pump them for info tomorrow. What about the owner of this place? The guy who invited everyone? Did you find out anything?"

At that question, Marcus shook his head. "*Nada.* Either no one knows, not even the staff, or they're not saying. I even talked to a few of the other bodyguards. They claim their bosses have no idea either. All they know is that their clients came because of some mysterious invitation." Weird thing, all of the security personnel seemed to have been outfitted in the same black security T-shirts meant to identify them. He had found extras on his bed when he returned from dinner. A not-so-subtle hint about their dress code while on the island.

"Are all these people stupid? Who the hell just drops everything to go somewhere to meet someone?"

"People with money to burn and power at their fingertips. The people on this island are loaded and span the nationalities."

"I noticed that at dinner. Or should I call it a snack?" She rubbed her tummy. "I could have eaten a whole tray of those little crab cakes and still had room for more."

Marcus grinned. "Hungry? Would it help to know they had steaks and baked potatoes for us big and burly men?"

"I hate you."

"Now, little pint, you know what they say about hate."

"What do they say, meathead?" The words might sound challenging, but the way she said them...

"It's not your fault you lust after my body. It is impressive." For some reason, despite being a usually low-key kind of guy with the ladies, with Kacy, he turned outrageous. He goaded her constantly, trying to get a rise out of her.

"Impressive if you're into giant rocks. I prefer my men slimmer, more finely toned than steroid bulky."

"I don't do 'roids."

"And I don't do meatheads. So if we're done, continue with your report."

"Only a few of the visitors brought wives. Most, like Darren, brought girlfriends. Two of them of are young. I swear that old dude has to be pushing seventy. He could be a great-granddad to his arm piece. I don't know how he can possibly keep her satisfied."

"Going to offer your services?" Her eyes sparked as she spat the query, and he held in a grin.

Is that jealousy I hear? "I thought maybe I could get close to her, you know, give her what she needs in exchange for information."

Kacy's fingers dug into the wicker armrests, and while she said in a cool tone, "Sounds like a good plan," he detected a subtle undercurrent of anger.

"Glad you approve. Hope I'm not too rusty. It's been a while since I've been with a woman. Touched and kissed."

"You kissed me."

"I did, but barely. And then, even though you owe me a kiss, you reneged, so I guess I didn't do it right." Funny, because he could have sworn sparks had flown between them.

"Your kiss was fine."

"Only fine?"

Her fierce scowl couldn't hide the red in her cheeks. "Great. Are you happy?"

"Not really, because if it was great, why won't you pay up?"

"You didn't technically fly the chopper."

"You're splitting hairs."

"Are you going to harass me until I kiss you?"

"Nope. I will just say I thought you were a woman of your word."

At that, she sprang out of the chair and stalked toward him, five foot nothing of bristling Latina fury.

And passion.

"I won't have it said I don't honor my debts. Bend down."

"Make me."

Instead, she jumped, once again climbing him and wrapping her limbs around his torso, and while she didn't need his help holding on, his hands still cupped her ass, cradled the fullness of it, hating the fabric of her skirt that stood in the way of his touching her flesh.

Her lips mashed against his, a fierce kiss meant to prove a point. Meant to pay her debt.

But the anger in it quickly softened. The embrace turned sensual. Soft. Sweet.

Standing there, their mouths fused, as did their tongues. Their panting breaths became one. One molten moment.

Marcus couldn't help but feel himself weaken as all the blood in his body and brain fled to a point south of his belt. His erection strained behind his slacks, swelled with need for this woman.

He managed to find a seat on the couch, sitting down harder than he'd meant to, yet despite the jarring movement, Kacy remained clinging to him, lost in the passion of the kiss.

She chose to straddle his lap and undulate against him, her heated core pressing against his firmness.

The skirt of her dress rode up, and his hands kneaded the smooth flesh of her ass. A part of him expected her to bite him or push away at any moment. Yet she seemed just as caught up as he was by the arousal flaring between them.

Just as needy and hungry.

While his hands explored the curves he'd been lustfully admiring, so did she check him out, her hands skimming under his shirt, palming the hard planes of his chest. She ground herself against him, making small sounds against his mouth, sounds that he absorbed.

With his long reach, he slipped his fingers under her and stroked against the damp crotch of her panties, a flimsy G-string that took only the slightest tug to move out of his way.

With her mound bared, he stroked her velvety petals, spreading them to insert a finger, wetting the tip with her honey.

He used her own slick juices to rub against her button, feeling her breath hitch as he pressed and circled that sensitive spot.

Losing herself to the coiling passion, her fingers dug into his shoulders, and she stopped petting his flesh while fiercely sucking at his tongue.

He stroked faster, alternately rubbing and then slipping a finger into her tight channel, feeling the hot walls of her sex clench. Her body bounced against his fingers, and he found himself panting for breath as he felt the pleasure coiling in her body, heard and smelled it.

He thrust his fingers inside her just as she came, her sweet sex clenching and squeezing him so tightly, his own hips arched in reply. She buried her face into the crook where his neck met his shoulder and bit at his skin, her whole body trembling with the aftershocks of her orgasm. Her breaths came in hot and fast pants.

For a moment, she collapsed against him, soft and sweet and sensual.

Mine.

Then, she bounced off.

Smoothed her skirt down.

And walked away.

"Where..." His voice emerged very husky. "Where are you going?"

She tossed a coy look over her shoulder. "I paid my debt, plus some. Now, I'm going to bed. 'Night."

Night?

But—

But—

His erection throbbed painfully.

And he might have jerked one off if he hadn't heard her screech, "Motherfucker!"

CHAPTER SIXTEEN

ENTERING THE BEDROOM, HER BODY STILL TINGLING, Kacy couldn't help but notice the empty bed. The stuff by the sliding door untouched. And yet, the glass itself was open, and only the screened part remained closed.

No signs of struggle, which probably meant that Darren had wandered off on his own. After being told not to go anywhere. Was it any wonder she yelled?

Marcus almost slammed into her as he ran to answer her call.

"Where's Darren?" he asked, easily seeing over her.

"I don't know, but he'd better hope he's dead because if he left this room of his own volition, I'm going to kill him."

Perhaps she should kill herself, too, for allowing herself to be distracted.

Is that what we're going to call my orgasm in the living room? A distraction?

What was she thinking?

The real problem? She *wasn't* thinking, not clearly at least. She'd allowed her needs to interfere with the mission. Let herself be goaded into pleasure before duty.

And now, she paid the price.

I lost my fucking client.

Grabbing her gun from the nightstand where Darren had left it, she emerged from the cabana onto the deck and, by the soft glow of a crescent moon, immediately saw Darren down by the water.

Alone.

Tucking the gun away, she motioned Marcus back as she approached. But Marcus didn't listen.

He never listened.

He took.

Took advantage of her weakness for him and exploited it—giving her extreme pleasure.

I should kill him.

Right after she murdered her client for being a moron.

"Do you have a death wish?" she hissed as she got close enough for Darren to hear her over the sounds of the waves lapping the beach.

"I wanted to see the beach in the moonlight."

"How about wanting to see your eightieth birthday?" she snapped.

"Give him a break," Marcus rumbled at her back. "I think someone's having a sentimental moment."

"Am not," Darren retorted.

"Really? Then tell me you weren't thinking of Francesca and how you met her on that beach in France."

"Who's Francesca?" Kacy could have sworn she'd heard the name before.

"The woman he fell for who ditched his ass."

"I am not pining for Fran."

"I warned you what would happen if you started moping about her again." Before Kacy could stop him, Marcus lunged at Darren and shoved him into the water.

Her client came up sputtering. "I was not moping."

Kacy held out her arm before Marcus could trip him again. "I can't let you hurt the client."

"Dunking doesn't hurt. What you did, though..." Marcus glared, and she felt a twinge of remorse.

Kacy had used him, let him pleasure her in an attempt to flush her attraction for him out of her system. He, on the other hand, got blue balls. Sucked to be him. Especially since she still tingled and felt great.

"Are you going to whine about it?" she sassed, hand on her hip.

"Nope. But I have no problem getting even."

She didn't expect the hands that grabbed and tossed her, because what girl who'd just been pleasured would think that same man would dunk her in the warm waves of the ocean?

She stood with a glare, hair streaming with water. "Why, you—"

"Come and get me, little pint. If you can," he taunted, fingers beckoning.

Darren called their rivalry to a halt. "We're being watched, children."

Those words froze Kacy from chasing after Marcus.

She pivoted to look where Darren pointed. "I don't see anything."

"Because I caught them watching. Someone on the rooftop had a telescope pointed at us."

"Maybe they were star gazing."

"That requires looking up, not down."

"We should head back to our room." Where she could browbeat her client without witness. Wandering out to stare at the moon. *Are you fucking kidding me?*

"If the person watching wanted me dead, they could have killed me. They had the perfect spot to play sniper."

"Just because they didn't splatter your brains doesn't mean there aren't others who won't. Let's go." Kacy laced her fingers with Darren's and flicked her wet hair in Marcus's direction.

Petty? Most definitely, and something she'd disparaged other girls for doing. However, she didn't know what else to do.

She'd let Marcus touch her. And then had the tits—big, brass ones—to walk away. What she didn't expect was the guilt. She'd hurt him and made him angry, and for some reason, that bothered her.

It also unsettled her that when Marcus laid his hands on her to throw her in the water, her skin had reacted. Her sex tingled, and she realized that one time wasn't enough.

I still want him.

As they entered the room, she toweled off while Marcus told Darren what he'd found. The dip in the ocean had erased the more obvious scent of her actions, but her flesh still throbbed, and hearing Marcus talk in that deep rumble of his didn't help.

Jerk.

Totally his fault somehow.

Dressing in the darkest shorts and top she could find, she twisted up her damp hair, stuck her special clip into it, and then frowned as she realized she couldn't tuck a gun anywhere unseen.

"What are you doing?" Marcus asked, finally noticing her actions.

"You had your turn to reconnoiter. Now, it's mine."

"You're leaving the cabana?"

She rolled her eyes. "Well, duh. I can't very well investigate while cooped up in here. You should be thanking me for trusting you to babysit the client."

"I'm not a child," Darren retorted.

"So you claim, yet you don't listen to instructions very well." To Marcus, she said, "Sit on him if you have to. No more walks on the beach."

"I don't like you going alone." Marcus's brow knit.

"I'm a big girl who can take care of herself."

"Until you run into something bigger and badder."

She shrugged. "It's a chance I'll have to take. If I'm not back by dawn, get Darren out of here any way you can."

Before Marcus could argue some more—and treat her like a girl—she left and didn't look back. She took the beach route since, if anyone asked what she was doing, she could claim she'd taken a walk to clear her head.

Explaining her actions if she got caught at the big

house snooping, though, might prove more complicated. She didn't let that stop her. Nothing ever stopped Kacy when she gathered information. Locked doors yielded to her picks. As for alarm systems, there were ways of disarming them, but she preferred to bypass when she could.

Sneaking around, she remained conscious of the fact that there were cameras and microphones watching and listening. Most observation devices tended to be motion and sound activated to preserve battery, so she did her best to remain quiet and kept to the shadows.

The lights in the main house were all turned off, with only the faint glow of the moon outside providing illumination.

A sweep of the first-floor common areas wasn't needed. She'd already gotten a good grasp of the layout during the reception party. She also avoided the kitchen. She doubted any secrets were kept there. What she was after was on the far side of the house, the private wing reserved for the missing owner, the one place on the island that had a locked door and panel alongside it that required a handprint. Since she doubted they'd placed her unique palm signature in the system, she opted to avoid that door and slipped outside via a window.

She didn't have much room to maneuver. The tall turret sat on the edge of a cliff, a precarious perch with an epic view of the island and ocean. The rooftop deck topping the two stories appeared to be the same section of the building where Darren had claimed he saw someone watching.

And yet, weren't they told the owner of the island had yet to arrive?

If indeed the owner was in residence, it would make her snooping all the more dangerous, especially if caught. But she couldn't sit idle.

Sitting idly would mean thinking about Marcus, and she was not thinking of him. Not at all.

Inching along the outside of the building, she quietly cursed the coral façade. Sharp-edged and not forgiving on skin. Climbing it would shred her without proper protection, so she kept angling around the rounded construction, hugging it as much as she dared, her bare feet gripping at the rock, hoping it wouldn't crumble at her added weight.

When she reached the midway mark, she finally found her opening. A patio extended out over the cliff, held in place by wooden beams buried into the rock face. A peek showed it empty of people, the lounge chairs vacant. She climbed over the glass panel half-wall and then took a moment to wipe off the smudge of her fingerprints. Subterfuge only worked if you covered all the bases.

Keeping to the side and out of sight, she inched over to the patio doors outlined in a pale glow from a light source inside. She stuck to a crouched position. People tended to look out of windows at eye level. They seldom looked down.

Slowly, so as not to set off any motion detectors, she peered in. The sconces on the walls emitted a low light and revealed that the vast first-floor space acted as an office slash living area, with a big desk to one side and a high-back leather chair and an arrangement of sofas and chairs on the other. A spiral staircase sat in the far corner of the room.

No sign of anybody inside.

A check of the door didn't show any wires, and a quick inspection with her compact showed no invisible threads to an alarm. Then again, who would expect someone to risk falling to get to this deck?

A true security team should have.

Perhaps when she finished this job, she'd have Bad Boy Inc. send in a list of recommendations—and a quote. Harry would be so proud of her.

When sixty seconds had passed, and nothing changed, she grabbed hold of the handle and turned it. Not locked. What a surprise.

She inched in and listened for an alarm. While her compact could detect a great many electronic things, it wasn't foolproof. A glance to either side of the doorframe showed no keypads of any sort. For a rich guy, there really wasn't much security.

Would that laxness extend to the desk?

Nothing marred the solid wood surface, the grain distinct and highly polished. Not a single pen or notepad. Drawers on either side, plus a long, narrow one in the middle, begged for exploration.

She opened each, displaying what you'd expect to see —office supplies, pens, paper clips, a stapler, file folders labeled *kitchen supplies, pool, winery,* etc. While the folders opposite had names in categories such as *kitchen staff*, *cabana staff*, etc...

But nothing about business interests, and nothing about the owner.

Speaking of the owner... Who slept on the second floor? Did she dare take a peek?

She glanced at the staircase in the corner and pondered how far she should go. She might never get a better chance. Or, she might ruin everything. Once she set foot on the spiral staircase, it would be hard to hide if someone entered, or descended.

If caught, she could get tossed from the island, leaving Darren vulnerable.

Depending on who owned this place, she might even end up as shark bait.

Going upstairs would nullify any excuses she might have. At this point, she could still claim she'd wandered in by accident. That someone had left the door open. They probably wouldn't believe her, but then again, those were the chances taken when indulging in cat burglar activities.

Breaking and entering wasn't for the faint of heart. She put her foot on the bottom step and a hand on the rail.

A husky laugh drifted from upstairs.

Shoot. Someone was home.

And approaching. She felt more than heard the staircase vibrate as someone set foot on it.

Time to get out before she got caught.

Exiting onto the patio, she couldn't have said who

was more surprised, her or the person dressed in black from head to toe, including a mask over their face.

"Who are you?" he barked.

"I could ask the same," she snapped back, using the conversation as a distraction to hide the fact that her knee rose to connect with his jewels.

He bent over with a grunt of pain, and she dropped a sharp elbow on the back of his head. He hit the ground, but her victory was short-lived as another body clad in black climbed over the railing. And then another. Two opponents plus one groaning on the ground.

A quick glance behind showed movement on the stairs, some woman in a robe coming down. Going back was no longer an option.

These guys probably wouldn't let her shimmy around the building.

Nor would she dare, given she'd make a ripe target.

That left only one choice.

Fight.

Kacy dropped into a half-crouch and beckoned.

Being men, their square frames making their sex obvious despite the masks, they obviously thought they could take the tiny Latina.

Cocky men were stupid men. Or, as the sergeant used to say, dead men.

When it came to fighting, she didn't think of who the men behind the masks might be, didn't care how old they were or if they had families. Sentimentality could get an operative killed, which was why she tempered her fiery

Latina side with the cold dispassion of a woman who'd killed before and would again.

Screw waiting for them to come to her. Kacy ran at them, drawing them off guard, jumping at the last minute to hit one of them in the chest with both feet. The blow hit him square in the torso and sent him stumbling back against the rail, where a roundhouse kick finished him off. He didn't have time to yell as he tumbled over the side.

That left one fresh opponent and a groggy one getting to his knees. She peppered the uninjured fellow with a flurry of punches, sharp jabs, and quick taps, moving so rapidly and erratically, he didn't know how to defend.

A leap and she grabbed his head, yanking it down to meet her knee. Crunch. He crumpled unconscious.

But she'd taken too long. Someone grabbed her from behind, lifting her off the ground.

Classic move.

Classic mistake.

Kacy smashed her head back, hearing cartilage crunch noisily and his bellow of pain. Fuck.

Would the woman inside hear it? Would she come to investigate?

Kacy jabbed her elbow into the noisy guy, and when his hold loosened, she whirled around and sucker-punched him. Then kneed him in the nuts again for good measure.

Grabbing hold of his head, she pushed him against the rail, bending him over it, and growled, "Who sent you? Who are you after?"

"Fuck you."

That answer never worked in the movies, and yet they always resorted to it.

She rammed her knee against him again, permanently removing his chance of procreation, and was about to ask him again when a woman exclaimed, "Who are you, and what are you doing?"

Since there wasn't really a correct answer as to why Kacy held someone pressed over the glass panel as she choked them, she decided to stay quiet.

Rather than turn around and face the music, Kacy hoped the balcony projected far enough and, using the body she held as a ramp, catapulted herself over the edge.

CHAPTER SEVENTEEN

SLEEP PROVED ELUSIVE AFTER KACY HAD LEFT.

Darren didn't seem worried at all that she'd gone off on her own.

"Are you just going to let her go?" Marcus asked.

"She's a trained operative. This is what she does."

Perhaps, but that was before Marcus had experienced the woman melting in his arms. Before he'd started to care for her.

A part of him wanted to chase after her, to provide the backup she might need. Yet...leaving meant abandoning the person he owed his life to.

It also meant disrespecting her.

The woman had trained with pros. She supposedly did these kinds of things all the time. To expect her to stop or change because he didn't like it was wrong. Marcus couldn't let misogyny control him. He couldn't let his burgeoning, mixed feelings for her control his words and actions.

He had to trust her, as she trusted him.

It sucked.

Especially since he couldn't sleep, not one wink. He spent the night on the deck, sitting on a chair, waiting for her to come back.

She eventually did a few hours later, looking worn out.

Despite all the words sitting on the tip of his tongue— *What happened? Are you okay? Are you stupid? Let me hug you*—Marcus remained silent when a very soggy Kacy dragged herself in. Held his tongue even if he wanted to ask why her shins bore angry scratches and how a clump of seaweed had gotten caught in her hair.

He clamped his lips shut.

Kept his hands to himself.

And sat on the back deck, watching the waves roll in as she showered—and trying not to imagine the water sluicing over her sexy, tanned skin.

His feelings for Kacy had gotten complicated. And by complicated, he meant he felt something for her that was more than lust. More than annoyance. He...gasp... cared for her.

How the fuck and when did that happen?

What happened to arming himself against emotion? Sure, Darren had weaseled his way in, the man just wouldn't leave Marcus alone, but he should have been able to repel Kacy. She certainly made no bones about the fact that she didn't respect him. She mocked him at every turn. Denigrated all his skills.

Melted in his arms.

When he saw her arriving weary and battered, his first impulse had been to wrap her in his arms and hug her tightly.

She probably would have gutted him for it. Little pint didn't like being treated as if she were weak. She had a chip on her shoulder almost as big as his.

So what to do about it?

Only once he knew she was in bed—*with Darren, who'd better count himself lucky he's my friend*—did Marcus finally relax. He fell asleep on the deck chair to the sound of Darren snoring and Kacy's tossing and turning. He fell asleep wondering what he should do about his Kacy dilemma. He still didn't have an answer the next morning. A peek inside showed Kacy asleep, and he heard the shower running.

The sight of her didn't help matters, especially as his body thought it would be a good idea to crawl into that bed and snuggle her. Instead, he chose to go for a swim. He emerged from the ocean to find his boss standing on the beach.

"Does Kacy know you're out here?" Because he somehow doubted she'd allowed it. She was adorably bossy in that way.

"Of course not. You know what she'd say. But we'll never know if anyone is targeting me on the island if I keep hiding away."

"And you'll never hear me call you a moron if a sniper shoots you in the head."

"If they're that determined, then it's only a matter of time." Darren shrugged. "I can't live my life in a cage."

"The President does."

"The President can't eat a cheeseburger without the press harping on it. It's not exactly a great comparison."

"Saturated fats will kill you," Marcus teased as he slogged through the damp sand, his toes sinking into the fine grains, and took the towel Darren handed him.

"This from the guy who says breakfast isn't complete without bacon."

"And eggs, with yolks, plus buttered toast. Mustn't forget the toast. The white kind, not that whole wheat shit."

"And you're worried about my well-being?" Darren shook his head.

Marcus laughed as he towel-dried his hair before wrapping the towel around his waist. "So, what's on the agenda this morning?" Marcus asked.

"Apparently, a nap, because you look like shit."

"I don't need to be pretty to do my job."

"Good thing because you have huge bags under your eyes. Didn't you sleep well?"

"Not really, but I'll get over it. I'll catch a nap later when Kacy wakes up."

"I heard her come in, but she didn't look in the mood to talk."

"I'm sure she'll tell us when she's ready." Or once Marcus snapped and shook her for answers.

"With her sleeping, you get to be my breakfast companion."

Food? His tummy rumbled. "Give me a minute to get changed." When Darren didn't immediately follow,

Marcus growled. "Don't you dare get me in trouble with little pint by staying out here by yourself. Get your ass inside."

"When did you get so bossy?" Darren grumbled, but he listened and followed Marcus to the deck, where he sluiced off the ocean water under the outdoor shower before they quietly entered the bedroom. Kacy didn't stir, but Marcus would wager she tracked their every step.

Inside the tiny shed, Marcus slid on a fresh security shirt and slacks. Darren stood just outside the door, making stupid commentary.

"This island is nice. Maybe I should buy an island."

"Maybe you should. With a yacht."

"I didn't take you for a sailor."

"I'm not, but at least out on the ocean I wouldn't have to worry that you're going to get killed." Unless Marcus tossed Darren to the sharks.

"Ah, bro, don't tell me you care."

Marcus gagged. "Ugh. Don't be an asshole. I'm more annoyed about all this overtime. Stop pissing people off, would you?" Marcus stepped out of the hut and found Darren leaning against one of the fat-boled tropical trees lining the path.

"Once we find who's behind the attempts, life will go back to normal."

The reassurance only caused a pang of disappointment. Marcus wondered at its cause until it hit him. No more attempts on Darren's life meant Kacy would leave.

He didn't want that.

Yes, he did.

The split in his mind made his lips turn down.

"Someone's looking grumpy this morning," Darren remarked as they followed the crushed seashell path to the main house.

"These past few days have made me realize something. I'm not really qualified to protect you."

"What are you talking about? You've done a fine job. I'm still alive, aren't I?"

"Yeah, but no thanks to me. Kacy's right. I don't know shit about bodyguarding."

"You know plenty. Keep in mind, these are extraordinary circumstances."

"In other words, I'm only good at my job when there's nothing to really protect you from."

Darren stopped and turned to face Marcus. "What's this really about? You've been working for me for years now. We've faced dangerous situations before."

"That's just it. We faced them. This whole sneaking around, bombing and snipers..." Marcus shrugged. "I don't know how to prevent and guard against it." Throw him down on the front lines with a gun and point him in the direction of an enemy, and Marcus could get the job done. Tell him to walk into a warehouse and use his fists to convince a guy that skimming profits was a bad idea, and he was your guy. But this subterfuge and coy attempts to kill Darren, he struggled with how to handle it.

Darren tried to alleviate his qualms. "Don't stress out about it, bro. Like I said, these are extraordinary circumstances, which is why we've got Kacy."

"But what about when she leaves?" What would happen when he didn't get to see her every day and struggled with his emotions?

"Is it me, or are you trying to tell me you'd rather we keep the girl on?"

What?

No.

Yes.

Um...

Marcus found himself flustered for a moment as Darren pinned the cause of his true turmoil. "Actually, I was thinking that maybe I haven't given the academy training thing a fair shake."

"I can arrange for you to get an expedited crash course if you'd like. I have connections, you know." Darren winked. "The academy would welcome you."

"But that would mean leaving you."

"Only for a short while."

"Or..." Marcus told his tongue to hold it back, to keep it in but he failed. "Or we keep Kacy on after we solve the contract on your life and she teaches me."

Give me a gun. I need to shoot myself.

Especially since Darren turned a knowing smile his way. "So there is something between the two of you."

"Yes. No. I don't know. But that's not why I'm asking."

"Sure it's not." Darren snickered. "So if I said, how about I instead get the best trainer the academy has to offer instead of Kacy, you'd say?" An expectant gaze turned his way.

Marcus clamped his lips tight.

"That's what I thought." Darren chuckled. "Poor Marcus. Pricked by the love bug."

"This isn't funny."

"No, it most certainly isn't. And yet, it's about time."

"What's that supposed to mean?"

"It means you shouldn't spend your life alone."

"I date." Sporadically and never for long.

"Fucking is not dating."

"Says the man who hasn't dipped his wick since a certain girl dumped him."

"My lack of interest in sex has nothing to do with Francesca. I've been busy."

"Now who's the one skirting the truth?"

"Francesca is nothing to me. I barely remember what she looks like. I couldn't care less where's she's gone off to or what she's doing."

"Really? That's good to know because, if I'm not mistaken, that's her on the far end of the terrace hanging off some dude's arm."

"What?" Darren whirled, and Marcus almost felt sorry for the man.

Darren could deny it all he wanted, but he'd had his heart broken by her. It had been a fling of only a few weeks when he'd gone to France on business. But an affair that had left him depressed for more than a year now.

The worst part about it all? No one could have seen it coming.

Marcus certainly hadn't. He'd thought Francesca was just as in love with Darren as he was with her.

So the note she'd left, and the empty apartment, a space cleaned out overnight, had taken them by surprise. Poor Darren had gotten so drunk that night, Marcus had to carry him to bed.

Marcus did that for seven nights straight before he forced him to get on a plane and head back home.

And now, here she was. In the flesh, with another man, looking as gorgeous as always with her tall, willowy figure, her long chestnut hair, and her exquisite features.

Why couldn't she have been sunburned and peeling?

Why did she have to be here at all?

Marcus recognized the glint in Darren's eye. Fire, the kind borne of pain that demanded satisfaction. Except the rich didn't fight like those of the lower classes did. Oh no, theirs was a war made of polite words and supercilious expressions.

Marcus could have applauded Darren's cool composure as he glided across the terrace, dodging tables covered in white linen, Marcus shadowing his steps.

Darren's smoothly purred, "Francesca, how nice to see you again," had all the right words, but Marcus could hear the undertone. *You bitch. Why couldn't you have fallen off a cliff?*

"Darren." She feigned surprise at seeing him. "How lovely to run into you again." Judging by her fingers clenched tightly around her glass, what she really meant was, *Fuck me, I heard you were here but was hoping to avoid you.*

"You're looking well." Code speak for, *You bitch, how dare you still be hot.*

Instead of returning the compliment, she turned slightly to indicate her companion. "Stefanov, might I introduce you to Darren Thorne."

The older gent, with more salt than pepper in his hair, smiled. "Very nice to meet you." The words emerged with a heavy Russian accent. "So glad you could accept my invitation."

"You invited me?" Darren couldn't hide the surprise.

Stefanov gestured widely to the area around them. "I invited everyone you see here."

"Why?" Darren asked.

"It is much too complicated to explain out here in the open. But trust me when I say we have many things to discuss."

"Are you sure about that? Because I don't know you, so I don't see what we'd have to discuss."

"And that is where the complicated part comes in. If you're not busy right now, perhaps we should adjourn to my office. I will have one of my staff bring us some breakfast to enjoy while we converse."

As the Russian spoke, Francesca slipped away, and Darren betrayed himself only a slight bit when his eyes tracked her movements.

Marcus wanted to slap him for paying her any kind of attention. The woman was obviously involved with their host. Darren doing anything with her might prove treacherous.

"I'll admit I am intrigued by what you might have to

say." As the men began to move, Marcus dropped in behind them.

Stefanov abruptly stopped and fixed Marcus with a cold, blue-eyed gaze. "This discussion is private."

Marcus bristled. "Where he goes, I go."

"Are you calling my hospitality into question?"

"Yes," Marcus growled. "I'm sure someone told you about the attempt on my boss's life on the way over."

"A regrettable accident. The original pilot was replaced without our knowing, but I assure you, the staff on the island is quite loyal to me."

When Marcus would have hotly retorted, Darren shook his head. "I'll be fine. Go back to the cabana and check on Kacy. Take her some breakfast while you're at it. Meet me back here in an hour."

"How do I know you won't wander off?"

"You don't." Darren smiled, and Marcus could only gnash his teeth as he watched the two men continue on their path, leaving him the choice of standing there staring like a slack-jawed idiot or reporting to Kacy—who might break his jaw for letting Darren go off on his own.

He rubbed his jaw. No matter what, he needed to tell her what had happened. Surely, she'd know what to do. To hopefully mitigate any damage to his person, he thought it prudent to bring her some food.

The plate he balanced in one hand soon found itself piled high with yummy tidbits—including lots of bacon. When a voice purred by his ear, he didn't whip around to smash the contents in a certain face but only because he hated to waste good food.

"Darren is in danger."

Not displaying any emotion, Marcus pivoted to face Francesca, her features as elegantly beautiful as always, but Marcus didn't find her at all attractive. He preferred someone a little more vibrant and tanned.

"You don't say. But don't worry. If he finds himself drawn to you, I'll kill you myself to save him the misery."

"I wasn't talking about danger from me." Francesca's eyes flashed with anger.

"Maybe not, but I was. Consider this your warning to keep your claws out of him. You've done enough damage. I won't see him hurt again."

At that, he noticed a flicker in her gaze, a shade of regret quickly there and then gone again.

"What happened between us was regrettable."

"Regrettable?" At that, he raised an eyebrow. "You shredded his heart."

Again, a shade of something passed over her face. "I am sorry for what happened, but it couldn't be avoided."

"I understand breaking up is hard to do, but to leave him high and dry, thinking you had a future..." He trailed off and shook his head. "That was cold. But the good news is, he's moved on. As a matter of fact, he's here with his new squeeze." A fake relationship, but, given the way Francesca's lips puckered in displeasure, it hit a chord. Good.

"I didn't come over here to speak with you to rehash my past with Darren."

"Then why did you bother coming over? I mean, other than to cause trouble."

"Darren's in danger."

"So you said. Aren't we all? I'm thinking I could eliminate a good chunk of it right now by making you go for a swim with the sharks."

"Resorting to threats now?"

"More like making promises for the well-being of a boss who is also my friend. You hurt him once. I won't let you do it again."

"It's not me who wants to hurt him. There is a contract out, demanding his blood."

How did she know that? Francesca obviously wasn't the woman Darren had assumed her to be. Then again, that had become obvious the moment they saw her on this island. More and more, Marcus wondered if Darren had known Francesca at all.

She fooled us all.

"We are aware of the contract and taking precautions."

"But are you aware that the person behind it is on this island with us?" Francesca turned from Marcus and swept her gaze over the spaced tables on the terrace, the people seated at them varying in age and nationality, but all having one thing in common, a subtle aura of power and wealth.

"How do you know the person who offered the contract is here?" Darren had also mentioned that possibility. Just how widespread was this supposed tidbit?

"I have my sources."

Yup, definitely more to Francesca than a beautiful model in France for a fashion show.

"Are you the person behind the hits?"

"It's not me." Said with hot indignation, the cool veneer crumbling for a moment.

"Then how do you know?"

"How I know is not important."

"I'd say it is. If you know who's threatening Darren, then give me a name, right now." Marcus moved so he stood closer to her, using his size to intimidate, except Francesca didn't back down. Much like Kacy, she had a backbone of steel, which made her running away from Darren in the night so much harder to understand.

"I don't have a name, nor do I know who it is. I only know they are present, and you must be vigilant."

"Tell that to your boyfriend who wouldn't let me join him and Darren." Hard to guard a body when his boss insisted on wandering off with strangers.

"You needn't worry about Stefanov."

"Says you. Who's to say he won't have a jealous fit when he finds out you and Darren used to fuck?"

Her lips pursed. "There's no need for vulgarity."

"I'll be as vulgar as I like. You treated Darren like shit. I'm just returning the favor."

"Your loyalty to Darren is commendable. One can only hope you'll be enough to keep him safe. Consider yourself warned. Be watchful." With those parting words, she slipped off, a slim figure in an elegant white pantsuit—an enigma he now wished he'd killed.

Just who was Francesca really?

More than ever, he needed to find Kacy. The plot had just thickened, and he could use her expertise.

Balancing the plate of food, he quickly made his way through the paths he'd memorized to the cabana. Entering, he crept quietly into the bedroom and stared down at little pint. She still slept, or at least feigned it, her face relaxed, her skin fresh and clean of makeup or artifice. Smooth of any scowl.

Utterly angelic looking.

Perhaps dropping a light kiss on her lips wasn't the brightest thing he'd ever done, but he didn't deserve the knife she pulled from under her pillow and held at his throat.

CHAPTER EIGHTEEN

Overreacting to simple things, that was Kacy, but then again, she didn't know what to do when Marcus kissed her.

Placed a light caress on her lips as if waking a princess.

And she'd allowed it. She'd heard him enter the room, so it wasn't as if he had surprised her.

The sweet and soft kiss most definitely did, though.

She opened her eyes to glare at him. "Why did you do that?"

"Because you were cute." He sounded as appalled as she was by the words tumbling from his lips.

"Cute?" Did he need a mental evaluation? She sat on the far end of cute with her unbrushed teeth, wild hair from her nocturnal swim, and the possible dried drool on her cheek from her exhausted nap.

"Should I have said sexy?" He pulled back from the

knife. "I have to say, it's kind of arousing to know you sleep with a weapon."

"I always have something under my pillow in case I need protection." She wouldn't need anything if she slept with Marcus. The man was beast-sized.

Hold on, why on earth would she even let her mind veer in that direction?

Struggling to a seated position, she noted the tray in his hand and the lack of client. "Where's Darren?"

"In a meeting at the main house."

"And you left him alone?"

She would have sprung out of the bed, but he placed the tray on her lap and sat on the edge of the mattress, pinning part of her thigh with his bulk.

"Calm down, little pint. Before you go rushing off, let me note that Darren made me leave. I didn't have a choice. He met the owner of the island, the guy who invited him and brought us all here."

"And you let them go off together?"

Marcus shrugged. "Like I said, I wasn't given a choice. He wanted to talk to Darren alone. But that's not the only thing that happened."

Since listening to Marcus—and imbibing some food— would be more valuable than running off half-cocked, she didn't throat punch the brute and shove him off the bed. Instead, she grabbed a slice of mango before asking, "Who's the guy Darren met? Describe him."

Marcus gave her the brief rundown, very brief, and then took a deep breath.

Uh-oh. "What else?" she asked.

"Darren's ex-girlfriend is here, on the island."

"And? Don't rich folk run in the same circles?" Kacy had watched more than her fair share of sitcoms and soap operas, enough to know that everyone slept with someone at one point. Sometimes more than once.

"*Rich folk*, as you call them, have a much wider circle and world than you'd think. Especially when they are from other continents. It's why Darren only vaguely knows the people here. As we've noticed, everyone present thus far seems to come from a different spot in the world. Darren is from the US. This Stefanov guy seems to be Russian. We've got that Chinese gal. The Australian. Some big dude from South Africa, and even someone from Brazil."

"And Europe seems to be two groups. One is definitely British, and the other is from Switzerland. Have you figured out what they have in common yet?"

"Other than the fact they're loaded?" Marcus shrugged. "Nope. But I imagine Darren's finding out right now."

Which meant Kacy would grill him once she got her hands on him—and shook him for, once again, being a moron. "Is this ex-girlfriend going to cause problems?"

At that, Marcus lifted his shoulders. "Yes. No. Probably. Darren really had a thing for her, and when she dumped him out of the blue, without any explanation, she fucked him up. Bad."

"With his resources, why didn't he hunt her down and ask for answers and get some closure?"

"For one thing, that would have been pathetic. For another, we couldn't find her."

"What do you mean you couldn't find her?" As owner of the academy, Darren had access to the most comprehensive databases.

"It's as if she only existed for that one month they spent together in France. Not a trace of her could be found, not by name, fingerprint, or DNA. All of our searches came up empty."

"That's almost impossible."

"Unless she wasn't who she said she was."

A spy? An agent for someone else? The plot thickened. "You said she appears to be with this Stefanov guy."

"That's the appearance they gave."

"I wonder if they arrived last night." Was that the woman Kacy had seen coming down those stairs, the one who'd almost caught her on the balcony? She'd have to watch herself around the woman.

"Doesn't matter when they got here. They're here now, and we'll have to be careful."

"You think they're behind the plot to kill Darren."

"Maybe. But that's not the biggest problem. I'm more worried that Darren still has a thing for Francesca."

"So?" The client's love life wasn't her problem unless this Stefanov fellow took exception. Then she'd have to protect Darren. "If her new boyfriend objects, I'll handle it."

"I don't think you understand. They can't get back together."

"Are you going to stand in the way of true love?" she asked, savoring freshly squeezed orange juice without the aftertaste that came from a store-bought carton.

"I won't see him hurt again."

At that, she eyed him and said, "If you don't want him to come to harm, then you should do your job instead of feeding me. Get back to work."

"You can't tell me what to do."

How many times had Kacy said the same thing? "You're very insubordinate for an ex-military guy."

A crooked smile pulled his lips. "Yes, I am. Guess all those years of taking orders left me with a need to mouth off. You gonna punish me for it?"

What she wanted to do was kiss him, and have him touch her again.

Instead of quelling her hunger for him, their brief interlude had only made it worse. Her body came alive around him, all her senses attuned to his presence.

How could she fight this insane attraction?

Maybe she shouldn't.

She didn't know who was more surprised, her or him, when her lips mashed against his.

He certainly did not object. Instead of shoving her away, his arms wrapped tightly around her, cradling her against his thick bulk. But the fact that he proved so much bigger than her didn't cause any panic. For once, she could relax in a man's embrace and feel safe. Marcus wouldn't hurt her. On the contrary, he made her feel all too good.

His mouth caressed hers with sweet fervency as he

took over the embrace. Engulfed her senses in hot passion.

He distracted her, and she didn't care.

A part of her insisted on a token protest. "This is wrong," she said in between nips of his lower lip.

"Feels right to me," he said, the low rumble of his words vibrating against her mouth.

He did have a point. It did feel right, and she didn't want to stop. Yet, the feeling of him sliding against her bare thigh, his skin slick and...scaly?

She shoved away from him and yelled, "I think there's a snake in the bed."

"Is the name-calling supposed to be foreplay?" he asked. Only to jump up as he noticed the moving bulge under the covers.

Marcus whipped off the comforter as Kacy tucked her legs to her chest. The sinuous yellow snake that had decided to join the party hissed at them.

"How the fuck did that get in here?" he asked.

Any number of ways. The question was, had it come on its own, or had someone placed it there?

Want to bet it carried poison in its fangs?

Oddly enough, while Kacy cringed at the forked tongue, Marcus seemed unbothered. His hand darted, fast enough to snare the snake just behind its jawline. He held it up and dangled its long body. "I have to say, this is the first time I've been cock blocked by a snake bigger than mine."

"Are you seriously making a sex joke?" she snapped,

inwardly shuddering at the realization that the viper had touched her.

"I wouldn't joke about something so dire as missing out on a chance to make out with you, little pint."

Hiss. The forked tongue waggled.

She cringed. "Get that thing out of here."

"If you insist. Come on, pretty girl, let's get you back outside."

Pretty girl? Was the man insane? Deadly vipers were only attractive as purses. Not that Kacy owned the real thing. Her only claim to snakeskin was a knock-off pair of boots that she'd needed for some undercover western thing she'd worked a few years back.

With Marcus taking care of the snake, she hopped out of the bed, knife in hand, gun in the other. Using the tip of the blade, she tugged the sheet completely off the bed, checking for more surprises.

She crouched down to peek under the bed, as well. Nothing scurried or hissed.

Still, though, she couldn't relax. She kept both weapons with her going into the bathroom. The gun sat on top of the vanity; the knife joined her in the shower.

Yet she didn't throw it when she heard Marcus rumble, "The snake is gone."

Maybe, but a more dangerous threat lurked just outside the shower stall.

"You should go back to the main house and check for Darren."

"He won't be done yet. I'll inspect the rest of the place for critters while I wait for you."

He left. She even peeked to make sure. However, knowing Marcus roamed nearby did something to her. Did something to her naked and slick body.

Her skin tingled, and between her legs, her sex throbbed. It still remembered how Marcus had made her feel.

Remembered the touch of his fingers.

The taste of his mouth.

Her hands couldn't help but stroke her skin as she lathered with the soap, sliding with sensual languor over her sensitized body. Slipping over her hard nipples, wishing his more callused hands were here to pinch them.

She couldn't help but slide a hand between her legs, finding her clit swollen and sensitive. She rubbed it, remembering Marcus and the bliss.

She must have made some noise, emitted some kind of indication of her actions, because, suddenly, Marcus was there, wearing only his briefs, his shirt and pants stripped, kneeling before her in the shower.

"What are you doing?" she gasped.

"Giving you what you need." His big hands clasped her by the hips, and he pried apart her thighs so he could push his face between them.

She might have argued more, but at the first lash of his tongue against her clit, she grabbed him by the hair and bucked.

He licked her, sliding his tongue across her sex, slipping it between her nether lips to probe deeper.

Dear God, it felt good. She fell against the cold tile of

the shower wall held up by his strength, awash in pleasure as he licked her and stroked her and bit down on her clit.

She cried out as bliss made her shudder, her orgasm coiling within, close—so close.

And then he stopped and stood. Stood and shadowed her, and she thought he would punish her, walk away at the peak of her pleasure like she'd done to him.

She could see now how cruel that was.

But Marcus wouldn't hurt her, not even for revenge. Instead, he had a simple request. "Touch me. Please."

She couldn't say no. She couldn't *not* act. She slid her hand inside his wet briefs, even as his hand slipped between their bodies to continue stroking her. His free hand cupped and squeezed her breast, and his mouth meshed with hers, the taste of her still on his lips.

All of that only served to heighten her pleasure, but what truly made her tremble and gasp was the sheer size and steel strength of his cock.

Long, so long, and thick, much thicker than her one hand could grasp. She caressed him, pulling his shaft free from his briefs, tucking it upwards and stroking it as he played with her.

The two of them, mouths meshed, hands working, pleasure building.

When he penetrated her with one finger, she clutched him tight. At the stretching of a second finger, pumping in and out, her grip turned deadly, and he caught her cry as her orgasm hit, but she wasn't alone in coming.

His hips bucked as he came, too, hot and spurting against her belly while her juices creamed his fingers.

It left both of them spent. Silent.

They didn't say a word as they rinsed off the evidence of their pleasure. They did so quickly and efficiently. She took the towel he handed her without meeting his gaze.

She wasn't sure what she'd see if she did. And what would he spot in her eyes?

Marcus kept making her forget why she was here. Kept making her feel like a woman. Kept making her break all her rules.

For once in her life, she didn't care. She'd never experienced this kind of passion. Never felt so sensual and alive.

If asked, she couldn't have said where this thing with Marcus was going. What she did know was that she couldn't ignore what burgeoned between them anymore. Couldn't ignore her feelings.

I'm falling for him.

Hard.

And, hopefully, it wouldn't get the client killed.

CHAPTER NINETEEN

As he kept pace with Kacy on their walk to the main house, Marcus could see the gears turning in her head. Could see those thoughts weren't really about Darren and the danger, but him.

She's thinking about me.

It wasn't arrogance that made him think that but rather her actions, such as how she barely said two words to him and wouldn't meet his gaze. Not out of regret. Her body language wasn't aloof or rigid. It appeared more as if their second bout of lovemaking in the shower had softened her.

And she didn't know how to handle it. Or how to handle him.

Neither did Marcus.

It had never been his intention to invade her privacy in the shower. When she'd left the bedroom, he'd actually searched the place top to bottom. Finding the snake had frightened him. What if he'd not arrived in time and Kacy had been bitten?

She could have died. With that scary thought in mind, he'd searched every nook and cranny and noticed Kacy taking longer than expected in the shower. So long he went to listen and see if she needed help.

What he heard were her soft moans.

As she pleasured herself.

Without him.

But because of him.

Usually, a man should wait for invitation. A man didn't just strip down to his briefs and join a lady in her shower.

But *usually* didn't apply with Kacy. With her, nothing happened as expected, and when it came to her siren call, he couldn't resist.

Couldn't stop himself from stepping into that shower, dropping to his knees before her perfect body, and worshipping her.

She'd let him. Let him taste her sweet perfection, and she'd touched him in return. They'd shared a moment together that neither could put into words but both definitely felt.

At some point, they'd have to talk about it. Figure out what it meant.

For now, though, he let her mull it over, as he kept an eye on her while they walked, her looking feminine in the long and loose gown that started as a halter on the top then fell in a skirt that hit her ankles. It effectively hid the scratches that she'd yet to explain and the gun she'd holstered to one thigh, while the other held a knife.

He wondered how she'd get to them quickly in an emergency. It was probably wrong to have a boner imagining her whipping up her skirt to pull one free.

"When we get to the terrace, remember to stand away from me a few feet. We hate each other, remember?" she murmured as they crossed the bridge over the lazy river.

"I hate that we can't lie in bed all day naked," he replied. Probably the wrong answer, but he said it anyway.

She shot him an open-mouthed glance over her bare shoulder, her cheeks pink. "Marcus!"

"I can't wait until you scream that when I'm balls deep." Again, not the most appropriate thing to say, but she licked her lips, and her reply emerged husky.

"Who says I'll be screaming first?"

With that sassy reply, she faced forward again, and her hips swished.

Damn.

How he loved her attitude.

What?

He paused, letting her get ahead as he realized that not only did he care for her and lust for her, but dammit, despite the brevity of their knowing each other, he was pretty sure he'd fallen in love.

Yes, love.

For those that claimed love took time, he said bullshit. As a military guy, he knew all too well the shortness of life. Not knowing what tomorrow might bring meant living for the moment. While he'd never thought himself in love before, he had experienced enough to know that what he felt with Kacy was different and special.

I'm in love.

But he couldn't let it show. He could just imagine what would happen if he declared it to little pint. He might get to experience her skill with a knife up close.

But what a way to die.

As Kacy climbed the steps to the terrace to mingle with the milling guests, he realized just how hard the next few days would be. This new thing burgeoning between them would have to be put on a side burner. In order for Kacy to protect Darren, hell in order for *him* to protect Darren, they both had to do their jobs and not each other.

At least, in public.

Once they put Darren to bed...

He couldn't let that fantasy occupy him, not knowing that, somewhere amongst these guests, someone had hired killers to take out his boss.

Who, though? Who among these rich and entitled pricks thought he or she could kill the one man Marcus loved more than himself?

Once I find you... They wouldn't live long enough to leave this island.

Or had he already found the culprit? Despite her arguments, he couldn't help but wonder if Francesca were involved. If not her, then perhaps her new boyfriend. It would explain a lot.

Except for the fact that the contract wanted to kill academy folk, not Darren directly.

Didn't matter. Marcus should do Darren a favor and kill the faithless bitch.

Francesca didn't appear to be on the terrace with the other guests. Marcus wondered if she'd joined Darren and Stefanov in their meeting.

He hoped not. Darren needed to stay away from her lest he fall into her trap again.

Hands tucked behind his back, Marcus wasn't the only one observing the gathering. Other security guys also stood on the periphery while their patrons conversed. It seemed all of them had tightened their security since their arrival. Had the others suffered an incident like the one they'd had with the snake?

He highly doubted the reptile had gotten into that cabana on its own.

Gradually, the people on the terrace divided. Those who were brought as dates congregated around one table, including Kacy, who seemed to have hit it off with the redhead who'd come on the arm of the British fellow.

On the other side of the large patio area slabbed in white stone, gathered around another table, were the men of the group plus the old lady. Marcus noted that her boy toy appeared missing.

Marcus couldn't help but stare at the latter group. The true power brokers.

What did they discuss?

Marcus wasn't close enough to hear. None of them were. But they seemed intent, their expressions not holding any of the fake humor and false smiles of polite conversation.

On the other side, the laughter rang out often as the women chatted. Some genuine, some fake, the arm candy banding together and pretending they had fun.

Movement caught his eye as Darren emerged from the hallway, alone. His brisk steps made a beeline toward the power group.

A subtle turn of her head indicated that Kacy had noticed his arrival. Marcus noted how she shifted to keep Darren in view, and probably the area directly around him. Knowing she watched low, he aimed his gaze high. Snipers preferred height. Now, if only he could see without squinting. Even with his dark shades, the sun proved too bright.

The powwow between the men and the old broad lasted until after the noon hour, when they broke to eat before, once again, huddling under the gazebo that provided shade. Meanwhile, Marcus had to move as the sun shifted and tried to bake his skin.

The majority of the women stripped down and dove into the pool. Lounging like mermaids and sipping cocktails brought in an endless supply. Only Kacy and the redhead remained sitting at the table, heads bent together, talking low and in earnest.

Bored, Marcus began to pace. More and more, the idea that someone would attack in broad daylight while they were all gathered seemed crazy. And yet he couldn't help a sense of unease, that feeling in his gut, the one he used to get before battle that said, "Get ready."

When a flash of light twinkled from atop the rooftop of the tower, a familiar glint he recognized from his sniping days, he moved—moved toward Kacy, not Darren, instinct causing him to throw his bulk in front of her.

Pain seared his bicep as a bullet tore through his skin. People screamed as the sharp retort of a rifle firing filled the air.

Bodies moved, the bodyguards throwing themselves in front of their clients. Marcus ignored the chaos and the seeping blood on his arm to whirl and check on Kacy, still using his bulk as a shield.

"Protect Darren," she snapped, the words sharp, but her expression ashen.

"They're shooting at you," was his reply before he grabbed her and took her to the ground a second before another bullet fired, hitting the chair dead center.

Amidst the screams and clatter of furniture getting tossed, Marcus covered Kacy as they scuttled for the shadows.

But no more shots followed them, and Darren, under the cover of the veranda that spanned the length of the terrace, soon joined them.

"Are you both okay?" he asked, dropping to his knees. "We're fine."

"No, we're not," Kacy said with a glare. "Marcus was shot."

"Better me than you."

Marcus should have known Kacy would make him pay for being chivalrous.

CHAPTER TWENTY

"What the fuck were you thinking?" Kacy snarled as she poured a disinfectant on his arm. On the hole in his arm, she should specify. A hole he'd gotten protecting her.

"Ow. What the hell are you doing? Dousing me in acid?" He scowled at her.

She glared back. He'd gotten hurt.

Taking a bullet meant for her.

The jerk.

Now, he'd suffer the consequences.

"It's peroxide, you big wuss. Suck it up. If you're going to act as a shield, then you should expect a little pain."

"A little? I do have a hole in me."

"A tiny one," she snapped back, dabbing at it with a clean wad of cotton.

"You know, Stefanov did offer to fly you to the mainland to see a doctor," Darren interjected.

"Ha, as if meathead would do something smart like go to a hospital."

Being a man, Marcus sneered at the offer. "I don't need a doctor. The bullet went straight through and missed the important parts. A long as I keep it clean, it will be fine. This isn't my first gunshot wound."

No, it wasn't. She'd seen the scars marring his fine skin. Still, the reminder of his toughness didn't excuse the fact that he'd fucked up. "You wouldn't have been shot if you'd done your job and protected the client."

"How about saying thank you for saving your life, seeing as how the shooter was aiming at you."

"You couldn't be sure of that at the time," she retorted as she threaded a needle.

"Actually, little pint, I could because, for one, the angle was totally wrong for the sniper to aim at Darren. That gazebo thing they were under meant he couldn't see Darren at all. You, on the other hand, were in his sights. I had a split second to decide. Apparently, I chose right."

"What I'm more concerned about is, why this sudden desire to take out Kacy?" Darren rubbed his chin. "First the snake, then the shooting. Why have they started coming after you?"

"Maybe your ex got jealous," Marcus remarked. He watched as Kacy sewed up his wound, the tools in the first aid kit familiar to her.

Everyone who went through the academy knew how to do field dressings and stitches. She'd just never done it on someone she liked before.

And he liked her, too. Enough to protect her.

Ugh.

She hated how it made her feel all warm and mushy inside.

"Even assuming Francesca is jealous, I highly doubt she's capable of hurting anyone. She's into the arts and classic works, not using my date as target practice."

"Marcus does have a point, though. She wasn't there when it happened. Not too many people were unaccounted for out on that terrace. And the shots were fired from the top of that turret on the rooftop deck."

"It doesn't mean it was Fran."

"Why are you so determined to defend her? The woman is a bitch who dropped you cold and is now dating some other dude."

"I'm not defending her," Darren huffed. "Just pointing out that it doesn't make sense. And she wasn't the only one missing. We're also assuming the shooter is one of the invited guests. For all we know, it was a stranger. Like one of the guys who attacked Kacy last night when she was reconnoitering."

Kacy didn't meet Marcus's gaze. He'd been less than impressed when she'd quickly filled them in on her adventure the night before on their way back to their cabana. When he'd heard the story of her excursion and attack, he'd clamped his lips tight, but she could read his expression—*You shouldn't have gone alone.*

The fact that she protected herself didn't matter. He thought he should have been there with her.

It was cute and, at the same time, annoying.

Kacy didn't usually work with a partner. *I can protect myself just fine. I don't need help.*

"Stefanov has assured me that they're combing the island and double-checking all the staff."

"Assuming the guy can be trusted," Marcus remarked.

She approved of his suspicion and added, "Our host and his minions probably won't find anything. The weapon is most likely long gone." Tossed off a cliff into the salty ocean waters.

"Even if it is, I'm going to go on the record as saying I don't think Stefanov was behind the attack. I've spent time with him. He doesn't seem like the type to sneak around. If he's got a problem, I think he'd say it to our faces." Darren shrugged. "I know his type."

"It's not hard to fake a persona. I'm doing it. For all you know, he and his girlfriend are, too. Don't forget, they were both missing at the time of the attack, and it came from their private tower deck."

"He claims both he and Francesca were in the kitchens talking to the chef about the menu for tomorrow."

That conversation must have happened while Kacy was busy ripping a tablecloth into strips to tie around Marcus's bleeding arm.

"He can claim whatever he likes. His staff will probably confirm it." Kacy pursed her lips as she peered at the wound to ensure it looked clean before applying a bandage. "Speaking of our host, what did you two talk about while you were closeted?"

"I can't say."

At that, she shot the client a dirty look. "Can't, or won't? Because I have ways of making you talk."

"I am sworn to secrecy, and my word means something."

"I fucking hate secrets," Marcus grumbled. "And this place has too many. If you ask me, the smartest thing we could do right now is get off this island."

"I agree," Kacy said. "We should go somewhere where we have access to the things we need and can protect ourselves."

"We should, but..." Darren shrugged. "I won't back down from threats or bullies. However, given the level of danger, I'm giving you both the choice of leaving. Stefanov has offered the use of his helicopter to anyone who wants to depart."

Marcus snorted. "You know I'm not going anywhere without you."

"Neither am I. The academy doesn't train cowards." Kacy half expected Marcus to protest her decision. To go all chauvinistic and tell her to get her womanly ass to safety.

Instead, he nodded at her. "Kacy and I will continue guarding your ass and guarding each other. Whoever is attacking will pay the price." Said so darkly and ominously that she couldn't help a shiver—of arousal.

He is so sexy when he talks badass.

"I commend your loyalty," Darren replied. "Given the day's excitement, I am going to spend the evening inside. Tomorrow night, Stefanov is holding a soiree that should prove entertaining."

"A party when we just had someone shooting at us?" she asked.

"Why shouldn't we celebrate being alive?" Darren asked with a smile.

"Because you weren't the one being shot at," she muttered. She tied off the bandage she'd wound around Marcus's wide arm. It would be sore for a while, but he didn't show any sign of the pain. Nor did he accept the medications she had offered.

"Since you won't tell us what you chatted with Stefanov about, how about dishing what you and the other dudes were talking about?" Marcus asked. "Things looked pretty intense, and yet I thought you didn't know them."

"I don't, not directly at any rate, but it turns out we have similar interests. And, no, I can't talk about that either. Not yet. Suffice it to say, I now understand why I was brought here."

"Secrets." Kacy made a face. "And people wonder why I snoop. I hate secrets."

"And yet, mysteries are what make the world interesting. Speaking of which, I've had enough interesting things for the day. If you two don't mind, I'm going to spend a quiet moment before going to bed. No need to join me. I'll yell only if I need you. Try not to be too loud." Darren winked.

Kacy almost threw a knife at her client as he walked

away and went into the bedroom. "He knows, doesn't he?"

"About us hooking up? Probably. We had a talk about you this morning."

"You did? What did you say?"

"Nothing bad." At her glare, he shrugged. "No, really, we were just kind of shooting the shit about this and that. I was thinking maybe after this is over, you could stay on for a while."

"Stay? Because of what happened between us?" Was he asking her in his obtuse way to be his girlfriend?

"I thought you could, um, teach me, you know...to be a better bodyguard."

Not the answer she'd expected. He wanted her to stay on as a tutor of sorts, and not as his girlfriend. For some reason, that irritated her. "I've got better things to do than train a meathead."

"Why do you have to be like that?" he asked.

"Like what? Myself?"

"No, acting as if you hate me when we both know that's not true."

"The fact that you're good at getting me off doesn't mean anything."

The frown on his face deepened. "Bullshit."

"What's wrong, meathead, did I hurt your feelings? Did you think that what we shared meant something more? That I would just swoon at your feet and turn into some doe-eyed geisha you could use at your whim for pleasure?"

"I don't expect you to change. I like you how you are."

"Then, if you have such respect for me, why didn't you do your job? Why did you stand in front of me?" She jabbed him in the chest with each query, her voice rising in pitch.

He glowered at her, grabbed her before she could move away, and slammed her onto his lap. "I did it because I didn't want to see you killed. Is it so difficult for you to comprehend that I like you? That despite your bitchy attitude, I've fallen for you?"

"You, what?" The words took her by surprise, and yet were exactly what she wanted to hear.

Also exactly what she didn't want to hear because if he cared for her, then she wouldn't be able to stop herself from caring for him. It would make her vulnerable.

Am I ready for that? Letting someone get close meant making compromises and catering to their feelings. Maybe even letting him handle stuff once in a while.

The very thought of not always being in control and at the mercy of someone else when it came to her heart brought a chill. But was she seriously going to back down from a challenge out of fear?

Hell no.

She grabbed him by the cheeks. "What is it about you that I can't seem to resist?"

"It's my charm."

"You have none."

"Exactly." He smiled, and she couldn't help but lean in for a kiss.

A kiss that went on longer than it should have.

An embrace that might have conveyed some of her relief that his wound hadn't been fatal.

A thank you that he cared enough to want to protect her, something she'd not often had in her life.

She kissed him and wished she knew how to say what she really felt.

And perhaps she might have found the words, or at least the right stroke of her tongue if her phone hadn't rung.

"Why now?" she grumbled.

"Ignore it."

"I can't," she said, sliding off his lap. "It's my mother."

CHAPTER TWENTY-ONE

SHE SAID IT WITH SUCH FOREBODING THAT MARCUS couldn't help it. He dove for the phone and snagged it from Kacy's hands before she could answer.

He held it to his ear and said, "Hello."

For a moment, all he heard was dead silence. Then a heavily accented voice said, "Is this Kacy's male friend, the one who took her away?"

"It is, and you must be her lovely mother."

"Give it back," Kacy hissed, reaching for the phone.

He pivoted away.

"Are you treating my daughter with respect?"

At the blunt query, he chuckled. "As if Kacy would let me do anything but. You've raised a fine, strong daughter. I'll bet she's just like her mother." The flattery came more smoothly than expected, and the more Kacy turned red and tried to punch him in the kidney, the more he found it fun.

"Such a flirt. No wonder my daughter is so taken with you. When do I get to meet you?"

Not if. When.

Marcus grinned as Kacy mouthed, "Never."

"Soon. We've just about finished with our business here."

"I thought she went away on pleasure?" was the sharp retort.

"A mixture of both, but it's almost done. I would be delighted to then come meet you in person."

The girlish giggle that came loudly through the phone made Kacy roll her eyes. She leaped one last time and ripped the phone from his hand.

"Ignore Marcus, Mama, he's a tease."

Not usually, but he kept making exceptions for Kacy. When she switched the conversation to Spanish and kept tossing him dark looks, he winked and walked into the bedroom, knowing he'd done his job. A job that involved driving Kacy nuts any way he could.

He found Darren staring out the window, a pensive expression on his face.

"Hey, boss, I know what you told Kacy and me, but are you sure we should stay on this island?"

"Yes. We have to, at least for a while longer." Darren's expression turned hard. "I have unfinished business."

"Why do I get the impression we're not talking about the assassination attempts?"

"They're only part of the puzzle."

"We'd better not be staying because of Francesca."

"I don't give a fuck about her."

"Good, because the moment you look like you're getting sucked back into her web, I'm clobbering you over the head and dragging you home."

A faint ghost of a smile tugged Darren's lips. "Speaking of home, I used Stefanov's satellite phone earlier today to make a few calls. The repairs on the house are going to take longer than expected. There was some structural damage to the floors and ceiling. We might need to find another place to stay for a while."

"And you're telling me this because?" Marcus arched a brow because he got the feeling there was more to this than just a temporary homeless situation.

"I'm telling you because this might be a good time for you to grab a vacation. I might have to go away for a bit. Alone."

"Like fuck you are," Marcus exclaimed. "Where you go, I go. It's a bodyguard thing."

"Listen, bro, I know we've been a tight duo for a while now, but I've got to do something, and I have to do it alone."

"You do know there are people still trying to kill you?"

"I do, and I am hoping to have that resolved before I have to leave."

"Take me with you." Marcus didn't like the thought of leaving Darren alone. They'd been through so much. It didn't feel right.

"I can't. You're going to have to trust me."

"I do, except when you're being a moron."

"Who's a moron?" Kacy asked, wandering into the bedroom.

"The boss is talking about going off on some secret thing after we're done on this island. Without me." Marcus glared.

"I agree, that sounds moronic. Why would you go alone?" she asked.

"Academy business."

With those two words, Kacy nodded her head and took Darren's side. "Good luck."

"That's it? Good luck? What happened to protecting the client at all costs?" He glared at her.

"That applies only if there is a client to protect." She shrugged. "If he decides to go off on his own and becomes an academy agent, there really isn't a damned thing we can do about it."

"You're not helping," Marcus snapped.

"Would you like me to play you a sad song on my little violin?" She arched a brow and rubbed two fingers together.

It was almost enough to make him smile. Almost, until he looked at Darren. "What am I supposed to do if I'm not taking care of your dumb ass?"

"Take the time when I'm gone as a chance to maybe relax a bit. Travel. On me, of course. Think of it as a long overdue vacation."

"I don't want a fucking vacation."

"I can see that. You are a bit of a workaholic. If you're worried about being bored, I could probably give my old pal Harry a shout and see if he's got something for you to do."

"We are not talking about this." Marcus stomped out of the room and onto the deck. Anger burned inside him, along with a sense of abandonment. Why, after all this time, was Darren cutting him loose?

Retaliation because he'd protected Kacy this afternoon instead of diving for Darren?

Surely Darren didn't hold a grudge because Marcus had made a split-second decision, the right one as it turned out.

Why is he trying to send me away?

The gaping hole of loneliness that he'd once fought free from inched closer, but he shut his mind against it. *I am not alone.*

Darren had said to trust him. Marcus could do that. He took a deep breath and watched the remnants of a spectacular sunset, the sky streaked in pinks and oranges, the vivid colors illuminating the clouds rolling in. The briny smell of the ocean filled his lungs and helped calm him.

Staring at the rolling waves, Marcus didn't react when Kacy came to stand beside him.

"Please don't tell me you're going to cry because your boss is dumping you for a bit after this gig."

He glared down at her. "He's not dumping me, and I'm not crying. This is me looking pissed because I think he's making a mistake."

"Darren can take care of himself."

"Really? Then why are you here?"

"You know what I mean. I'm assuming if he's planning to go off and do his own thing it's because he figures we're close to resolving the hitman-for-hire business."

"You'd like this to be over, wouldn't you? Then you can run back to your place and forget we ever met." Bitter words, but at the same time, he suddenly felt betrayed. Betrayed by Darren, who talked of leaving him behind. And soon, abandoned by Kacy before he had a chance to show her how he truly felt.

"What if I don't want to forget you?"

The soft words caught him by surprise. A sharp look aimed her way meant he caught Kacy looking down at her feet as if uncertain.

He could understand that because he wasn't sure he'd heard her right.

"Exactly what are you saying?"

Her toe scuffed at the weathered wood of the deck. "Well, if Darren's planning to go off for a bit, and with the house still a mess, then, uh...maybe you could, um..." In all the time Marcus had known Kacy, he'd never heard her hesitate, which was why he could only listen in disbelief as she stammered her way into saying, "...you could stay with me. For a while. You know, if you'd like to."

A bright warmth blossomed in his chest. "Why, little pint, did you just ask me to move in with you?"

Her cheeks flamed. "Visit. I asked if you wanted to come visit my place."

"And sleep in your bed?"

She nodded.

"Meet your mom?"

A moue twisted her lips. "Yes. But don't be too excited about that. Chances are she'll harass you about your intentions toward me."

A slow grin tugged at his lips. "So I shouldn't mention the fact that all my intentions are dirty and involve you naked?"

"Don't you dare!" Her cheeks couldn't get any pinker. Kacy, the woman who could take on assassins without batting an eye, blushing when he talked about sex.

So fucking awesome.

What he found incredibly more awesome was what she'd proposed. She wanted to spend more time with him.

She's not ready for whatever is happening between us to end.

It made him ridiculously happy.

"Don't think this invitation means—"

Whatever she meant to say got muffled by the crack of a gunshot.

Taking off, his bare feet digging into the sand, he bellowed, "Take care of Darren while I go see what's happening."

He smiled when she yelled, "Get back here. You're still injured."

Barely, but it was nice to know she cared.

CHAPTER TWENTY-TWO

THE WORST PART ABOUT HEARING A SHOT BEING fired was sitting around waiting and babysitting while a guy—a guy she cared entirely too much about and had actually invited to come and stay with her—ran off to check it out.

If Marcus had not reminded her to guard Darren, she would have gone with him. Actually, had she managed to trip him—throwing herself on his legs and felling him like a giant tree—she would have left Marcus to guard the client while she checked things out.

Instead, she found herself stuck inside, sitting in the bathroom, with Darren tucked in the shower where the tile provided added protection from possible bullets. The client grumbled about her overreacting and didn't shut up until she loaned him her satellite phone, which he tapped on furiously.

The noise of it irritated, but at least it indicated that Darren lived.

Did Marcus?

She'd heard three more gunshots after the first one.

Three. More. Shots.

And she didn't know who the gunfire targeted. Worse, she couldn't help but wonder if her stupid meathead had thrown himself in front of someone else using himself as a shield.

He'd better not. She kind of liked to think he only did that for her. And maybe Darren since they were good friends.

Sitting cross-legged by the bathroom door, she kept her knife and gun on the floor on either side of her within easy reach. Her gaze remained trained on the screen since she'd kept the sliding glass portion open to the beach, the better to hear anyone approaching.

The pocket door separating the bedroom and living area was shut. She'd wound a necktie through the handles to keep it that way. If anyone tried to bust in, she'd have plenty of time to shoot them.

I hope someone tries. She really wanted to shoot someone.

As time passed, she became aware of the exterior commotion—more than seemed normal. The helicopter appeared to be in use, the sound of its whirring, rotating blades distinctive. She could also hear the growl of a boat engine. Even distant yells as people chatted with each other.

No more gunfire, though.

She also noted a lack of screaming, which she counted as a good sign. Just not good enough to let

Darren out of the shower. However, she did relent enough to throw him some cushions for his soft butt.

Eventually, the outside fracas died off, much at the same time as the natural light did. The thick twilight passed into darkness, unalleviated by any moon or stars. She wouldn't light a lamp, though. Let anyone outside think the cabana sat empty. She kept vigil and eschewed even speech with her bored client lest she miss a hint of sound.

Where is Marcus? The nagging worry irritated, especially since she didn't often experience it. The only person she usually worried about was her mother.

When a shadow suddenly filled the doorway to the beach, she had her knife in her hand, poised to throw it when she heard Marcus sing, "Honey, I'm home."

Just for that, he almost got the blade in his throat.

"That is the worst Jack Nicholson impression I've ever heard," Darren announced from behind her.

As for Kacy, she couldn't speak. For some reason, her throat felt tight. Warmth flooded her veins, the icy chill of worry fleeing with her relief.

Despite knowing that Darren would see—would notice her weakness—she couldn't help but launch herself at Marcus, flying at him and knowing he'd catch her. She hit his solid body, relieved he appeared unharmed.

He hugged her tightly with one arm. "Nice to see you, too, little pint," he murmured against her hair.

"I wasn't worried," she lied, embarrassed at her uncharacteristic display of affection. She untangled herself from him and would have moved away, utterly mortified by her actions—*shoot me now*—but he grabbed hold of her hand and kept holding it as he chose a chair to sit in. He tugged her onto his lap.

Given Marcus didn't appear concerned about more danger, Kacy allowed Darren to move into the room. He kept to the outer edges, out of direct sight of the door.

Smart boy.

"What's happening?" she asked. She thought about moving off Marcus's lap, her spot was highly unprofessional, but any plans to hide what she felt for Marcus seemed stupid at this point. Darren knew they were involved. They even had his blessing, or so he'd said to her at one point when she'd gotten up for like the fiftieth time to look for signs of Marcus.

"He'll come back," Darren had said. "He now has a reason to." The implication was clear.

"You heard the gunshots?" Marcus's voice rumbled, dragging her back to the present.

"We did," Kacy replied, leaning over to flick on a light. Time to get out of the dark.

"Anyone die?" Darren asked.

Marcus shook his head. "No, the bullet only grazed Manuelo."

"The Brazilian fellow?" Darren's tone held a musing note to it.

"We heard several shots," Kacy pointed out.

"That was his bodyguard returning fire."

"Did they get the shooter?"

"They did. One of the newer staff brought to deal

with the extra guests. They think he was responsible for the shooting this morning, too."

Working alone? Or did they have to worry about more of the staff being assassins in disguise? "I thought I heard the chopper taking off, and a boat."

"Stefanov had Manuelo flown off the island with his girlfriend and security guard. The dude apparently wasn't staying a minute longer."

"That only explains the helicopter."

"Because you're impatient and didn't give me a chance to finish," teased Marcus. "Given this was the second incident today involving a newer staff member, Stefanov decided to not take any chances and fired everyone who's been with him less than two years and sent them back to shore."

"All of them?" The query emerged on a high note, and Darren looked surprised. "That must have been quite a few."

"It was. He's only got a skeleton staff left. A handful by the sounds of it, plus a few of his own security."

But would the measure be enough? She didn't imagine Stefanov had mentioned those who had invaded the island their first night here. Anyone with a boat, or even a parachute, could drop in. "While the gesture is nice, getting rid of most of the staff might not be enough. That's two shootings that we know of now while in his care. We never even told him about the snake, and I have to wonder if others are having similar issues. With all that's happened, I imagine, by morning, this place will be almost empty. Everyone will want a ride out of here."

She felt more than saw Marcus shrug. "Possibly. Although Manuelo was the only one demanding. Everyone else just kind of came out for a peek and then went away."

"You think they'll stay? But it's not safe."

"Even the most loyal can turn," Darren said.

"Not me. Money doesn't interest me."

"But what if they threatened someone you cared about?"

Darren's pointed look made her squirm. "If you're implying we won't do our job—"

Darren cut her off. "No, I have no doubt you both would die rather than betray me, but not everyone is so loyal."

About time Darren recognized it. "In other words, we can't be sure Stefanov's rid himself of all his problem employees. Will we be leaving in the morning then?" she asked.

"Maybe."

"What do you mean maybe? This trip was obviously some kind of setup." Kacy thought about launching herself off Marcus's lap to slap and shake some sense into Darren.

"I won't deny that there's some manipulation going on, but at the same time, the attempts thus far have been rather inept."

"Bad aim isn't incompetence. It's luck," she groused.

"I think what Darren is saying is if someone really wanted us dead, they would have done a better job by now."

"Is the fact that the gunmen so far can't shoot a reason to stay? Are we waiting for someone to actually die?"

"Aren't you at all curious as to why we're here?" Darren asked.

"No, because obviously you have an idea and you're keeping it secret."

"It's academy—"

"Business," she finished with a sigh. "Yeah, you said that before, but that only works so far as an excuse."

"I don't want to say anything yet until I gather more intelligence. What I will say, though, is we are under attack, and by *we*, I mean everyone associated with the academy."

Brow furrowed, she queried, "And what does that have to do with Stefanov and the others?"

At first, she thought Darren wouldn't reply, his lips clamped shut, but Marcus joined the conversation, not willing to let his boss and friend keep this secret.

"I might not be academy trained, but I'm gonna go out on a limb and guess that all these folks gathered here either run or work for academies of their own."

At that leap of logic, her mouth rounded. "Is he right? Do they also run their own schools?"

Darren's mouth pinched. "Yes. More or less. Some have schools. Others are a little more covert and specialized. But Marcus is right. In essence, we all train elite operatives."

"Stefanov, too?"

At her query, Darren frowned. "I would assume so. Though he hasn't confirmed it."

"Why gather you all in one place? Is someone looking to take the schools down?"

"Yes, someone seems to be targeting us, but that's not why we're here. This meeting was supposed to be about collaboration and joining forces. We've had some incidences with academy operatives clashing with others on missions. We want to avoid that in the future."

"A NATO for assassins." She shook her head. "Unbelievable."

"And top secret. These people wouldn't be happy if they knew their secret was out. I'm not the only one who's been threatened recently."

"And that threat appears to have followed us here. I still think we should leave."

"Not yet. Let's see what the dawn brings," Darren announced. "And speaking of dawn, I'd like to see at least one before we leave, which means, bedtime for me."

But Kacy was too wound up to go to sleep yet, and Marcus sensed it.

"Come on. We'll go into the other room so his majesty can get his beauty rest."

As Marcus went to drag her, she pulled back. "But what if—"

"Don't argue, little pint. It's been a long night," Marcus growled.

"Listen to Marcus," Darren interjected. "If it makes you feel better, pull the drapes, throw down your noisy booby traps, and go. I'll be fine."

She might have protested more, except being in the same room as Darren wouldn't stop a bullet, and she'd hear an intruder before they managed to get in.

Despite the smirks she knew the men wore, she did weave a layer of items across the door and windows. She also made Marcus check the bed inside the sheets and under for snakes.

Only once she was satisfied the room was secure did she untie the sash keeping the pocket doors closed to pull them apart and enter the other room. Marcus shut them most of the way, leaving them open only a sliver.

He then flopped onto the wicker couch, which creaked alarmingly, and she feared for its life when he yanked her down on top of him.

"We're gonna break the couch," she warned.

"I'm okay with that."

"We should do a perimeter check."

"I already did before I came in."

"We should probably—"

Kiss. Or so Marcus thought, given his lips silenced hers. With her worry over him now turned into relief, it wasn't hard to fall into the pleasure of embracing Marcus. She wasn't used to worrying about a man. Her mother, yes. Even her aunt and her cousin.

But this fear that Marcus wouldn't return to her... He'd come to mean so much to her, so fast. *What would I have done if he'd actually died?*

Gone on a killing spree—and cried.

Kacy hated crying, so it was a good thing he didn't make her do it. She clutched his face and showed him how happy she felt that he'd returned without any new holes.

He reciprocated his happiness at seeing her with an erection that butted against her bottom. The evidence of his arousal was all it took to wet her panties.

How could she desire him again so soon? He'd pleasured her earlier that day, and the night before.

Yet, once again, her hunger for him knew no bounds.

Did it really matter how he managed to get her so aroused?

She should be more concerned about the fact that his hands roamed over her body and pushed up her skirt.

"What are you doing?" she whispered.

"Hopefully, you," was his reply.

Another guy would have gotten slapped for saying it. Marcus got a kiss, and yet when he fully shifted her so she faced him, straddling his thighs, she said, "We can't go any further."

"Why not?"

"Because Darren is in the other room," she hissed. When she would have pulled away, he tightened his arms around her.

"So what if he is? He's sleeping. I can already hear him snoring."

So could she. Still, though... "What if we wake him up?"

"Then you'll have to be quiet."

"We shouldn't let ourselves be distracted." She tried to be a good girl.

"What's distracting me is the thought of not sinking into you."

Her breath caught. "We could be attacked at any minute."

"Doubtful. Anyone watching will wait until they think we're all asleep. So instead of wasting time talking..." He winked.

"We wouldn't have time to get dressed, and I hate running after criminals while naked. It's hard to get them to take you seriously."

"That statement screams of a good story, which you're going to tell me someday. But not now. And I might add, we don't have to get naked to make this work."

True, she did wear a loose skirt, and his pants had a zipper.

The snoring from the other room was constant. If it stopped, it would provide ample warning.

"I guess since there's nothing else to do..."

"Brat," he growled before taking her mouth in a fierce kiss. His hands tugged her skirt up her legs, and she lifted herself enough so that he could bunch it around her hips. It revealed the holsters strapped to each thigh, both once again filled with weapons.

He sucked in a breath. "Damn that's sexy, little pint."

Funny how that name used to bother her; yet now, coming out of his mouth with such reverence, it only served to melt her.

"You think I'm sexy wearing weapons?" Any other man would have dropped to his knees and begged for his life while blubbering. Really unattractive, she might add.

"You're fucking sexy wearing anything. Or nothing. But the weapons...yeah, they add an extra element to it. I've never been with a woman who could handle herself like you."

"You will never be with another woman like me." Because Kacy was beginning to realize Marcus was the man for her. The guy her mother said would one day come into her life and sweep her off her feet. She just hadn't expected a man who could literally pick her up one-handed and not strain while doing it.

"I'm okay with spending my life with you."

The husky admission saw her kissing him. She clutched his face and devoured his mouth, fusing her lips to his, tasting him and squirming against his rigid cock, a cock held back by only a thin layer of fabric.

He moaned as she wiggled on him, rubbing her mound against him for friction. She nabbed his lower lip between her teeth, nibbled on it as his hands cupped her ass. The callused tips abraded her skin in a nice way, sensitizing her to his touch.

Made her crave more...

As Kacy kissed him, she savored his flavor, tasting the gum he'd recently chewed, the minty taste lingering. She skimmed the tips of her fingers through his hair, the strands longer than she'd expect from an ex-military guy.

Her hands stroked down his muscled arms and then skipped over to his torso to tug at his shirt, pulling it off him.

"What happened to keeping our clothes on?" he asked.

"I changed my mind. Let them be distracted by your body so I can shoot them," she teased, admiring the hard strength of him.

She explored his physique, skimming her palms over his flesh, learning his shape, loving the feel of his hard ridges. She discovered what made him catch his breath, pinching his nipples; and what made him twitch, raking her nails down his abdomen. Kacy touched and explored as much as she could reach while his fingers dug into her ass cheeks and he ground her against him.

Someone was ready. And she didn't mean him.

The crotch of her panties was drenched in her juices. She more than wanted him; she needed him. Now.

With deft fingers, she undid the zipper to his slacks, pulling his erection out and, once again, marveling at its size. Long. Thick.

Mine.

The possessive feelings only heightened her arousal for this man.

She stroked him, and his breath caught.

The element of discovery and danger should have made her want to move quickly, and yet, instead, it added an extra component to the excitement.

A taboo bit.

She slid off his lap, and he protested with a, "Where are you— Aaaaah."

He stopped questioning when she knelt between his legs and gave him a lick.

A long, wet lick from base to tip. The glistening pearl

on the head of his cock beckoned, and she swiped it with her tongue, feeling the shudder that went through him.

She swirled her tongue over the mushroomed tip before licking her way down the length of him. Then back up. Drawing him into her mouth, not as far as she would like, he was much too big, she suctioned and tugged and pulled.

He just enjoyed, his hands loosely threaded in her hair as he moaned and groaned, enough that she said, "Shhh. Don't wake the boss, or we'll have to stop."

He went rigid after that, and while she sucked, she looked up to see the strain on his face, the way the cords in his neck went taut.

Seeing his enjoyment only served to increase her own. Her sex clenched and grew wetter, the flesh pulsing in arousal, waiting impatiently for its turn.

She did debate letting him come in her mouth, sucking him until he couldn't hold back anymore, but Kacy needed him inside her.

Needed him to claim her with his big, beautiful body.

With one last hard suck, she released him and rose to her feet. He stared at her, his eyes at half-mast, looking utterly sexy.

Still standing, she lifted her skirt, high enough for him to see the holsters around her thighs. She reached under and grabbed the edge of her panties, giving them a yank so they fell to her ankles. She stepped out of them before positioning herself over his erect shaft.

Hovering in mid-air, she let her nether lips brush against the tip of him. A quiver went through her.

His hands grabbed her around the waist, holding her steady. She eased herself onto him slowly, taking him inch by inch, feeling the stretch as he filled her completely. He felt so gloriously big.

And she wondered if he'd fit all the way, even as she kept sinking onto him, impaling herself on his length until he was fully sheathed.

Dear God, it felt incredible. Her flesh throbbed around him, and when his hips moved, pushing him deeper, her head flung back, and she let go of her skirt to grab hold of him, digging her fingers into his bare flesh.

He moved again, stretching her to perfection. Filling her up so tight that she couldn't help but squeeze him. Every slight movement brought pleasure. The wiggle of her hips drove him deeper. The upward push of his cock touched her in that special spot that caused such a sweet jolt.

She couldn't help but want more and more, so she ground herself against him, rocking in a steady but languorous rhythm.

Her orgasm coiled within her, pulling tighter and tighter, each push, each stroke, each grinding pressure bringing her closer and closer...

When she teetered on the edge, she buried her face against his shoulder and set her mouth on his skin.

Just in time.

As ecstasy rippled through her, she bit him rather than crying out and kept biting him as wave after wave swept through her.

The intensity was shocking.

The pleasure more than she could have imagined.

Spent, she would have collapsed on him in a heaving and boneless mess, except Marcus wasn't done with her.

He still rested inside, rock-hard.

With his hands spanning her waist, he began to lift and push her down on his rigid length. Slamming her sensitized flesh, reigniting her passion, making the waves that had subsided wash through her anew as he managed to roll her into a second orgasm, the sound of which he stole by kissing her, drawing the scream that hung on the tip of her tongue into his mouth, just as her body drew his cream inside her, the muscles of her sex pumping him and giving him his own climax.

And it must have been good because, for a long while, they both just lay cuddled against each other, breathing hard, his hands lightly stroking her back.

"Are you okay?" he whispered at one point.

She managed a grunt of some kind. And then, because she was a smartass, said, "We didn't break the couch."

"Is that a challenge?"

She laughed. "Maybe it is. But can we try to wreck it later? I'm kind of comfy right now." And she was, snuggled on his lap, sheltered in his arms. So secure she might have slept.

Possibly drooled.

But that didn't stop her from slugging him when she awoke not long after the dawn to his teasing, "Think we have time for a quickie while Darren is in the shower?"

CHAPTER TWENTY-THREE

THE MORNING DAWNED BRIGHT AND BEAUTIFUL, despite the dark clouds on the horizon. Marcus couldn't stop grinning, and so Kacy kept slugging him, but he didn't mind because he caught her grinning more than once, too.

Despite the danger they might face until they left the island, Marcus had never been happier or more optimistic about the future. He'd found a woman who didn't mind his rough edges and who could handle him, scars and all.

It was almost enough to make him forget that Darren wanted to ditch him.

But that hadn't happened yet, and Marcus wouldn't dwell on it. Not when he had an invitation to Kacy's to look forward to.

Despite the commotion from the night before, a trip to the terrace for breakfast showed no one else planning to leave. Only Manuelo couldn't handle the idea of danger.

Given the staff was down to a skeleton crew, breakfast was served buffet style. Since everyone ate out of the same dishes, Kacy didn't taste Darren's food; instead, she made them wait a few minutes for everyone else to take a few bites before allowing them to dig in.

Feeling a bit smart-assed this morning, in between mouthfuls of fluffy scrambled eggs, Marcus said, "What if it's a slow-acting poison?"

"They'd still show signs first." Kacy waggled a piece of bacon. "And, quite honestly, slow-acting poisons usually require numerous applications over a period of time. Everything else reacts fairly quickly."

"Speaking of quickly. The window for leaving the island is fast departing. According to Gerard"— the manservant who'd greeted them on the dock—"the winds are too rough for flying out or even taking a boat." Darren had spent a moment speaking to the man before sitting down to eat.

"So, no matter what, we're stuck here?" Kacy asked.

"What a hardship, stuck on a tropical island," Marcus griped. "Whatever shall we do?"

The kick under the table? Totally expected, as was the glare Kacy shot him.

He grinned because he knew she was now thinking of the things they could do—with each other.

"If we're going to be stuck here at least one more day, then we should be cautious. Just because Stefanov evacuated the island doesn't mean everyone left." Kacy stuck to business.

"Or that some didn't come back," Marcus added with an ominous tone.

The paranoid statement earned him a smile. "Exactly. We need to stay on guard."

Ding. Ding. Ding. The rap of a utensil against a glass drew attention to the center of the terrace, where Stefanov stood, his cream-colored slacks looking slightly rumpled, as did his open-necked white shirt. By his side, wearing big sunglasses in spite of the shade from the gazebo, was Francesca, her lips puckered in disapproval, an expression that turned into outright annoyance as Kacy deliberately placed her hand on Darren's arm and smiled at him.

Knowing she did it on purpose was the only reason Marcus didn't jab his fork into his best friend. Seeing his woman—*yeah, she's mine*—touching Darren didn't send him into a jealous fit, but only because he trusted them both.

The moment Darren strayed over that line, though... It shocked Marcus to realize there were some things he wouldn't forgive his best friend for.

But he doubted he had to worry overmuch about Darren putting the moves on Kacy. The idiot man couldn't seem to stop his gaze from fixating on a certain brunette.

Did anyone else notice the heated intensity in Darren's watchful eyes?

"Dear guests," Stefanov said when he'd gotten their

attention. "I regret the incidents of yesterday. I take full blame for not realizing my staff posed such a risk. As you must have heard by now, I had all but my longest employed and most loyal servants removed in order to assure your safety." Stefanov looked genuinely bothered, and Francesca squeezed his arm and softly said something to him.

A drink held to his lips went unsipped. Darren's grip on his mimosa tightened until the thin stem snapped. Before Marcus could act, Kacy discreetly grabbed the broken glassware and disposed of it under the table while Stefanov continued his speech.

"I appreciate the trust you place in me by deciding to stay so that we might further our friendship. Which is why, tonight, even though I've canceled the band originally scheduled to come, I hope that you will join Francesca and me for an evening event where we shall dance and eat, a celebration of what we are about to accomplish with those remaining."

"So much for keeping it secret," Kacy muttered.

"And now I've said too much." Stefanov smiled, and a titter went through the group, not all of it genuine, some of it tinged with nervousness. "So, enjoy the day before the rain comes, and I shall see you this evening, hopefully able to make a grand announcement."

With that, everyone raised a glass in silent acknowledgement, Darren's being water since no one was around to replace his missing drink.

In spite of Marcus not seeing any signal, Darren, along with the other power moguls in the group, rose from their tables and congregated around Stefanov, following him to his inner sanctum, leaving those brought as plus ones and security detail alone.

Being alone didn't mean Marcus could slide closer to Kacy. They both still had a role to play.

The redhead who'd come with the British fellow slipped into an empty chair at their table.

"Morning," Kacy said. "Interesting night."

"I don't think we've seen anything yet," said the woman called Willow. At least that was what Marcus thought Kacy had said her name was when she reported about her.

"I was told the helicopter and boat were out of commission," Kacy noted, the glass she lifted to her lips hiding her words.

"So I heard, and yet it's not that bad yet."

"A storm is coming," Kacy remarked.

"Something's brewing, all right," Willow said, the words serious, and yet her expression showed a bright smile to anyone watching. "And I am not talking about the weather."

"Do you think we're in danger?" Kacy asked from behind her napkin, both women careful to not let anyone see their mouths.

Were they worried about someone reading their lips?

"Keep your eyes open. I don't trust our host."

Funny thing, neither did Marcus.

Despite the gloomy day, and the way each group kept to themselves, with Willow not spending much time with them before opting to go off, Marcus and

Kacy stayed on the terrace. Well, Kacy did. Marcus, on the other hand, left her on a few occasions to scout around. The island was like a ghost town. The many gardeners he'd gotten used to seeing now missing in action, the servants fetching towels and drinks notably absent.

Only Gerard, an older woman who acted as housekeeper, the chef, and a pair of security dudes in white shirts—unlike Marcus and the others in black—seemed to be left of the island staff.

The lack of people should have eased his mind. Instead, he could feel the knot of worry getting thicker.

When Darren emerged late afternoon from his meeting, he appeared quiet and withdrawn. He wouldn't answer any questions as they returned to the cabana, but he did insist on borrowing Kacy's phone.

He closeted himself in the bathroom with the water running, leaving his two bodyguards to pace outside.

"He's not telling us something," Kacy grumbled for like the hundredth time.

"Because he's the boss. If it's important, he'll let us know."

"He might not realize it's important until too late," she snapped back. Then sighed. "Sorry, I shouldn't be a bitch to you."

"I've got big shoulders. I can handle it."

"We should have left last night while we still could. I don't like this, Marcus. I don't like this at all. Something's wrong," she said, reiterating Willow's earlier words.

"We're here because Darren thinks we need to be. So,

we'll handle whatever happens and shoot anyone we don't recognize at this point."

For a moment, she gaped at him then smiled. "Yes, we will."

He held on to that smile as the evening event approached. Kacy elected to dress in a lovely halter dress with her hair pinned up. She looked elegant and sexy. Not dangerous at all.

A quick frisk of her body while Darren got ready meant Marcus could assure himself she was armed—and wearing boy shorts instead of a lacy thong.

"What happened to the dental floss you had on yesterday?" he asked.

"Have you seen the wind outside? I am not flashing my ass to everyone if it happens to flip up my skirt. And besides, if shit's going to happen and I have to run or climb, I'd like to not show everyone my papaya."

"Good plan. I'd hate to have to shoot them."

"For looking?" she queried.

"Yup. It's mine." He dragged her close for a kiss and didn't let her up for air until she was good and flushed.

Darren cleared his throat. "Ahem, if you're both done, shall we get going?"

The walk to the main house was done in silence, mostly because Kacy and Marcus, even Darren, kept a close eye on their surroundings. The lush foliage didn't appear so lovely and tropical now, not with the gloomy skies overhead.

Despite the quiet of the walk, once they reached the terrace, with the music from hidden speakers sending out a pulsing, rhythmic beat, smiles appeared on faces as everyone remaining on the island as a guest converged and pretended that everything was okay.

Perhaps it was. Perhaps Stefanov had eliminated the problem plaguing his guests. And maybe no one else had landed on the island, hiding and biding their time.

Maybe...

Or this was the calm before the storm.

In either case, everyone faked it. Especially their host.

Stefanov held center stage, spinning Francesca in a rapid-fire dance that drew Darren's eye.

Kacy did her best to distract him, constantly tugging Darren this way and that, trying to turn his attention from Francesca. To no avail.

The man couldn't help himself. Just like in France, Darren found himself sucked in by Francesca.

Since Marcus couldn't exactly punch his boss in public and call him an idiot, he had to content himself with surveying the room.

With the storm approaching, and the winds outside gusting, the soiree was being held indoors, but the room proved more than spacious. The high, vaulted ceilings with their wooden beams and the boards between them painted white, gave an impression of vast space.

Along the wall closest to the kitchen, a series of long tables were covered in white linen and laden with food. Platters of fresh fruit cut into bite-sized chunks. A chocolate fountain bubbled for those who wanted to give their fruit some added pizazz. Shrimp on a bed of crushed ice appeared plump, pink, and fresh. Brochettes held spiced meat charred on a grill, while salads and couscous added a variety of side dishes.

Most only nibbled at the fare, just like the majority only sipped at their drinks. He saw more than one person dump a full glass into a potted plant then refill, pretending they'd drunk it.

Marcus didn't eat or drink at all where he stood on the outskirts of the room. He kept his back to the windows overlooking the terrace and intently watched the couples circulating, noting their fake laughter and smiles filling the air. Everyone had his or her public masks in place.

There existed a certain tension among them, an anticipatory air. If there was a hint of fear or nervousness, no one showed it. They'd chosen to stay, chosen to accept the consequences. Curiosity drove them to find out what happened next.

It made Marcus wonder if perhaps he and Kacy should have pushed harder for information. Demanded that Darren give them answers. Didn't he owe it to them? *To me, his friend?*

What did it mean when Darren had said they were planning to combine their resources? Why did they have to meet in such a clandestine location?

So many questions. It drove Kacy nuts that Darren had declared the talks confidential, but Marcus had spent time in the military, a long time, where those higher in the ranks made the decisions, and the foot soldiers followed orders.

But that was before he'd met Kacy. Now, he couldn't

wait to get off this island, to drop this charade so he could openly explore their burgeoning relationship. He couldn't wait until they could spend more time talking and sharing, not just their bodies but also their thoughts.

She's the first person since Darren that I've let get close to me. The first woman to ever see past the hard shell he'd encased himself in.

A new experience for him. For them both, actually.

While their childhoods had taken different paths, there were similarities in the fact that they didn't trust many people, were loyal when they did, and had a love for war movies—especially critiquing them.

Despite the danger on the island, he couldn't regret the time spent here, not when it had resulted in a sharing of bodies and minds that he'd never imagined possible.

He didn't want it to end.

But it couldn't last.

The calm before the storm had arrived. Everyone could feel it. It crackled in the air, the ozone in the very atmosphere building and amassing over them all.

A real storm darkened the sky overhead, but, surely, they had nothing to worry about. The island sat high, and even if the waves crashed close to the cabanas, they could flee to the security of higher ground at the mansion.

As for fearing another shooting, Stefanov proved determined to assure them that the incident wouldn't repeat itself. After firing his staff, Stefanov had supposedly searched the island, turned it upside down. Nothing had been found.

Apparently.

Kacy didn't believe it for one second. Marcus agreed with her. It was too neat. Too tidy.

Not to mention, if Francesca was to be believed, the true culprit behind the money for the hit was one of the guests.

A snake still moved among them, hiding his or her true nature. Was it any wonder they all eyed each other with suspicion?

Crack.

The sharp retort of thunder had Marcus's gaze straying from the room at large to peek outside. Dark clouds covered every inch of the sky and brought early shadows to the grounds. With no staff left to do storm preparations, the lighter furniture on the terrace rocked in the wind, a few chairs sliding across the stone but not yet flying. The strong winds gusting did find some loose items.

With his spot by the window, Marcus caught glimpses of the occasional item as it went flying by—loose leaves, flipping and twisting, a plastic bag that hadn't gotten secured in a trash bin, even a scrap of fabric, the dangling strings of a bikini top, couldn't resist the strength of the gust that had caught it wherever it had hung to dry.

The rain hadn't yet started, but the humidity in the air kept climbing. Even inside with the air conditioning, the dampness in the air made his skin slick with sweat.

Seeing nothing but debris moving outside, Marcus turned his gaze back inward. An angry Kacy stalked toward him.

Alone.

"What happened to Darren?" A glance around didn't show his boss anywhere in the vicinity. Perhaps he'd visited the men's room, but if that was the case, why didn't Kacy linger close to him?

"Our boss decided he wanted a private word with his ex."

"Why the fuck would he do that?" As far as Marcus was concerned, Darren should stay far away from her. Picking up the pieces for a second time didn't appeal.

"I don't know why he did it, and I don't like it. He's blowing our cover."

"Or he's acting right in character. He and Francesca have history."

"That most people don't know about. So what they're seeing is him ditching his current girlfriend for another guy's girl."

"I think it's fairly clear that Stefanov and Francesca don't have much of a relationship."

"Doesn't matter if they do or not. Darren is being disrespectful."

"Jealous?"

"If this relationship were real, he'd lose his balls."

"Does that mean I shouldn't let my gaze wander?"

"The moment you disrespect me is the instant you end up dead and decomposing somewhere no one will ever find you."

"You say the hottest things." Marcus couldn't help but grin at her snarl of annoyance. But he'd come to know that her growl was part of who she was. Part of the toughness he liked about her.

Hands on her hips, she surveyed the scene unfolding in front of them. "This party, this island, this whole thing is a recipe for disaster."

"Worried about the storm?"

"More like worried that we are all in one place with no means of escape."

"You think there's still an assassin among us."

"I'd wager on it. I think whoever is behind the attacks is just waiting for their chance to strike."

"So soon after the last incident?" he said, not hiding his skepticism. "People are more on guard now than ever."

"Exactly, which makes the situation ripe for an accident."

"If that's the case, then I'm surprised you let Darren go off on his own."

"It wasn't my intention. But he pulled rank." Her lips turned down.

"Where did they go?"

She shrugged. "Off in the direction of that tower she's staying in with Stefanov."

"I wonder what her Russian boyfriend will think of that."

"Good question. Especially since he's now looking around for someone. Wanna guess who?"

Indeed, the host of the island craned to peek around, and a frown knit his brow when he didn't find what he wanted. With long strides, Stefanov took off in the direction of the tower.

Not good.

"I think we should follow," Kacy murmured, moving in the direction the man had gone.

Marcus began to follow at a discreet distance, keeping to the outer edges of the room instead of directly behind her.

Crack. Crack. Crack.

The rapid-fire thunder and lightning strikes shook the very house, and the bright flashes illuminated the space with high-intensity light.

So high that a shadowy corner lost its protective, dark cloak, and Marcus did a double take as he saw a figure clad in head-to-toe black, and masked.

He blinked, and when he looked again, he couldn't see the person, but he knew he hadn't imagined it.

Taking long strides through the room, Marcus headed toward the spot where he'd seen the concealed intruder when suddenly something came smashing through the windows, drawing everyone's attention.

Only a branch, but the nervous titters turned to a few screams when the music stopped and the lights went out.

CHAPTER TWENTY-FOUR

CLINGING TO THE EDGES OF THE ROOM, KACY followed the big Russian. Amidst the crashes of lightning, she vaguely noted that Marcus didn't follow, but it didn't concern her.

She could handle one guy, a guy who never once looked over his shoulder. Did he have no sense of self-preservation? Then again, what did their host have to fear on his island?

Stefanov had orchestrated everything from their transportation to clothes and accommodations. The staff who'd shot at them? His staff. Just like he claimed the island was clean.

Darren didn't seem bothered that they were at Stefanov's mercy. She thought that had to do with that Y chromosome boys were cursed with, the one that made them sometimes stupid.

Anyone could see that something about the big Russian was off. How could they all be fooled into thinking he was some big-shot mastermind? But if Stefanov wasn't really the boss, then who gave him his orders?

Francesca? Or someone else...

Kacy thought it past time they found out.

Shadowing the Russian discreetly, she could have cursed at the loud crash of breaking glass from behind her, followed by screams. The commotion halted Stefanov and drew his gaze. His eyes narrowed as he saw Kacy.

"Why do you follow me?" he barked a moment before the music cut out and everything went dark.

Power failure, also known as a disturbing turn of events. Now some might think losing power during a storm was normal. Nothing to worry about.

On the mainland, perhaps it *was* normal, where electricity relied on poles and wires, easily taken down by storms. But here on the island, generators controlled all the power fed to the house. Generators and backup generators. There were even some solar panels feeding batteries to ensure a seamless operation of the most crucial items. As to how she knew? Kacy had discovered this during one of her excursions because she liked to know how things ticked.

So when a place powered by several levels of electricity safeguards suddenly went dark, it could mean only one thing. Sabotage, or as she was sure Marcus would elegantly put it, shit was about to hit the fan.

Sweet. Kacy hated the waiting. She preferred to act.

Forgetting any pretense of being a lady—about

fucking time—Kacy hiked up her skirt and reached for her gun as she ran down the now dark hall. She could only hope her training in the box—a lightless space where the academy students were expected to call upon senses other than sight—would keep her from crashing into anything.

Feeling her way through a dark space worked a lot better when she was walking slowly, not running full tilt. The table Kacy slammed into dug into her hip and spun her around, leaving her disoriented for a moment. The point of impact on her side throbbed and was sure to be a nice color in the morning.

If she survived until then.

If we all live through the night, then Marcus can kiss it better.

Lightning flashed, enough to show she'd veered in the direction of the main living area. The excited chatter and flares as the smokers in the group clicked their lighters helped orient her.

A jagged streak of light outside illuminated a window enough for her to see Stefanov fumbling at the door, the keypad dark, meaning he had to resort to using a key, which hung from the long chain he wore around his neck.

The door opened.

She ran toward him but didn't make it in time. The door slammed shut, and she heard a click.

Locked out. Good thing Kacy knew another way in.

Slipping off her shoes, the heels impractical for climbing, Kacy shimmied through the same window she'd used the last time she went looking for a way into the tower.

Her bare toes clutched at the thin rock ledge. She kept a hold of her gun and relied on her free hand to grip the coral wall, wincing as it bit into her flesh as she sidled around to the balcony.

The wind whipped at her, tugging at her loose skirt, and she was glad she'd chosen to tie back her hair because the stray strands that escaped tickled her face.

The heavy feel of the storm pressed on her, the humidity thick, the ozone electrifying her skin. She realized just how precarious her perch was as she side-stepped around the curved tower and could have cursed when the rain chose that moment to come down.

It immediately soaked her to the skin, plastering her gown against her and giving it a leaden weight. The cool raindrops, their temperature a direct contrast to the hot air, slanted into her face, blinding her. But at the midway point, she didn't have a choice but to go on.

Shuffle. Slide. The trip took too long. She tried to quicken her pace and gasped as her foot lost purchase on the slippery rock. She slammed herself against the rough surface, hard enough that she lost her grip on her gun. It fell from her hand, clattering against the rocks before disappearing from sight.

Shit. For a moment, Kacy stood there clutching the coral wall, panting.

That was close. Too close. Falling wasn't an option.

She kept moving, not allowing herself to think past putting one foot down over and over.

When she saw the balcony appear out of the gloom, she could have cheered. Instead, she clambered over the railing and hit the solid stone floor of it with an inaudible sigh of relief.

The double doors held a flickering light within. Someone had lit a candle. Given the weight of her dress and the inability to smoothly move, Kacy pulled free her knife and hacked at the skirt, dropping the sodden mess of it to the ground, leaving her in something thigh high and thankful she'd worn her boy shorts. Her holsters were revealed, but at this point, she didn't care.

Blowing her cover no longer mattered. Only the safety of her client did.

Holding a knife in one hand, hoping she didn't have to face a gun, she dropped into a crouch and made her way to the edge of the door.

Slowly, she peeked inside and saw Stefanov holding Darren by the shirt and shaking him. Her client didn't appear bothered, and neither did the woman they fought over. Francesca stood off to the side, arms folded over her chest, looking as cool and composed as ever.

Let's see how long that lasts when I throw my knife at her head.

Time to step in before something happened to Darren.

Kacy gripped the door handle and pulled it open, only to lose her grip on it as a strong gust of wind ripped it from her grasp. The door slammed against the wall, the glass pane in it shattering, the combination of noise drawing attention.

All eyes turned on Kacy, only for a moment before,

once more, the lights went out, the candle extinguished by the sudden air swirling in the room.

Despite the howling of the storm, Kacy could hear a struggle, the grunts of men engaged in battle, the thud of fists meeting flesh.

Her knife did her no good without a visible target, and so she tucked it back into its holster.

Since she assumed Darren had the Russian, she decided to make her way over to the woman. Too often in a guy-on-guy battle, the girlfriends were ignored, and yet they were the ones who usually did something like grab a vase or a lamp and bash someone over the head. Not everyone had to be a trained killer to be effective.

Inching her way into the dark room, Kacy kept straining to see in the thick darkness, but in the absence of light, even the differentiation of shadows within shadows proved impossible.

As for listening, between the whistle of the wind, the crashing of waves on the rock, and now the pounding at the door, it proved impossible to distinguish anything.

Except for one thing. A voice.

"Open this fucking door!"

Marcus. He'd come to help her.

I don't need help.

However, there was a time and place for pride, and that time wasn't when a client's life might be at stake.

Kacy heeded the *rat-tat-tat* of a big fist pounding wood. She could hear the thuds of the fight as her hands skimmed over the wooden portal looking for the lock. She cursed the fact that she'd not put a flashlight under her skirt. She should mention that to the developers who made her other gadgets. Maybe they could do something with her next pair of shoes.

The thumb bolt yielded with a click, and she yanked open the door, only to blink as a beam of light blinded her.

"Are you all right?" snapped Marcus.

How cute. Concerned about her. But misplaced. They both had a job to do.

"Help Darren," she yelled, grabbing the slim penlight from Marcus. She dabbed it around the room until she found the struggling pair.

It was hard to tell who was winning. Both Stefanov and Darren bore bloody lips and fierce scowls.

Their wrestling match had taken them out to the balcony. Marcus headed after them, and Kacy meant to follow, only she heard the thump of feet on stairs. She looked over in time to see Francesca disappearing upstairs.

To do what?

Would she grab a gun and maybe shoot from above to save her lover?

Which lover would she choose?

Kacy couldn't take the chance. Marcus would have to handle the things on the balcony on his own. She dashed up the stairs after the woman, her bare feet hitting each tread hard and reminding her of each cut and bruise she'd acquired.

Kacy hit the last step and burst into a massive bedroom, the king-sized, four-poster bed huge. Surely big enough for two people, so who was the rollaway cot by the window for?

It didn't matter because she noted trim ankles disappearing up a second set of stairs as Francesca headed for the rooftop deck.

Kacy sprinted across the room, the tiny penlight bobbing. As she hit the bottom steps, she switched it off and tucked it between her teeth before climbing. No point in making herself a target.

Emerging onto the rooftop deck, Kacy came face to face with the barrel of a gun.

"Keep away." Francesca snarled the warning as she aimed the gun.

Kacy grabbed the penlight from between her teeth. "I'm not here to kill you," Kacy remarked. "Just making sure you aren't planning to shoot Darren."

"I should. It would make things easier," Francesca snapped. "He wasn't supposed to be here. He ruined everything."

"What's wrong? Did your new boyfriend not like the one you dumped showing up?" The wind snatched the words from Kacy's mouth, but they stood close enough for Francesca to hear them.

"You don't understand. No one does. There's more at stake than you know."

"Then perhaps you should explain."

"I was trying, but then Stefanov arrived. He didn't take kindly to Darren's treatment of me."

"So was that the plan all along? To have Stefanov lure Darren to this island so he could kill him?"

"What? Of course not." The other woman sounded genuinely puzzled. "You shouldn't speculate on things you know nothing about."

"I know that someone is trying to kill Darren, and right about now, you and Stefanov seem like the most likely suspects."

"I'm not trying to kill him."

"Weren't you the one claiming the killer was on this island? How else would you know unless it's you or your new boyfriend?" Kacy kept Francesca talking, waiting for an opening, but the woman held the gun steady, steadier than a bimbo girlfriend should have been capable of.

"Francesca isn't the one behind the murder attempts." Darren's voice cut through the storm, and Francesca angled the gun away from Kacy and pointed it at Darren.

Bad choice.

Lunging forward, Kacy felt no compunction about punching Francesca in the tit. And when the woman gasped, Kacy knocked the gun from her hand.

Before she could do further damage, Darren stood between them. "I'll take over from here."

"Go ahead. Toss her over the side." Kacy stood back, but Darren shook his head.

"I'm not killing her yet. I need to speak with Fran. Alone, please."

"The girl just had a gun pointed at you. You can't seriously expect me to go."

"I do."

"What about her boyfriend?"

"Marcus took care of him. So you can leave us alone. I assure you I can handle Fran by myself."

He couldn't seriously be falling for the frightened look on her face? The fake shaking and hunched shoulders?

Kacy didn't believe it for a second. "She's fucking with you."

"Leave, Kacy. That's an order."

Insubordination wouldn't achieve anything, but her muttered, "If she kills you, expect me to say I told you so," made Kacy feel somewhat better as she clambered down the stairs into the massive bedroom and ran into Marcus.

He grabbed her and hugged her tightly. "Are you all right?" he asked.

"I'm fine. But Darren's up there with that viper."

"Let me guess, he kicked you out. I swear he turns into a moron whenever she's around."

"I don't trust her."

"Me either," he admitted with a shrug. "But he's the boss. And you can't cure stupid."

"Speaking of stupid, where is her boyfriend?"

"In the office. Don't worry. I took care of him."

By take care of she thought Marcus meant he'd knocked Stefanov out, so Kacy found herself more than a little surprised to see, by the light of a candle someone had relit, the Russian on the floor, eyes open and staring, a puddle of blood under his head, his throat slashed wide open.

"Damn, meathead. When you said you took care of—"

"I didn't do this," he swiftly interrupted.

But it didn't look good for either of them when a shocked voice said, "Oh my God. What happened? You killed our host."

The boy toy, a twenty-something named Benoit who'd arrived with Adele Bouvier, the older French lady, walked into the office wearing skintight pants and a mauve silk shirt unbuttoned to his navel.

Benoit stood over the dead body, exclaiming, "I can't believe you killed him."

They hadn't, but explain that to the idiot. They couldn't. And he'd blab. Witnesses were never a good thing. The academy taught a whole segment on what to do with witnesses. Good witnesses were protected. Bad ones...well...

Kacy moved toward Benoit with her hands raised and tried to divert his attention. "We didn't do this. We found Stefanov like this. The gunman from yesterday must have been in cahoots with someone else. Quick, we must warn the others."

"Warn them that there is a new killer on the loose? Or is he in this room?" Benoit said slyly, shooting a look at Marcus.

"Marcus didn't do this. Stefanov must have missed the gunman's accomplice when he cleaned house," Kacy retorted while trying to hustle him out.

But the kid wouldn't budge.

Marcus shouldered himself between them, acting as a shield, but Kacy wasn't about to let him do that again. She moved to his side to form a better wall lest Darren suddenly decide to appear and make the situation even stickier.

As Marcus explained, "Let the grownups handle this, kid," she noticed a glint of silver in Benoit's hand.

A blade still stained red.

Knowing she didn't have much time, Kacy did the only thing she could to save Marcus. She threw herself at the guy.

And got sliced as a result.

CHAPTER TWENTY-FIVE

As soon as Kacy yelped—because she bloody threw herself on a knife-wielding asshole for no good reason—Marcus moved. He grabbed hold of Benoit and bounced his head off the wall a few times.

And even when the boy's eyes rolled back, he slammed it again. Just because.

Then he turned to Kacy and, through the panic seething within, managed to ask, "How bad is it?"

"It's nothing. A scratch."

He didn't care if it was only a pinprick. She'd gotten hurt.

"Let me see." He pulled her hand from her side and noticed the rip in the fabric and the stain of blood. A thin thread of blood, not thick and gushing. Still, though, the fucker had hurt his little pint.

He glared at Benoit's limp body. "He dies."

"Not yet. We need him for answers. Could be his boss is the one we've been looking for, in which case, we'll need him as leverage. Drag his ass back to the great room, would you? I want to use him to make an entrance."

"My pleasure." Reaching down, Marcus grabbed hold of the guy's collar and heaved him up enough that he didn't have to hunch while walking.

He let Kacy lead the way, little pint looking adorably violent in her raggedly trimmed dress, her sodden hair, and the holsters strapped to her thighs.

Halfway up the hall, she stopped and turned so fast he almost bumped into her.

She held out her hand. "I need your gun."

"What happened to yours?"

"I might have dropped it when I almost fell off the cliff."

A vein in his forehead started twitching. "Are you trying to kill me?"

"Don't worry. I'm pretty sure I would have hit the water and survived. I did last time."

"Last time?" The words emerged faintly as he realized little pint embraced danger.

Kind of like me.

Which meant he couldn't chastise her for it, even if his heart might stop beating one day because of her antics. He handed over his gun.

She cradled it with a smile. "My, what a big gun you have." And yes, she winked at him as she said it, the gloom in the hall not as thick given, farther ahead, flickering lights alleviated the shadows.

"Let's get this over with," he grumbled, because the

sooner they took care of business, the sooner he could have her cradling his even bigger gun.

Before they entered the main room, she halted again, this time whispering, "Why is it so quiet?"

An eerie silence permeated the space. No music. No voices. Nothing.

"Maybe everyone took off to their cabanas after the power failed." Marcus peered around, the two flickering candles set on the buffet table not really enough to light the vast room.

"Hold on, let me grab the penlight." She yanked it out and turned it on, shining its narrow beam around. On her first sweep, they saw nothing. On the second, the narrow band of light caught a foot.

Kacy stopped moving the flashlight around to illuminate their find, an older woman's foot, which, when followed, led to Benoit's lady friend, Adele. Dead. Not of a knife wound but a garrote to the neck, the red line gouged into her pale skin easily visible.

"What the hell is going on?" Kacy muttered.

"Did he kill her, too?" Marcus asked, sounding just as puzzled as he held up the limp body.

"No, I did." The words came from Willow, who stepped from behind a drape.

At her voice, Marcus dropped the body, and Kacy aimed her gun, but the redhead held up her hands.

"Don't shoot."

"You just admitted to killing her," said Kacy.

"Because I had no choice. It was the only way to get my boss off this island alive."

"She was the one behind the hits?" Frowning, Kacy looked down at the body and thus missed the redhead pulling out a knife.

Marcus saw it, though, and grabbed Kacy, throwing them both to the floor. The thrown blade narrowly missed them.

"What the fuck? She just tried to kill us." Kacy shoved up from the floor, head pivoting from side to side to look for Willow, but the woman had disappeared.

"I think we have a problem," Marcus rumbled.

"You think?" she snapped. "Why would she try and kill me? Is everyone on this island insane?"

"They're in survival mode," said Darren as he came striding down the hall. Alone.

"I told you to stay in that room!"

"I never was one to listen to orders I didn't like." Darren smirked as Marcus heaved Kacy to her feet.

A scowl crossed Kacy's face. "Then I won't be held responsible if you get killed."

"I should hope not given everyone on this island is out to get us."

"Explain," she demanded, and not very nicely.

From her expression, Marcus could tell the temptation to murder Darren was strong. Secrets. Always with the secrets, making everyone's job harder than it should be.

"This meeting was a setup."

"I told you from the get-go this whole thing stunk. But did you listen? Oh, no. You just had to be a man."

Marcus snorted. "Feel better now that you got that out of your system?"

She shrugged. "Not really. If you ask me, our client needs a good shot to the head to make him think straight, but I'll hold off until we make it out of here alive."

"Good plan because we'll need to be in top form if we want to survive the night."

"But Stefanov is dead. Surely any plot he planned will fall apart now," Marcus replied.

"*If* Stefanov was the mastermind behind it all." Darren played devil's advocate.

"It's his island. His invitation," Kacy remarked.

"So he said. Just like he claimed he manipulated us into coming here."

"You think he lied?" Marcus queried.

"Maybe. Without having my usual resources to check him out, I can't be sure. I do know he didn't have us brought here for the reason he claimed."

"You mean he wasn't trying to make everyone join some kind of Assassins United group?"

"He might have used that as a pretext to bring us here; however, I'm not sure that was entirely his idea. He could have been just as much a victim as we are. Apparently, I wasn't the only one dealing with assassination attempts. The other guests were also being targeted."

"And we are just finding out about this now?" Kacy snarled. "This would have been useful information to have."

"What would it have changed?"

"Well, for one thing, we might not be standing here in

the dark wondering why everyone has gone bat-shit crazy," Kacy yelled at Darren, making some excellent points.

A shake of his head and some tsking showed Marcus's displeasure. "Dude, not cool. You should have told us about it."

"If I had, you would have bundled me off this island, and I wouldn't have had a chance to gather information."

"Damned straight we would have kidnapped your ass and taken it back to shore. It's our job to keep you safe," Kacy said, exasperation in her tone.

"But playing it safe would have meant not knowing what happened, or why." Darren rolled his shoulders. "Sometimes, you have to take risks to get ahead."

"Yes, you do, but you should let those around you know so they can better help you."

"I'm telling you now. Now, we deal with it. Starting with the latest update, which is everyone you've met has been targeted. And—"

"By whom?" she interrupted.

Darren shrugged. "No one seems to know, and it's part of the reason we've not fled even when given the chance. We all are looking for that answer. Why does someone want to kill us and in such a strange fashion? Why not assassinate us at home? Why bring us here to this island and then deliver instructions to—"

"Instructions? When? How?" Kacy barked.

"A note found in my toiletries. A discussion with a few other guests let me know that everyone guesting on this island found a note."

"I didn't get one," Marcus replied.

"Me either," said Kacy.

Darren's nonchalant expression had him practically eyeing the ceiling and whistling in false innocence.

"Holy shit, I had a note," Kacy said in a breathy exclamation.

A nod by Darren. "You both did."

"And you didn't tell us?" This time, Marcus couldn't contain himself. "That is seriously fucked up."

"When I found mine, I went looking for yours, and found them. I thought it best to hold on to them until needed."

"And what was on these notes? What instructions did they have?"

"Not much. To escape this island, eliminate...and then a name."

"Please tell me they had your name for mine," Kacy said, her tone low and growly. "I am in the mood to kill something."

"You didn't get me or Marcus. Your target was Willow."

"No shit." Kacy gaped. "That's cold."

"Are you saying after what she's done you wouldn't kill her?"

Kacy blew a raspberry. "Please. I'd kill her without blinking. But, seriously? I am more pissed that the *hombre* pulling our strings thought he should pit the two women against each other. As if we're not capable of taking out bigger prey." Kacy tossed her head, and Marcus wished they were anywhere but here in the dark with a storm howling outside and dead bodies popping up everywhere.

"You are assuming Willow got your name," Darren said.

"She tried to kill me."

"Or was she protecting herself?" At her glare, Darren shrugged. "We are in an odd situation where we are being pitted against each other. Our fears, our need for survival, trumping the usual rules. We can't trust anyone right now."

Despite wanting to change the subject, Marcus couldn't help but ask, "What name did you get?"

"Aren't you curious about the one assigned to you? You had Lee, Ming's bodyguard," Darren replied, skirting the answer.

It took Marcus only a moment to clue in on who Darren had gotten. "Your note said Francesca, didn't it? You were supposed to kill her."

"Who else but Fran would be on my missive? Although I don't know why they thought it would be hard. I feel nothing for the woman." Darren's short, clipped words might have been meant as dismissive, but Marcus could hear the falseness of them.

"Did you really kill her?" Kacy looked up at the ceiling, and even Marcus had to wonder if Darren had the coldness needed for a dispassionate kill of someone he'd been intimate with.

That would take some seriously cold balls.

"I didn't kill her. Not for lack of wanting, I assure you. But the very fact that someone thought I should kill her and not Stefanov was why I sought her out. I was more curious to see the purpose in demanding such a thing. Stefanov was behind the attempts on Kacy."

"Hold on, Stefanov had a note, too." Kacy's brow creased. "But he was the one organizing this shindig."

"And like I said before, I don't think he is the mastermind behind it all."

"I can see going after you and the other honchos, but why go after the girlfriends and bodyguards?" Marcus asked.

"To start a war? Because they could?" Darren shrugged. "The why of it doesn't matter. Someone is playing games, and this entire island is a trap."

Marcus cracked his knuckles as the severity of their situation sank in. "It's a death island."

"More like a gladiator ring," said Kacy. "The strongest survive."

"Or we refuse to play the game." Darren gestured to Adele's still body. "Someone is forcing us to dance to their tune, and we're letting them. It has to stop."

"How, though?" Kacy asked. "If you've got people ready to kill on the vague promise they won't die, how do you convince them not to act?"

"Are you whining because your redheaded friend tried to kill you?" Marcus arched a brow.

"I'm mad because I know better than to trust someone I just met," Kacy grumbled, looking very insulted.

"To err is human," Darren quoted.

"To err means being buried six feet under because

you were stupid." Crossing her arms, she confronted her boss.

Time to get them back on track. While they were yapping and catching up, there was a killer, possibly more than one, on the island. They needed to make a plan.

First, Marcus needed to tell them what he'd seen. "I think there's someone else on the island. Just before the lights went out, I saw someone in a mask."

"Which means it could be anyone. A current guest, a new player," Darren remarked. "Perhaps the one manipulating us all. Not that it matters. If the others on the island decide the only way out is to kill, then we have a problem."

"Only if they get to us first."

Kacy grinned at him. "Exactly. How many each do we get? I call dibs on any tie breakers." Kacy pulled her knife and checked the blade.

"You can't call dibs," Marcus retorted. "It's whoever finds them first."

"Well, that doesn't seem fair." She planted one hand on her hip. "You're taller. You can spot them from farther away."

"Are you really going to play the I'm-too-short card?" Snort. He smiled, slow and smirking. "Are you making excuses because you're not a man?"

Her eyes fired, and her lips curved. "I accept the challenge."

Whereas Darren bobbed his gaze between them. "You're both insane."

"No, we're good employees," she stated. "This kind of thing is where we really earn our paychecks."

"Should we ask for bonuses now on the people we take out?" Marcus asked.

"We are not killing people willy-nilly," Darren snapped. "Or have you forgotten these are power players in the world? Their deaths would not go unnoticed or unpunished. Not to mention killing is playing into the hands of whoever is manipulating us. I would prefer to make the other guests into my allies."

Kacy sighed. "I figured you'd say that, but"—her lips curved—"pretending I was going to pull some kind of *Hunger Games* on them was fun."

"Speak for yourself. I was serious." Marcus was ready to do what it took to keep little pint and his brother by another mother alive.

"Don't worry, meathead," Kacy said in an exaggerated whisper. "I'm pretty sure we'll have to kill a couple."

"Only if you have to. If someone is targeting the academies around the world, then we might need to save our strength and unite rather than fight one another. But if it comes down to kill or be killed..." Darren shrugged.

"I guess we could call this a killer tropical vacation." Marcus grinned.

She scowled, only to shake her head and smile. "You're impossible, meathead. But a decent partner to have. And we've also fucked around enough. Unless our client here has some more secrets he'd like to share, such as the fact that we're sitting on an active volcano?"

Darren shook his head.

"Okay, so here's the plan. We need to get the client back into the tower and barricade the doors. Then we wait until morning and call Harry for an extraction."

"Coast Guard would be quicker if we run into an emergency."

Kacy shook her head at Darren, but Marcus replied for her.

"We can't have the Coast Guard show up, too many questions. With the number of bodies lying around, we'd never convince them we weren't involved somehow."

"Then what do you suggest? We can't exactly hide that people died here."

"We could if we got rid of the bodies." It was Marcus who pointed out the obvious. "No bodies, no crime. And this storm is the perfect cover."

Darren shook his head. "Are you suggesting we toss them all into the ocean, claiming what? That they went for a swim in a storm and died?"

Kacy pointed out the most obvious flaw. "Not even mob mentality could make that many people so stupid. We need something a little more unexpected. Something that would take a bunch of people out at once."

"Falling off the cliff?" Marcus suggested.

"Only plausible if the balcony falls down." A slow smile curved Kacy's lips. "I have an idea. But first, we need to find all the bodies and pile them in the tower."

"And then what?" Marcus asked. "Set it on fire?"

"In a rain storm?" She shook her head. "Nope. We're going to put them on the balcony, claiming they went out to watch the storm, and blow that fucker up."

CHAPTER TWENTY-SIX

WHILE KACY'S PLAN WAS QUICKLY APPROVED BY THE men, it did require a few things to make it work. First off, they needed to gather all the bodies. Not just Stefanov and Adele, but any other bodies that might be around.

Marcus made quick work of the ones they knew about, putting them out in the rain and leaving the balcony doors open to flood the inside of the office, washing most of the blood clean.

Benoit remained unconscious, and Marcus eyed him with hands on his hips. "What do we do with this little shit?"

"Eliminate him so he can't talk." Kacy was taught not to leave the enemy behind.

Darren eyed Benoit dispassionately. "He's probably a guy for hire, so I doubt he'll talk to the authorities. However, he is dangerous. So, keep him tied."

"The academy doesn't recommend compassion," she reminded.

"The academy isn't usually under attack," Darren retorted. "Besides, we might need him to answer some questions."

"As the client wishes." Kacy might not agree, but she had been trained to obey the client. They trussed Benoit like a turkey and stuck him in the office for the moment.

Kacy eyed Darren and asked, "What about Francesca? Did you leave her on the roof?"

His expression turned cold. "You don't need to concern yourself with her."

"As long as you took care of her." Hopefully, in a way that would cover his tracks.

"What next, little pint?" Marcus asked, deferring to her.

"Now, I go and see if I can find some more bodies." Because Willow was still out there, and if she'd decided to hedge her client's odds by killing everyone else, then they'd have to deal with her and whatever mess she created.

"What do you mean you're going? We're all going," Marcus argued.

She shook her head. "We can't risk Darren like that. Not with a killer or more on the loose. You're safest staying here with him, locked in the tower, with a gun. If anyone but me enters, shoot."

"You need Marcus," Darren interjected.

"I'm capable of killing on my own." The hot retort was a familiar one. Men always felt a need to treat her like a girl.

"I know you can kill, but you won't be able to carry the bodies back. You need muscle for that."

Good point. However... "We can't leave Darren unprotected."

"You will if I order it." Darren crossed his arms over his chest. "And I am ordering it. We don't have much time before the storm blows over and people come looking. I'm sure I'm not the only one who put out a call for reinforcements."

Tossing a look at the raging storm, Kacy pursed her lips. "We have a few hours before we need to worry."

"Which isn't long to secure the island and set the stage for any authorities. You and Marcus need to work together. I'll be fine. The door still has its lock."

"I came through the balcony," she pointed out.

"And you're nuts. Not everyone can climb like a ninja squirrel," Darren retorted.

Marcus snickered, totally earning the elbow to the ribs.

"I guess, if you parked yourself in that corner"—she pointed to the one farthest from the stairs and patio —"then you could shoot anyone trying to come in."

Placing a hand over his heart, Darren swore, "If anything moves, I'll shoot."

Kacy didn't like it, but even she had to admit, if she wanted to sweep the island and hide any evidence of foul play, then they had to do this. "Fine. But I swear, if you leave this room—"

"I know. You'll kill me yourself," Darren said with a roll of his eyes.

"I'll kill you twice," she growled. She handed over the gun she'd borrowed from Marcus. It still miffed her that she'd lost her own pistol. However, she still had her knife and some mad *ardilla rabiosa* skills. "Ready, meathead?"

"After you, little pint." Marcus gestured.

Not liking the plan, but not having much choice, Kacy left Darren in the tower room, but she didn't move away until they heard the click of a lock.

She'd warned him about how someone could access the balcony, even in this weather. Also, while doubtful anyone could get on the roof in this storm, she didn't discount it. Professionals always found a way.

Darren knew to keep watch on all three points of egress into the room. Hopefully, they wouldn't find out if Darren shot as well as he boasted.

Re-entering the large room, struck anew by the silence in it, she did find some comfort in having Marcus with her. Back to back, they swept the house. With the guests scattered, she wondered what had happened to the skeleton staff.

Kacy found the chef behind the island in the kitchen, cleaved with his own knife. "Blowing up the tower won't hide this," she remarked.

Marcus looked at the pooling blood staining the tile and shook his head. "We might need to think bigger."

The whole house would have to go.

Fire? But so much of this place was tile. The walls were stone. Only the ceiling boasted wood of a sort.

Worry about it later. Marcus motioned to her by the back door. Knife in hand, she approached as he slipped outside. She followed him, the humidity just past the barrier of the house enough to make her skin heat. A step out from the protection of the porch cooled her with the heavy drops of rain.

Marcus stood to the side of the small garden path, staring at something on the ground amongst the growing vegetables, the tomato vines tall and lush, heavy with fruit.

"I found Stefanov's security," he stated. One garroted to death, the other shot point blank between the eyes, the sound probably hidden by the vicious storm that still whipped the island into a wet frenzy.

"Grab their weapons." No point in leaving them behind to be used against them.

She waited while Marcus lifted the bodies out of the garden and dumped them inside before they set off on the path.

Their trail was dimly lit by moonbeams, their solar-based power unaffected by the outage at the house. But even their illumination couldn't fully penetrate the maelstrom. The rain and fog made it hard to see, the squall itself so noisy it masked anything else.

The foliage around made dark sentinels that loomed suddenly through the torrent. She kept in constant motion, moving and shifting to see everywhere at once.

Nothing moved.

Not a sound overshadowed that of the pouring rain.

A few twists into the path, she smelled it.

Smoke. She ran, Marcus at her heels, and burst

around the curves to discover even the rain couldn't stop a fire if it blazed big and hot enough.

A cabana burned. While the wet thatched roof of the guesthouse contained most of it, Kacy could see the flames dancing within. She knew who guested here. Banele, the giant man from the South African nation. If he hadn't escaped before the flames took hold, then he'd surely perished. No one cried for help or answered her when she called out, only the steady snap of things burning answered.

"Should you be announcing our presence?" Marcus asked, guarding her back, the gun he'd filched from the security guard's holster getting wet as he held it out in front of him. Here was to hoping it was well kept and would fire if the time came.

"Don't tell me you're scared."

"No, just wanting to be part of the plan. Didn't we have a bet?"

"Not officially," she remarked as they left the burning cabana and moved down the path to the next. "But maybe we should. Despite what Darren thinks, I don't think we're going to have a 'We Are The World' sing-along moment."

"So you think we should employ deadly force?"

"If attacked, yes. If you can subdue, then that's better. If we bring one or two back to Darren alive, then maybe he won't be too pissed about the ones who don't make it."

"Do you have any idea how sexy it is when you talk tactics to me?" Marcus rumbled, gun out in front of him as he eased around a bend in the crushed-shell path.

Did he have any idea how sexy it was that he respected her and treated her as an equal? The guys in the office treated her as one of them, but she didn't want to bang them until something crowed.

Moving past the next curve brought them to a cabana that appeared fully dark. Shoving at the door didn't budge it. Someone had barricaded the entrance.

Signaling to Marcus to flank the opposite side, she leaned against the wall before pounding on the door. "Is anyone alive in there?"

At first, she thought no one would reply.

"Go away, or we shoot!" a woman yelled. Kacy recognized the voice of Ming, the Asian woman who'd not spoken to many in the group, preferring to keep to herself.

"We know about the note. We're going to do something about it."

"You mean kill us like you killed Banele?" was the shouted reply.

Arguing their innocence was a pointless waste of time. "Just stay inside," Kacy shouted back. "We'll take care of the assassins on the island."

The reply was something spat rapid-fire in Chinese, possibly rude, but Kacy couldn't blame her. At this point, no one could really tell who was friend or foe.

The next cabana had the shutters closed, but the seam running along them showed a flickering light from a candle or two. A brisk knock was greeted with a bullet through the door. Good thing they weren't standing directly in front. The shots fired let them know the Swiss contingent was safe.

Which left Willow and her British date unaccounted for, as well as the Australian couple.

Marcus corrected her. "You forgot Gerard and the housekeeper."

She had, and she also assumed no one else had landed on the island before the storm. She hadn't forgotten the incursion from the other night by those determined killers. The possibility of running into more, while slim, existed.

The rain proved relentless, a heavy deluge that soaked them to the skin, bringing a deep chill from within. The wind whipped around them, driving the rain into them with needle-like force. Visibility proved impossible. Even the solar lights barely managed a muted glow. She could see in only a small radius around them.

Anyone could be hiding within feet, and they'd never know.

It made their task almost impossible. But Kacy wouldn't give up, and, she'd bet, neither would Marcus. He shadowed her, his expression grim but determined.

Traversing a small bridge over the lazy river, the wood slats slick with moisture, Kacy had turned to ask Marcus if perhaps they should return to check on Darren when something rose from the waters and grabbed her by the ankles.

Caught off guard, a sharp cry escaped Kacy as she slammed down hard on her ass before she was yanked off the small bridge, whacking her head on the edge in the process.

The blow stunned her, as did the submersion in the subtly chlorinated water. Under the surface, she kept her eyes open but could see nothing. She kept her mouth closed lest she breathe in fluid.

The slow-flowing stream pulled at her body, but she quickly found her footing. Only she couldn't push up. Something held her down!

Lashing out with her feet, the movement sluggish because of the current, she managed to hit flesh. But it didn't free her from the hands currently meshed in her hair, pushing her down. Trying to drown her.

Panic threatened as the pressure in her lungs demanded she breathe. But she couldn't. What she could do, though, was stop flailing like a ninny.

Reaching for her knife, she pulled it from the sheath and slashed blindly in front of her. When that didn't hit anything, she slashed beside her, the edge of the blade hitting flesh.

The grip on her hair loosened.

Pushing against the bottom of the lazy river, Kacy rose from the water and heaved in a lungful of air.

Rain still slammed down, and she could hear Marcus yelling for her. She couldn't see the bridge, and the river current tugged at her. Instinct made her duck just as a fist came flying.

She whirled, expecting to see Willow. Instead, she confronted Betty, the Australian cattleman's wife.

The round-cheeked woman blinked at her, and for a

moment, Kacy hesitated. The other times she'd seen this woman, she'd exuded a maternal, matronly air, always smiling.

Betty still smiled as she lashed out with a fist. Kacy managed to turn enough that the blow struck her in the shoulder. It hit a nerve, though, and she found her fingers opening, the knife falling from her grip into the water.

Whap. She blocked a right hook, only to miss a quick follow-up on the left, which took Kacy on the edge of her jaw. Her head snapped.

Ow.

All hesitation and reservation evaporated. If the bitch wanted to fight, then so be it.

Gaze narrowed, Kacy dropped into fighting mode. Snap. Jab. She felt nothing but grim satisfaction with each blow that hit.

"Why," Kacy snarled in between punches, "are you doing this?"

She danced in the water, ignoring the rain and anything else to focus on her opponent.

Betty had her hands up too, looking fierce in her gaze. "The note said, only one faction can survive. Ours." The older woman rushed Kacy, and Kacy slipped when she sidestepped.

Down they went, the current sweeping their unbalanced bodies, sliding them farther downstream. It took a few bobbing moments to find her feet, dancing on tiptoe a few strides before controlling her momentum.

She'd barely stood when a blow to her back sent her

staggering. Whirling, she noticed Betty right behind her, hand raised, clutching the knife Kacy had lost.

There was no blocking the sharp blade arcing. But Kacy tried, throwing herself backwards into the current.

Bang.

Betty's eyes widened, and the arm stopping moving. Floating on her back, Kacy saw the perfect, dime-sized hole barely fill with blood before the woman's body sank in the water.

Thrashing to get her feet back down, Kacy whirled to see Gerard, soaked to the skin in a dark suit, his gun kept dry in a plastic bag.

"Thank you."

Her smile quickly faded, though, as the gun didn't lower but aimed at her.

"Don't thank me yet." Gerard smiled, not the vapid grin of a servant but of someone used to being in charge. "Is now a good time to mention I'm the one who arranged this fantastic event?"

"I thought that was Stefanov?"

Gerard snorted. "A simple minion playing a part. As the true owner of this island, I'm rescinding my invitation."

CHAPTER TWENTY-SEVEN

CRACK. THE BRANCH HIT GERARD ON THE BACK OF the head with a satisfying crunch before the lying prick could put a hole in Kacy.

The body fell into the lazy river and bobbed merrily away, but Marcus let it go for the moment, more concerned about the woman standing drenched and alive in the current.

Kacy blinked at him. And then smiled. "Nice timing."

"I know."

He held out his hand, and she gripped it, trusting him to pull her to safety, which, in this case, meant in his arms for a crushing hug.

He couldn't stop himself from holding her, his relief immense. "Stop trying to give me heart attacks. I thought my chest would explode when you were yanked off that bridge."

"Remind me to never go cliff diving with you," she quipped.

"Do not joke about this." Not when his pulse still raced in fear. Seeing someone standing over the woman he loved holding a gun did things to a guy.

"Get over it, meathead. You're just jealous because you were afraid I would get ahead in the kill count."

"Too late. I'm pretty sure I'm beating you."

"Did you run into someone while I was wrestling Betty?"

"Two someones. Your pal, Willow, who, as it turns out, was in cahoots with the Aussie couple. Her British employer never knew."

"Is he dead?"

Marcus nodded. According to Willow, who'd cackled as she struck Marcus from behind, "That snooty bastard never even saw it coming."

"I almost died, too. When you got taken off the bridge, I was kind of distracted." More like terrified that he was about to lose Kacy. "While I was searching the water, they snuck up on me and clocked me in the head."

Her fingertips touched the wound at his temple. "Good thing it's made of rock."

"Yes, it is a good thing, and also a good thing they underestimated the density of my skull. I pretended to fall, and when she came close, I tackled her around the knees. Her head hit the ground, and she was out cold. Then I showed Outback Tom why he shouldn't bring a knife to a fist fight."

"And then you found me before Gerard could kill me." She squeezed him. "Thank you."

"Don't thank me. We should have stayed in the tower and let these idiots kill each other. I thought the wars I fought in were crazy and stupid, but this is..."

"Evil. I know." She tilted her head back to look at him. "This is why we train at the academy. So we can fight against this."

"But someone is trying to turn the different schools and groups against each other."

"From the sounds of it, it might have been Gerard, except he was no manservant."

"He played us." Marcus couldn't help but feel disgusted. He'd never even seen it coming. "Do you think he's dead?" The body had fallen into the water, unconscious. But...

Kacy shrugged. "Maybe he is. Or maybe he isn't. Just like we can't be sure Willow's out of commission. Either way, we should get back to Darren and check on him. I think it's time we hunkered down and waited shit out. We'll have to take our chances with the Coast Guard if they get here before we can clean this shit up."

Except, before they could make it to the house, it exploded. As in a giant fucking *kaboom*, ground-shaking explosion.

Bits of the house—wooden beams, glass shards, even chunks of stone—blew outwards and rained down on the island, hitting the ground like a dense meteor shower. The rain chose that moment to taper to a fine drizzle, which meant some of the smoldering debris burned where it landed. Burned even the wet thatch of the cabanas.

Lit up trees and roofs in a bright, hot blaze that stank of smoke.

Gathered on the beach, the ragged survivors stuck close to the waves, lest they have to escape the hot flames.

They could only watch as everything—clothes, furniture, and the bodies that couldn't run, like Darren's —burned.

Burned to ash, leaving nothing behind. Nothing but the gaping hole in his heart.

When dawn broke, brilliant and sunny, the Coast Guard arrived to find the survivors huddled on the beach, shell-shocked and dark with soot. There weren't many of them, only those who'd barricaded themselves in once the violence started.

As they were herded onto the ship and given blankets along with warm drinks, Kacy huddled close to Marcus and remarked on his lack of emotion.

"Are you okay? You must be shocked about Darren."

Shocked? Maybe. Disbelief was more like it. He had a hard time believing his friend had died so ignobly.

It didn't feel real. And he said so to the men in uniform who questioned him. He'd told them he was taking the boss's girlfriend for a walk on the beach to watch the storm when everything exploded.

To his surprise, they didn't question him much. The authorities on that boat and those who met them on the dock didn't really delve deeply into the island explosion, the consensus being that the generators got hit by lightning, and the fuel tanks feeding them somehow exploded. Then burning shit took care of the rest.

No bodies. No crime. Just a horrible tragedy. But because those involved were rich—and special—it never even made the news. Those with power knew how to hide things, and the next in line stepped in to take their place.

In short order, the survivors were released. Marcus and Kacy were bundled off to a hotel, paid for by Kacy's company, Bad Boy Inc.

Tired, dirty, and still damp, Marcus couldn't wait to strip and get into a hot shower.

The show would have to wait because waiting for them in the room was a man. Harry.

At the sight of him, Kacy squealed and threw herself at him, hugging him tightly before pushing away and staring at her toes, shoulders hunched.

"I failed the mission."

They both had. Marcus, in keeping Kacy safe, had failed his best friend.

The numbness permeated every part of him. It didn't seem real that Darren was dead. Surely Marcus would feel it in his heart if it were true? And yet, they'd found no more survivors.

No Darren.

"You hardly failed. You're here in one piece, as is Marcus, I see. Darren is quite happy about that."

"Darren is dead." Marcus uttered the words and wished they didn't feel so wrong.

"Not exactly dead," Harry corrected. "He sent me here to let you know."

"What?" Kacy's head snapped up. "What do you mean he let you know? Darren's alive?"

"Quite."

She snarled. "Where is he?"

"Now, Kacy—"

"Don't you *Kacy* me. I'm going to kill him. How dare he make us all think he died?"

How dare he make Marcus think he'd been abandoned?

The soothing words from Harry didn't placate. "Don't be too mad. He had to do it and make it look real in order to go into proper hiding."

"How about I help him by sticking him in a box six feet under?" Kacy didn't even try to hold in her rage.

He could understand it. "Where is he?" Marcus asked. Because he kind of felt like Kacy right then. Itching to wrap his hands around someone's throat for a good throttling.

"I can't disclose his location. And neither of you can let on that he's still alive. But he thought you should know before you began spending everything he left you in his will."

It took a moment for the words to sink in. "He made me his heir?" Marcus whispered, his throat closing up.

"You should know by now you're like family to him," Harry said. "Just like Kacy is family to me, which means hurt her and—"

"I know. No one will find the body," Marcus interrupted.

"Do you really think I'd merely kill you? That would be too simple. I'd make it hurt first." Harry smiled. A cold smile. But one Marcus didn't mind because anyone who cared for Kacy was a good shit in his books.

Harry handed them a wad of cash plus some plastic cards. "Replacement identification. Money. You'll find some clothes in the bags I left in the closet. I've arranged for a flight back in the morning. Kacy, I'll expect you in the office on Monday."

"Are we hiring by any chance?" she queried.

Harry's calculating gaze swept over Marcus. "I think we can find something for your boyfriend to do."

It wasn't Harry's offer of a job that stunned Marcus most, but the fact that Kacy didn't deny the claim. As soon as the other man left, Marcus swept her into his arms.

"What's got you so happy?"

"Other than the fact that you sort of called me your boyfriend?"

"What else would I call you? I mean, you're a boy. I think we're friends."

He plastered his mouth to hers but couldn't help a chuckle. "He's alive! Darren's alive."

"Only until I get my hands on him." Said with an ominous undertone.

"I'll hold him for you. Especially since we're now partners."

"Who the hell said that?"

"You want me to work with you."

She grumbled, "Well, I doubt you want to stick around my place cleaning and cooking all day."

"If you'll cook, I'll clean." Old military habits died hard.

"Are you negotiating terms?" she asked.

"Best to have ground rules if we're going to be together."

"No one said that was permanent."

"Then how long were you planning?"

"Until you annoy me and I toss you out." The words sounded feisty, and yet, she still hugged him. Was it his imagination, or was she tugging off his clothes?

His lips twitched. "I love you, too."

"I never said that."

"Maybe not yet, but you will. I love you, even if you're the most infuriating woman ever."

"You love that I'm a bitch?" Her brow arched.

"I like that you don't take any shit. That you know how to kick ass."

"Say it. I can kick your meathead ass."

"Anytime, little pint."

For some reason, it caused her gaze to smolder. "You know, you're not too bad either."

"Not too bad?" he growled, squeezing her until she gasped with laughter.

"Okay, maybe I'm fond—"

Squish.

"Very fond, of you, too. Maybe." She squealed when he lifted her off her feet and swung her around.

"We're gonna make a great team, little pint."

"We'd better, or you'll have to deal with Harry."

"I will make you happy."

"You'd better." She grinned. "So when does the making-me-happy part start. I could use a shower and more."

"Can't we skip to the 'and more' part?" It didn't take much to strip the poncho off her and rip the ragged remnants of her gown.

Looking down at herself caused her nose to wrinkle. "Only a man would think this"—she gestured to her grimy body—"is sexy."

"I told you before, I like you as you are, little pint. Now, give me a kiss."

"Ordering me around?"

"Begging." He dropped to his knees. "Please."

"Get up, you meathead. Let's go get clean."

She drew him to his feet before turning to lead the way into the bathroom. The water took only a moment to get hot, and as she stood under the spray, Marcus joined her, nestling into her body from behind, arms loosely laced around her.

He rubbed his jaw against the top of her head, smelling the smoke in it and not caring. What did he care about her hickory scent when his cock pushed hotly against the crevice of her ass?

Turning in his grip, she lifted her lips for a kiss, and he bent to meet her. Her touch never failed to electrify him.

They stood under the spray, locked in a kiss, bodies

pressed together, his pulsing cock trapped between them. Her arms twined around his neck. She hugged him to her tightly. The feeling of her skin against his, silky smooth, drove him mad with lust.

He skimmed his hand down her side, pausing when he felt the gauze.

The white bandage served as reminder of her wound. They'd cleaned and dressed it on the boat, and here he mauled her instead of letting her get the rest and care she needed. He pulled away, angry at himself for being so selfish.

"Don't you dare leave this shower. I'm not done with you."

"You're injured."

She leaned out of the shower and poked him in the arm, smack-dab in the center of his own gauzy bandage.

"That didn't hurt."

"You know what will," she said as he reached for a towel, "is you leaving me and yet knowing I'm going to be in here touching myself, thinking of you."

His hand froze.

"Why do you insist on making things hard?" He turned around, hands on his hips, his erection pointing right at her.

She smiled.

She bloody well smiled and crooked a finger at him.

So much for being a gentle-fucking-man and letting her heal. With a growl, he dove back into the shower and took her lips in a passionate embrace.

For all his roughness and passion as he devoured her

mouth, he was also gentle, steering his hands clear of her wounded area.

She wasn't as tender, nipping and biting at his mouth. Hips grinding against him.

The passion beat fiercely between them. He dragged his lips down the column of her throat, drawing sweet moans from her.

His tongue licked its way to her breasts, and at long last, he got to play with them. He circled a nipple with the tip of his tongue, teasing her while he cupped her ass. That sweet fucking ass.

Bending her back, he leaned in and took the other nipple between his lips, sucking the puckered nub into his mouth. Switching breasts, he lavished the same attention on the first nipple, tugging on it with his teeth before sucking on her flesh.

This time, she didn't have to stifle her passion. She was vocal about it, her cries merging with hot pants, her pleasure not just loud and wonderful but rough as she dug her fingers into his shoulders. The sharp pinch of her nails drove him crazier.

He dropped to his knees, uncaring of the water sluicing down. He nuzzled her belly with his face before tickling the curls covering her mound.

"Marcus." She said his name on a low moan, clasping his hair.

Grabbing her ass cheeks, he squeezed them and pushed at the seam of her thighs, getting them to part.

With the first flick of his tongue against her sex, she

cried out, her hips bucking hard, almost knocking him back.

"More."

Definitely more. He stroked her again, parting her lips to lap at her. Suck. He flicked his tongue against her clit, and she arched. Cried out.

Did all manner of things as he held her and licked her and made her crazy.

Tugging at her clit with his lips, he worked it, sometimes flicking his tongue against it back and forth, other times biting on it gently with his teeth.

It made her come. Come with a strident scream that saw her bucking in his grasp.

Standing, he hoisted her high enough that the tip of him could find the entrance to her still-quivering sex. He thrust into her, sheathing his cock with one shove that stretched her and triggered a second orgasm.

"Marcus!" She screamed his name then moaned as she clutched at him. Trembled and groaned her pleasure as he pumped into her sweet body.

When he did finally come, his hips heaving hard one final time, she sighed his name.

"Marcus."

"I love you, little pint."

Softly said but he still got punched.

Not hard.

He knew it.

She loved him, too.

CHAPTER TWENTY-EIGHT

After sleeping all day, when they weren't doing filthy, dirty things or eating, they finally dressed and boarded a plane on Saturday night, meaning they were in her bed early Sunday morning and still lying in it when someone walked into her house.

Someone with a key.

Kacy had only enough time to snatch Marcus's gun from his hand and slide it under the pillow before Mama walked into her bedroom. She didn't have time to put on clothes, and neither did Marcus.

Her mother's eyes went wide. "*Dios.* Now that's what I call a lot of man!"

Kacy screeched, "Mama, would it kill you to knock?" She scrambled to pull a sheet over them both.

"Would it kill you to call your mother?" she retorted. "I had to rely on the neighbor to call me and tell me when you got home. With a man." The pointed stare covered Marcus, who grinned.

"Hi. I think we met on the phone already. I'm Marcus." He held out his hand, and Kacy wanted to hide under her bed as her mother gripped it and turned it over, inspecting it.

The appraising gaze inspected every aspect of Marcus before her mother said, "Bring him to dinner."

And with that, her mother sailed back out and slammed the front door.

Kacy groaned. "Oh, God. I can't believe that just happened."

"It's not that bad. I was bound to meet her sooner or later."

She gave him a side eye. "I had hoped for more time."

"Why? She seems nice."

"She can be. Just be prepared."

She just wouldn't tell him prepared for what. He'd soon find out.

Later that day, at her mother's house for dinner—which wasn't an option—they were seated at the table, a table laden with food. There was homemade salsa and guacamole with fresh tortilla chips—homemade, not store-bought. Mama had gone all out making spicy enchiladas, the smell heavenly when they'd walked through the door.

Marcus's eyes had lit up at the sight of all the dishes. The only time Kacy had seen Marcus look happier was in bed.

Now, Mama soaked in his praise as he hummed and groaned with almost every single bite.

"Delicious." He took another bite, this time trying a

chip slathered in fresh dip. "Dear God, you made this? I don't suppose Sunday night dinner is a tradition."

He laid it on thick, but damned if she didn't think he was sincere.

Mama noticed and reveled in it.

The doorbell rang, and her mother sighed. "I'll get it. It's probably that man for Tito again."

"I thought Harry was going to take care of him?"

"He offered, but I didn't want to bother him. This is a family matter. Your employer should not be involved."

Silly given who Harry was, but Mama didn't know what Bad Boy Inc. really did.

"What's going on?" Marcus asked, pausing in his feast.

"My brothers owe some money, and some thugs think they can shake down Mama for it."

Being predictable, he said, "I'll handle it." Marcus rose from the table and left the room. Kacy wanted to follow, wanted to so badly, but she could see Mama watching her.

"I'm surprised you're letting him answer the door. You don't usually let men do things for you."

"Marcus is different." For one, Kacy didn't feel a need to constantly prove herself around him.

"He's a nice boy."

More than nice. He also had a bad streak she really liked. And he made her smile. Made her mad. Horny. She sighed. "I think I love him, Mama."

Words she could admit to her mother but still hesitated to say aloud to Marcus.

The squeal of tires from outside had Kacy burning to know what had happened.

Marcus stepped back in, looking just as calm as before.

Mama eyed him. "Do you need ice for your fist?" Kacy's brothers always needed tending after their scraps.

Marcus smirked. "I'm not hurt. His jaw was soft. As was his reason for visiting. He *won't* be back."

Kacy shivered at the implied "or else" in his words.

"More enchiladas?" Mama pointed a serving spoon at the dish.

"Yes, please."

"And come back Tuesday. I make tacos."

Since when? In that moment, Kacy knew she'd never get rid of Marcus. Mama approved.

And so did this pint-sized killer.

EPILOGUE

WEEKS LATER...

"You know when I said I didn't mind mixing pleasure with work, I didn't mean on our honeymoon," Marcus grumbled.

"Don't be grumpy, meathead. Just think, not only are we getting paid to go on a cruise, you get to see me in a bikini." Kacy reached down and pulled the hem of her cover-up over her body, revealing the bikini that Kacy swore was too tiny but that Sherry claimed contained just the right amount—more like lack—of fabric.

His eyes widened as they roved her body. "Good God, little pint. Put that back on."

A frown creased her brow. "Don't you like it?"

"I do, and so will every man on board. It might look kind of suspicious if we arrive in port and most of the males are dead."

A coy smile pulled her lips. "Only most? I'm disappointed."

"I wouldn't have to kill the gay ones, but if it makes you feel better, I might toss the women who eyeball you off the ship, too."

At that, she laughed. "And then I'd have to get rid of the rest for daring to ogle you."

"You think they'll ogle?" He flexed, her big, beautiful, burly husband. Yes, husband. Because Mama adored him, and when Aunt Juanita asked, "Why you bring that *gringo* into my house?" Kacy had finally said the words he'd been waiting to hear. "Get used to seeing him, because HGet usI love him."

Of course, her mother and Marcus had then used those words against her, conspiring to put together the quickest wedding ever, minus her brothers, plus Harry and the crew at BB Inc., also minus Darren, who was still off on his secret adventure.

His loss.

They hadn't wanted to wait. She loved Marcus, and he loved her. Besides, as he'd claimed...better to nail her down before she changed her mind.

She wouldn't have. Kacy wasn't a quitter, and she hadn't minded taking those vows, not even the *'til death do us part* part because, if Marcus ever dared to fall out of love, she'd kill him. And he knew it. It made him smile. Crazy meathead.

My meathead. Now and forever.

———

IT SEEMED as if he'd waited forever for this chance. Ever since Francesca had left him, despondent and without a real reason, Darren had wondered what he had done wrong. Why? Why had she set out to hurt him?

Not that he cared.

Not anymore.

This wasn't about revenge, but something else.

She stirred, her long lashes fluttering against her pale skin. Her body undulated as she tried to stretch her limbs and found them caught.

It wasn't the first time Darren had had her tethered to furniture. Of course, the last time he'd been in lust and they were both naked.

Things had changed since then.

Her brilliant blue eyes opened wide in shock. "Darren. What's happening?"

"Hello, Fran. Have a nice nap?"

She pulled, and her gaze narrowed. "Untie me at once."

He would.

Eventually.

But first, he held up a knife. "We need to talk."

ARE YOU READY FOR DARREN'S STORY? HITMAN WEDDING.

For more Eve Langlais books see www.Eve-Langlais.com

Lightning Source UK Ltd.
Milton Keynes UK
UKOW04f1537031017
310312UK00001B/84/P